ALL THE
BEAUTIFUL LIARS

All the Beautiful Liars

The Fictional Memoir
of Katrina Klain

Sylvia Petter

Published in 2020
by Lightning Books Ltd
Imprint of EyeStorm Media
312 Uxbridge Road
Rickmansworth
Hertfordshire
WD3 8YL

www.lightning-books.com

British Library Cataloguing in Publication Data
A catalogue record for this book is available from the British Library.

Printed by CPI Group (UK) Ltd, Croydon CR0 4YY

ISBN: 9781785632174

*To Margaret Kennedy
in appreciation of years of
support and encouragement*

*– cocoons of words
that lived in our chests but did not fly
to our lips*

– 'Those Things We Do Not Say', Angela Readman

All I have written here is true; except the lies

– *Famous Last Words*, Timothy Findley

Dear Editor, and, I hope, dear Reader,

A 20-hour voyage to the other side of the world to bury the last remaining member of your family can play havoc with the mind. Sleep dreams are shaken by film snips and time-travelling memory blasts of sometimes wishful thinking... and you might even find yourself becoming a 'person of interest' in the Panopticon of a lonesome tabloid hack.

The journey is long and so, in your mind, you write, write, write; you must complete and deliver your story if it is to be read, and if you are to escape from that Panopticon to pursue your quest on landing. For how do you know where you're going if you don't know where you're coming from?

You may also find that the telephone that rings three times has changed from a tolling bell into a new chance, and that your inflight experience has prepared you for facing the reality that will confront you on arrival.

Forgive me if I include you in my adventure; it is, after all, a fictional memoir, where silence recounts 'true' stories as fictions, and truths can finally be told.

So if your interest is piqued, do take my hand and enter with me the Panopticon of *All the Beautiful Liars*, where we shall transform the last chance into a new reality.

Sincerely,
Katrina Klain

PART ONE

INFLIGHT PANOPTICON

I

Chapter 1

I am Jaimie, Jaimie Stadler, the keeper of lost endings. A life in Limbo is my lot: the price I must pay for my worldly delving into the tales of others, their scandals and secrets.

My job entails servicing The Panopticon in that period between death and the rest of the journey to God knows where. God, perhaps, may not even know where; and none, I am told, have come back to give the exact coordinates.

I may be new at this game, but I have work to do. Not that such work is evident, but there is a certain amount of opening doors, and closing them, pressing the play button – I am not always responsible for the stop button – and providing a fresh cup of tea, or glass of brandy.

Ah, someone is knocking at the door. I must release the lock and let them enter. But first let me click the play button so that you see what my visitor was going through. It is a woman of late middle age. I shall put the kettle on.

Click.

Labelled already?

Name & origin:	Katrina Klain, Australian citizen
Location:	Morgue of the Medical Insititute of the university of Vienna
Cause of death:	slit throat

What a clean sweep. And such neat stitching. The human head, it is documented, remains conscious for ninety seconds after decapitation (footnote 1: *Severance* by Robert Olen Butler, an American writer). But that is the view from the other side.

In fact, it can take days, even weeks, before beginning the journey down that tunnel of which one speaks. Not many get to the light, I might add, most end up wandering the corridors, the proverbial loose end having slipped from their grasp. But some are curious by nature. My guest, I suspect, is one of these. Let us then move into her mind. I always find that letting the 'interviewee' speak can liven up even the deadest reportage. (Do excuse my little joke.) So, over to Katrina Klain for a first-person account of the situation.

Shoot. Or should I say, cut?

Cut. My throat was cut! But when the blade slit through and I asked 'Why now?' I realised that I still had some unfinished business. I must find the story. It is not just my story, it's my family's, too, or what I can make of it. We must have been a family of liars, making up everything.

Except the bits that are true.

They say there's a light at the end of a tunnel. Warm, fuzzy, strangely welcoming. But I've learned not to believe what they say. It's not that they lie. I can see through lies. It's all the things they don't tell you. All the things you can't tell.

I didn't go down the path straightaway. But I saw a light flickering just after they wiped away the blood and pulled out the pipe. It got a little stronger when they brought me to the morgue to await the next step. It is quite pleasant lying here under the sheet, nothing to do, nothing to say, just remembering. My mother had lain the same way in a morgue in Australia except that her throat had been intact. I'd stroked her cheek and kissed her forehead; and I'd whispered, 'my beautiful liar'. The words surprised me then, and they haunted me for the rest of my life.

So this is Katrina Klain. Quite short. A metre and a half, I would say. Well-proportioned with the beginnings of an embonpoint. Little grey in that short hair. A straight nose. Not unattractive for a corpse. Let me look at her file.

Ah, it says that she was the daughter of Bettina and Alfred, who brought her to Australia from Vienna in the early '50s.

It is interesting that her question was neither, 'Why?' nor 'Why me?', but 'Why now?' which is perhaps an uncommon spin when one seeks reasons for gratuitous actions.

Her story cannot be a memoir. Even I could not presume to ghost-write such a thing. There are too many holes. Big holes of silence. And there are dreams, some coming from nowhere, yet they also become a part of the puzzle. What can one do if there are just bits and pieces to go on, held together with slipstitches, and a rosette here and there, to make them look almost beautiful? I, too, can add my – how do you say? – two cents' worth, although two is an unsightly number, the way it curls and drifts off. Sometimes into memories.

Memories. The bits one feels and the bits one is told, and they all come together as snapshots in one's mind. Some are lost, and some become parts of someone else's memories. And some bits just disappear and one ends up looking for them for the rest of one's life – even beyond it. And so they become part of an unfinished business; a business that can only be settled with the help of Yours Truly.

The light Katrina Klain saw was not from the end of a tunnel, but from a side passageway. It was not fuzzy or welcoming, but an open, matter-of-fact sort of light, like a 60-watt bulb, although there were no lamps. She got up and took one of the green gowns hanging on a peg on the wall, slipped it on, opened the morgue door and walked out. Drawn by the light, she came to my door. The plaque said: *The Last Chance*.

She had to take it.

Chapter 2

Katrina Klain pushes the door open and stands agape in green hospital scrubs. The room is round, and there are no windows. A large television screen covers a segment of the wall in a home-cinema curve; a large high-backed couch upholstered in brown velvet faces the screen. The only other furniture is an armchair in the same brown, in the corner next to a Biedermeier side table.

A small loudspeaker box – a little like the one with the dog – from where my voice will emanate, stands on the table. Katrina takes tentative steps towards the armchair and, with a hand on the table to steady herself, sits down. She sees the exercise book next to the speaker box and traces a finger over the childlike handwriting on the cover: *The Rules.*

More rules. *Even after death?*

There would have to be, of course. Even Lucifer needed

some sort of middle managers in Hell.

'Welcome to The Last Chance,' I say.

That is what I always say. Of course they wonder where they are. This one is different. I could tell. She is unable even to utter a word, and her hands tremble, but I can see a will there. Hmm. The others hardly had any left by the time they came through the door. They just gave up. That, of course, made it much easier for me to pack them off to the archives to languish forever with their unfinished stories. I would have to try another – how do you say? – tack?

'Just call me Jaimie,' I say. I pronounce the 'J' quite forcefully so that my name comes out as 'Tchaimie'. I try some French. 'A sweet name, n'est-ce pas? Bittersweet.'

She looks around. Stares at the box. Says nothing.

I must admit that I am surprised at her reaction. She, of course, does not know what to expect, and it is quite natural for me to presume she is wondering where she is. Old habits die hard. A legacy from my tabloid hack life: presuming for the sake of finishing the story. I should have known, of course. I mean, I can read her mind. The facts are there. It is me she is wondering about.

She rubs her forehead. Her head starts to throb. *Pain after death?* She stands up. Her knees tremble. She has to sit down. *Not here. The couch?* I cough. The loudspeaker crackles. She thinks she is dreaming. *Dreaming in death?*

She spirals slowly towards the couch. Grips its high back with both hands. 'Who are you?' she says, breathing the 'you'.

'I am dead, just like you, Katrina. Like you, I am also quite newly dead, but I have a mission. I am the keeper of this place where you might take your last chance. I see you are wondering about where you are.'

I press the switch. Click. The screen snows zigzags.

She looks at the screen. She turns and listens for sound from the loudspeaker. She looks for cameras. There are none. *Oh shit.* Play this cool, she thinks. *Ha!* She pulls back her shoulders, strides to the front of the couch, and sits down as if she has been invited to make herself comfortable.

'Yes. Do make yourself comfortable,' I say. 'It will be a long ride.'

She leans back in the couch. My accent? Yes! Schwarzenegger characters jostle through her mind: *Terminator, Barbarian.* She shudders and sits up straight. *Kindergarten Cop? Let it be Kindergarten Cop.*

Arnold Schwarzenegger? Peleeease! *I* have studied journalism at the University of Vienna, and have even spent six months in London. I do *not* have an accent! Ah, of course, the Mr Austria semi-finals when I was 18. Perhaps that comes through in my voice. I may have been a hack, but I was a damned attractive one, if I do say so myself. Hmm. It is perhaps a pity that she cannot see me.

The pitch is higher than I intend. I pause and drop the timbre. 'No, I am not Arnie, although I might meet him one day.' I pause for gravity. 'I am the keeper of lost endings.'

She stares at the screen. Sees just the snow. Then looks at the loudspeaker on the table.

Click.

She looks back at the screen. A banner appears: *Have you seen the rules?*

So what are these Rules? Know them and break them is what life taught me. But life has gone now and we are in this intermediary annexe, not unlike those bays for emergency in a long tunnel: under the Mont Blanc or the Arlberg, or perhaps even beneath the Great Wall of China.

Katrina gets up and goes to the table. She opens the exercise book.

Rule 1: Tie up all your loose ends.

'It is really the main one,' I say.

Her hands tremble. She wills them still. Shuts the book and goes back to the couch.

'A cup of tea?' I ask.

Her eyes are wide and her lips take on a quizzical bend. She straightens on the couch. She thinks she must be careful with her thoughts. She suspects that I can read her mind. My God, she thinks, if this is limbo, what's hell like?

'There is no hell, Katrina. It is not a matter of good and bad. There is only here and the hereafter. A much better binary.'

'But you can read my mind.' *There's nowhere to go, even in my thoughts?*

'It has always been like that, Katrina. You just did not notice, or did not want to.'

'What do you mean?' She looks at the screen, then at the loudspeaker box. She purses her lips.

I pause before I say: 'Data retention, Big Brother, or, closer to home, NSA, Five Eyes. Ring a bell?'

Bells have been ringing in her head, it seems, since she walked through the door of *The Last Chance.* 'So if you know everything, what's your interest in me?' she says and pulls at her earlobe.

'Ah, but I do not know everything. I only know from those who have died whose stories are buried forever in my archives.'

And, of course, there is the material that has just checked in, much of her own…shall we say…patchwork.

She stares at the loudspeaker box from where my voice emanates. 'What time is it?'

She had me. She had not thought why herself yet, so there was nothing for me to read in her mind.

'I could do with a drink,' she says, stretching her legs out before her and surveying her ankles.

Nice ankles. I do not answer. She thinks she has me flummoxed. I do not get flummoxed. I did not in my other life, and I will certainly not get so now.

She crosses her legs leisurely. *Spontaneous thought. That was the answer. Don't give him time.*

'Time, my dear Katrina, is something you need to worry about,' I say in a measured tone.

'You don't scare me,' she says.

'It is not about scaring you. It is about the rules. There are only two, anyway. But did you read them?'

'I only saw something about loose ends.'

That pursing of lips again. Headstrong? 'Something?' Make her find the answer.

'Tying them up.'

Ha! But is she sulking now? 'I must say that that book is a bit of a joke, since people always want rules.' My voice slips into hypnotic mode. 'But, nevertheless, it is there in case of need. And in your case there is need. You want to know. Do you not?'

Her eyes close. It is working. 'We are situated in a variable time zone. Some never knock on the door and are destined to roam the corridors in search of a glow that remains little more than an eternal refracted light-play. They may see it as a never-ending Son et Lumière, sometimes without the sound. Some may enter, but then give up. Others may take that last chance. You did.'

Click.

'Where were you just now, Katrina?'

I scratched the itch of a familiar sadistic streak running down my back – old habits and all that – but some of the players in Katrina's story are not wholly unfamiliar to me.

'Shall we start with Bettina?'

Here is her chance to hear more about her mother, Bettina Klain. She nods.

I remember Mum saying how it was better to know nothing, better that than watching yourself fall apart, one sense at a time. First it was her sense of smell, then taste – the two are really one – then hearing and sight. Touch was still there to pick up her marbles, she'd say. She'd been lucky. Had a long life. What hadn't she known?

'Not so easy, Katrina.' I am in my element as I turn invisible screws on her thumbs. 'What was the last thing you spoke to her about?'

She has nowhere else to go, so leans back in the couch and stares at the screen. Is that a glare in her eyes?

(For my 'to do' list: get her out of those awful hospital scrubs.)

Click.

Chapter 3
Katrina Klain

2009. Geneva. The phone rang three times. I'd picked it up.

'Your mother has had a massive stroke. She is alive, technically. We need your permission to remove the breathing tube.' The accent was broadly Australian.

I'd left my contact number with the home on Sydney's upper North Shore. In Europe? they'd asked. I can be there in thirty-six hours, I'd said. It's not as if I lived in the Never-Never.

Now all I had were memories, and a long, painful flight to Australia to bury a woman I perhaps never knew. To bury my mother, Bettina Klain.

***

I boarded the Qantas flight at Heathrow and settled into a window seat near the rear of the plane. They say that's where you're more likely to survive. Snort. Survival was what it was always about. We just get lazy. Forget. Give up or just plain get tired of it all.

I hadn't slept since the phone call the day before, stayed up to get the early flight from Geneva to London, cross town and then wait at Heathrow for flight QF 002. In the toilets I jabbed my belly with the syringe weeping my anti-blood clot shot and carefully placed the rubber nozzle back over the needle before dropping it into the bin for used pads. The last of the druggies. Ha! Every seven hours my doctor had said. Next loo stop was Singapore. No way could I go on the plane. Don't forget the support stockings, he'd said. I hated the support stockings that never wanted to stay up on the long lug walking to boarding. I hitched through the fabric of my light linen pants at the elastic stay-ups.

A Bloody Mary, my favourite on flights, a bit of a film. Schwarzenegger oldies came up three times. No blood and guts, please. *Kindergarten Cop.* Yes. Something funny. Arnie never could disguise his Austrian accent. He was home more often now that he'd given up on politics and his wife had given up on him. So much giving up, all round. I just couldn't yet. But what did I have? I thought of the last time I'd spoken to Mum just before getting her into the home, six months earlier. I'd been shocked. Angry.

'I am reminded of Nazi Germany,' she'd said.

'Mum!'

'Just look at the TV. This time it is to put up a fence around the pool so that toddlers cannot fall in and drown.'

'What's wrong with that?'

'There are no toddlers anywhere near our house.'

'But there could be.'

She shook her head. 'It is more than that. The government is taking away our own sense of responsibility. It wants to control everything.'

'You're exaggerating.'

'Warnings on television about this and that? We are living in a nanny state. I know where that leads.' She turned her head. 'Disempowering citizens. Making sheep of us all.'

'That was another time, Mum. Another place. Not Australia.'

'I am an old woman,' she said. 'I am glad that I do not have to live through it all again.'

I remember stroking her fingers, gnarled from years of arthritis.

Memories. The bits you feel and the bits you're told. They can haunt your dreams and become stories that ghosts tell. Some bits disappear and you end up looking for them for the rest of your life.

The stewardess poured tomato juice over crushed ice.

'Lemon please.' She nodded as she handed me a plastic cup and a small plastic bottle of vodka over the two empty seats by my side. I'd been lucky. All alone by the window. I'd been able to put my feet up in cattle class. I leaned back, put on my earphones and clicked on a video channel. Maybe I'd be able to sleep now.

Click.

The film started.

Indeed it has, Katrina.
It's just a film, Jaimie.
Do you really think so? We shall see.

Chapter 4

Bettina Klain

1921. Gorenzen, Thuringia. A small town in Germany.

I am Bettina Klain, née Strasser. I am the youngest of thirteen of whom two died even younger than my four years. My parents and siblings are out in the fields. I am alone. I run to my favourite tree, a tall elm behind the back of the barn where the sheep are kept through the long winter. There is a hollow in the tree that I can just reach. That is where I hide my treasures: two bits of brown glass from a bottle of malt beer my brother, Alvin, had inadvertently dropped on the rough stone kitchen floor. The bottle had been empty, but it was an accident my family could little afford. My mother collected all the pieces of glass to use for re-melting. All, save two tiny triangles. I spied them in a dark corner and secretly made them mine. I hold them up in the sunlight and feel a tiny thrill. I can make the brown earth glow.

Other treasures are the odd strands of flax that have fallen from my mother's spinning. I make a nest of the strands to cradle my glass jewels. Then there is a folded page carefully extracted from an old copy of my father's *Bauernalmanach*, the only reading material in the household and dedicated to farmers of the region. At first, I was drawn to the pictures of dancing.

Later, when I was able to read, I devoured the serials – stories of forbidden passion to enliven the hearts of the farmers' wives – ignored by my father. These, though, I did not extract, but after reading, replaced each issue carefully in order in the pile.

I learned early to keep secrets and to stay silent. Silence became my way of navigating the telling or not of what were considered to be lies.

When I spoke, however, I would embroider things in my mind, breathing life and excitement into stories of what was in fact a difficult farm life in that period following the loss of a war. 'You have to learn, Bettina,' my mother would say. 'Learn the land for a husband.' I would nod and close my eyes. A prince would come, and he would take me over a sea to a land where the earth glowed like gold.

But the land in Gorenzen was dry from a lack of rain. It was a time of hardship. A year earlier, my father and brothers had buried the greater part of the potato harvest deep in the ground to hide it from straggling marauders spawned by the defeat of a nation. The whole family would pee into buckets kept in the barn to be used in the spring to scour the fleeces of the twenty head of sheep kept inside over the harsh winters. Electricity had just come to Gorenzen, but Father monitored the one light switch. Electric light was too expensive to be wasted on women's work like darning and spinning. I did not mind. I loved sitting outside in the summer with my mother and sisters as they spun wool and flax in the moonlight. Summer evenings were dream times.

On the morning of my fifteenth birthday my mother said: 'So fortunate you are.' She had placed a small vase of field daisies next to my bread and butter plate. Her gift was the news that cousin Hildegard had agreed to take me on as a 'maid'. 'They have a big house in Mansfeld and you will have work. Hildegard has married well. That side of the family has always moved in good circles.'

Early spring 1934, each day, after the dusting and the tidying, the mopping, the washing of windows as needed, and the buffing of the silverware, I would withdraw to my room at the back of cousin Hildegard's two-storey house to work on my wedding dress. Gunmetal grey was not ideal, but the silky sheen of the rayon left over from Hildegard's curtains would make for a special outfit. Hildegard had allowed me to sew the straight seams on her Veritas sewing machine, but the rest, she said, had to be done by hand. I suspect Hildegard was fearful that I might damage the contraption when it came to the setting-in of sleeves, although the racing sound of the clickety-click did have the advantage of alerting her to the completion of my duties.

I, too, will move in good circles. I hung the long-sleeved dress with the dropped waist on a wooden coat hanger and hitched it onto a brass hook on the back of the door to my room. Just the hem left. The wedding was to be the next week. I could not wait. I could not wait to leave Hildegard's house after almost three years of being little more than a servant, hearing that as an uneducated farm girl I could not hope to expect more, and that as it stood, I was already lucky. But I did expect more, so much more.

And when I met Heinrich Rippenstein at a midsummer dance in my home village of Gorenzen, I knew there would be more than the life of a farm girl, a servant, destined to be married off to work her fingers to the bone and bear hordes of children like the ones my old mother had borne before I came along at number thirteen. I knew it from the moment he came towards me and asked if we might waltz. He looked very smart in his grey uniform with the high shiny boots. He would come to Mansfeld, he promised. We might stroll one evening.

And we strolled, and we danced. And I knew that my life was about to change. I could not wait to be with Heinrich in our little cottage reserved for him as an officer of the leftover army of the Weimar Republic.

Change was in the air, with a young, dashing politician promising a better life after years of inflation. But change also came in the form of a telegram delivered to Hildegard's home.

'It is addressed to you,' Hildegard said.

'Give it to me,' I said as my cousin held it an instant longer in her hand.

'Bad news?' she said. 'Telegrams are always bad news.'

I turned my back and with trembling fingers opened the telegram. Words jumped out at me: regret to inform you... unfortunate...death.

Heinrich was dead. He had fallen from his horse during manoeuvres and broken his neck. I repeated the words and dropped to my knees, my head almost touching the floor, as if my body could form a shell into which I might crawl. Hildegard stretched out a hand, then withdrew and left the room. Of course, I was devastated. My world crashed.

Click.

'That's enough for the moment,' I say. 'Have a cup of tea. You'll need something stronger a bit later.' I see that Katrina is agitated. She had not seen anyone bring tea, but there is a steaming cup on the table next to the exercise book. She puts out her hand. Stops. Stands up.

A cup of tea? Where did that come from?

She sits down again. Sips.

Sweet. Am I Alice looking for the Mad Hatter? And that other madman? Maybe it was thanks to a madman that we ended up in Australia.

She shivers at the thought of giving that man any credit. A nerve in her neck twitches. She puts the cup down.

It wasn't Hitler's fault that Heinrich broke his neck. Hitler may even have saved my mother's life.

'Yes, Katrina. Hitler, you might say, Hitler enabled Bettina to go to Austria and even on to Australia, where she would live happily ever after among the slipstitches of her memories and silences...'

Katrina shivers again and takes a large gulp.

Is this a bloody tea party? Bad was not bad and good was dead.

'It was a time of mixed messages, Katrina. We have that today, but it is much more subtle now. Then there was only one sort of information. Today there is a flood. The effect, however, is the same. Yes, she was devastated...'

Katrina closes her eyes.

There is more?

'There is more, Katrina. More on Bettina.'

Click.

Snow on the screen.

'Did you know, that your mother tried to commit suicide?'

That's a lie. She would never have done that.

'Why not? She was just eighteen. She was devastated. It is quite normal to have thoughts of ending it all when there is such despair. Did not you yourself want to start a new life at that age?'

I didn't want to kill myself. 'This is not about me,' Katrina says. It is almost a hiss.

'Not yet,' I say and let it sink in. 'But back to our clip.'

Click.

I took the savings Heinrich had left me and boarded a train to Garmisch at the foot of the highest mountain in Germany.

The Zugspitze. Almost 3,000 metres of unyielding rock at the border between Germany and Austria.

I had wooden skis that I would wear on my few free days in winter to traverse the flat land between Gorenzen and my cousin's house in Mansfeld, a distance of about ten kilometres. They were old hand-made skis with nail heads clamping on winter boots. My brother, Alvin, had made them for me as a Christmas gift three years earlier.

I rode the rack railway to the Schneefernhaus, the summit hotel, and took a single room for one night. Tears brimming, I carried my skis to the highest spot and pointed them downhill. Just let go. That's all I had to do.

'She crouched, took a deep breath, and sped in a straight line downhill, the wind and cold making her tears mingle with the snot from her nose.'

You are disgusting.

'Facts sometimes are.'

I tore towards a group of trees, their crowns rising up from the side of a crevice. It would soon be over. Let me fall. Let me not feel it. Knock myself out, fall like Heinrich, die in the snow.

Just before the trees, a young woman turned smartly, spraying snow in my face and breaking my flight. I bounced and rolled, one ski came off, the other came back to hit me on the head. It is over, I thought. The young woman knelt by my side. She wiped the snow from my face. The top of my head was bloodied, she said, from the errant ski. The young woman took off her scarf and wrapped it around my head. 'You'll be all right,' she said. 'Help is on the way.' Two skiers braked before us, bundled me into a sling and sped with me between them down to the valley. The young woman skied down after them. Her name was Gertrud Müller. All this I found out when I came to.

Click.
Click.

'Look, Katrina. Bettina in Berlin.'

My dark hair plaited over my head in a wreath, a long green apron covering most of my navy-blue shirt and trousers, I stood behind a long wooden bench potting seedlings. Above the bench, a long banner: *Gartenbau Müller.*

Gertrud Müller had not only saved my life, she had also taken me in, and persuaded her father to give me work in the family nursery. 'You will now have additional skills,' Gertrud said. I had no qualifications, and the times were such that papers were required for any movement.

'They need people like you. It is your chance,' she said. She was already big with her first child, and suspected twins. 'You can teach girls to run their households, and to support their husbands and brothers on the farms, just like you used to do yourself in your family. But now you will get a certificate. This is an idea of Hitler's. And when you are married you can have babies. Babies for Germany.' She patted the life growing inside her.

'This is my chance!' A certificate! A new life. This Hitler had such good ideas. Not just big roads. Hitler's plans for an *autobahn* were not realised until 1939, but all his speeches spoke of unifying all Germans, physically and emotionally, and giving us jobs for a better life.

What about the Jews?
  'She didn't know any Jews, Katrina.'
  But she must have heard. Kristallnacht.
  'That wasn't until 9 or 10 November 1938; I am not sure of the exact date. Nobody listens until it is too late. Just look at what is happening today. Did you learn about *Kristallnacht* at school? It was only much later.'
  Katrina shakes her head.
  'See?'
  Why should we, in Australia?
  'There were many things not taught at that time; when was it? The Fifties and Sixties? I imagine that other things were more important. .'

Click.
  Click.

I did well and received my certificate. I also got work. I was in charge of girls from the cities, teaching them how to bake bread, shear and spin the fleeces of sheep and even angora rabbits. I was in charge of eight young women from German cities: Munich, Hannover, Potsdam and Kiel. I wore a uniform with a brooch at my throat. There was a skewed cross on the brooch, but entwining leaves softened the edges. The girls loved me, I felt. I was at last somebody. And then I met Alfred Klain.

Click.

'I can give you a hint of what may come next.'

I don't want to know.

'Really? I do not think so.'

Katrina rides her hands through her hair and blows air out in a loud sigh.

'We must attend to Rule 2, Katrina.'

'Rule 2?'

'Do not waste time.'

That's a stupid thing to have as a rule.

'There is a use-by date on everything, Katrina. Even on the time to tie up your loose ends.'

She stares at the screen then back at the box, her eyes wide. Tears well in their corners.

'Under the book there is a tissue,' I say. I would so hate to see her cry. 'All this is just background for your own story. You cannot dwell on it. You might reflect on what you know about the Klain boys before we continue.'

'The Klain boys?'

'Alfred and Harald.'

Hell! This place is turning me inside out. Bad was not bad and good was a coward. I won't cry. Not here. Not with this know-it-all voice. What do I bloody well know about the Klains? About anything any more?

'Perhaps it is time for something a little stronger? A brandy, perhaps? Just a small glass?'

Chapter 5

Let me think. What do I know about my father's side of the family?

'Don't take too long, Katrina.'

She takes a sip of the brandy and shudders. I must admit it is not my best brand. No point in serving the best at this stage.

She cradles the bowl of the cognac glass in her hand. 'Lousy brand,' she says. 'Rough.'

'I was unaware that you were such a connoisseur,' I say.

Ha! So he doesn't know everything.

'I never said I did know everything. Just the facts, and some more. As we all know, the facts are never the full story.'

'Very well,' she says. 'Here's what I know. Can I click?'

Cheeky of her. Maybe it will work.

Click.

As far as I know or can remember being told, Alfred Klain was the eldest of three sons. Then there was Harald and Fritz, the baby.

Once when I was exploring my mother's jewellery box I found a brooch, a green insect on a golden leaf.

It's a beetle,' I said, running my fingers over the raised shell and feeling the tiny ridges.

'A scarab,' Mum said. 'From Egypt. Very old.'

'How did it get here?'

Mum took it and turned it over. 'This belonged to your grandmother. She gave it to me when I arrived in Vienna after the war.'

'She liked you?'

'I do not think so,' Mum said.

'But she gave you the beetle.'

'The scarab,' she said and tickled me, pretending to be a beetle, fingers crawling up my arm.

I squirmed and giggled. 'From Egypt.'

'Yes,' she said, and tickled some more.

'How did she get it?' Now it was my turn. I tickled her back.

'From your grandfather,' she said, laughing.

'He went to Egypt?' Tears of laughter welled in my eyes. 'Did he meet Cleopatra?'

'Don't be silly,' she said, pulling a straight face.

I copied her. 'He went to Egypt?' I said in a serious voice. 'Yes.'

The giggling was over as suddenly as it had started, but I kept pestering her until she told me that my grandfather had worked for the Prince of Thurn and Taxis. I thought he had taxis, but that was his name. I giggled again. And he lived in Cairo, she said. They had to leave Egypt and went to Trieste. She stayed serious now.

'That was where he met your grandmother,' she said. 'She worked as a chambermaid in the prince's hotel. Your grandfather was his major-domo.'

'Major-domo?'

'The person in charge of everything.'

Click.

'May I continue,' I say, and she nods. I try and keep the sarcasm from my voice. This is, after all, *my* show.

Click.

Even a prince had to let go of things and so he let go of your grandfather. But as a gift he put him in contact with a brewery, and soon Otto Klain was selling beer in Austria, with three restaurants in Vienna.

Years later one still has his name painted on a list at the entrance. He had not owned it, but had been the manager from 1926 to 1939.

The Klains were well-off between the wars, and when Alfred was born it had already been decided that he would take over the running of the businesses. The second-born, Harald, would become a lawyer, and Fritz would be given to the Church. That way, business, body and soul would be adequately looked after. The boys went to the Theresianum, the boys' school par excellence attended by sons of leaders who themselves would become leaders, the Viennese old boys' club for young ones.

Only a year separated Alfred and Harald. Alfred preferred sports to study and wanted to build bridges. Harald was good at languages and literature, but weak in maths and science. The brothers would share homework and tests, and both graduated, passing in all subjects with the help of a certain sleight of hand.

But Alfred's dream of building bridges came to naught. He had to learn the hotel trade, for he was to be able to run the three restaurants, the brewery, the small hotel, and whatever other properties his father had procured through the good connections he had established as a security for the future of the family.

As was the custom, Alfred was sent to London on an exchange, to work in the renowned Hotel Rembrandt. The young Kenneth Browning from the Rembrandt Hotel would come to the Gösserhof in Vienna.

Click.

'Years later you met Kenneth Browning in London. He was then already in his eighties. He gave you a tape he had made to acquaint you with the time he had spent with your grandparents in Vienna in 1938. I think I may have a copy of that tape in my archives,' I say. 'And the visuals that go with it.'

'But?'

'I am, after all, the keeper of lost endings, am I not?'

Her head is spinning. I was able to fill in some blanks. But I see she wonders if I have the whole picture.

There's something controlling about him and the place he's running. How long is it all to take? I knew the tape off by heart, but it'd led me nowhere for years.

'There is more to it than just a tape, Katrina. We must fit all the pieces of the puzzle together.'

The meeting with Kenneth Browning. Uh oh.

Chapter 6

'You remember. Tears in your eyes, Katrina? For a stranger?'

'He's not a stranger,' she says.

'Oh, yes. You met him. As an old man.'

She stiffens and reaches for the brandy glass. It is empty.

'Another drink?' I say.

She shakes her head. Rests her cheek in the palm of her hand. I am enjoying this. It is really the only way. 'Very well. We shall leave all that till later. Perhaps you will tell me.'

She clasps her hands and rocks slightly.

'Are you not curious about another old man? It has all been done before, of course, and could well be a sitcom. Is that the word?'

'I haven't a clue what you're talking about,' she says and brushes imaginary fluff from that awful green smock. (I must get her into something else.)

'How I met your mother?'

She starts. Sits up. 'You met my mother?'

'Ha. Just the *Zeitgeist*, Katrina.'

He's mad.

'Not mad, Katrina. I just know more than you do. More than most know.'

But I know things, too.

'What was that, Katrina?'

'Nothing.'

Click.

'Da-dah! Alfred Klain.'

Chapter 7
Alfred Klain

When I came to work in London at the Rembrandt Hotel, I was eighteen. The Rembrandt would lease its staff to service private dinners as a forerunner of the catering industry. My first outside position was to be one of several servers who, at the signal of a baton against the floorboards, would lift large silver lids from the main-course plates of a dining table for twenty. Guests wore dinner suits and long evening dresses.

I was lonely in London, and that may explain why I soon fell into the arms of the ten-years-older Agnes, sister of Kenneth Browning who had taken my place in Vienna. She, too, worked at the Rembrandt and was in charge of the parlour maids. But let me tell you about my first Christmas.

Austria is a very Catholic country, where Vienna's St Stephen's Cathedral opens its doors for the needy of prayer.

A country run by Roman Catholic republicans some called fascists. And here I was, Christmas alone in a protestant land with a king. I sought out a church and found the doors barricaded. Rain ribboned on the streets, the night glowed damp. Nowhere to go on Christmas Eve, no festival of home and midnight mass that I was used to. In my despair I stared at the Thames, its roiling water calling me in. It is not clear why I did not jump. Fear perhaps. A coward? Or the universe readying me for Agnes Browning, a young Jewish woman, the first love of my life?

Agnes and I would stroll on our days off; but just round the time her brother Kenneth was due back from Vienna, my father had a stroke. This was hardly surprising considering his embonpoint and the times. But the timing was bad and so I was called back to Vienna, and shortly after, war broke out. I never met Kenneth Browning, and never saw Agnes again.

'The Brownings had certainly made an impact on the Klain boys, had they not? Kenneth and Harald, now Agnes and Alfred. Do forgive my insinuations. Life, I suppose.'

Years later, Bettina and Katrina would laugh about Agnes. Well, not laugh, but they would tease me. I do not think Bettina minded. Agnes had been an 'older' woman, so, for someone young, she did not really come into the equation. It was no secret. I did not know about the Jews, and anyway, Agnes was in England.'

'I knew about Agnes,' Katrina says. 'It was no secret. Dad didn't know about the Jews, and anyway, she was in England.'

'Have you ever considered the arms into which one runs when one loses all?'

She is puzzled. Is silent. Perhaps it will come to her later.

'Let us move on,' I say.

Click.

Just before the outbreak of war, one still had a choice... We boys were called up. Harald, because of his language skills, went to intelligence. I, at last closer to my dream of building bridges, enlisted in the *Luftwaffe*. It is ironic that I would later bomb the objects of my childhood dreams. Orders are orders. But I saved a comrade. Was awarded a medal. Not by the *Führer*, but in his name.

'It is ironic that he would later bomb the objects of his childhood dreams, *n'est-ce pas?* Orders are orders.'

But he saved a comrade, a mate. Got a medal. Not by the Führer, *but in his name.*

'Did you ever see that medal?' No matter.

Click.

Spool back.

Click.

Training for the young pilots took place near Stuttgart. Nearby were fields and the compound where young German women learnt to care for the land, or at least its fruits, so as to be able to replace hands to be sent to the front. This was where Bettina was in charge. *Arbeitsdienst.*

Click.

(Here is what it says on Wikipedia: 'In the course of the Great Depression, the German government of the Weimar Republic (...) established the Freiwilliger Arbeitsdienst ('Voluntary Labour Service', FAD) on 5 June 1931, two years before the Nazi Party (NSDAP) ascended to power. (...) The concept was adopted by Adolf Hitler (...) to provide service for mainly military and to a lesser extent civic and agricultural construction projects. (...) It was the official state labour service, divided into separate sections for men and women.')

Click.

The young women would till the fields, harvest potatoes, and beans, pumpkin, whatever would grow. And they would sow cornflowers, blue, pink and white ones. One day, after the harvest, the women were walking back down the furrows, picking a cornflower here and there, when we flew so low that the women had to drop to the ground. Bottoms up. When we had gone, a woman stood up and shook a fist at the tail ends of our disappearing planes, or so she told me much later. Her girls had been in shock, shaken.

We came right down low. It must have been terrifying. Having to lie face down on the ground. And then everything spilled. No wonder she was mad.

We slipped out of our overalls and back into uniform. It had been fun. Watching the milk bottles hit the ground. Ha! What sport! Time for a beer.

Yes, it was horrible. Stupid.

We got hauled before the top brass. The woman in charge of the compound had made an official complaint. I, as the most senior, together with one of my men, was to go to the compound and make formal excuses for our behaviour.

Chapter 8
Bettina Klain

Yes. I had shaken my fist. Those hooligans had flown down so low. They terrified my girls. Later in my rooms, I prepared a table with cups of coffee and shortbread biscuits. I was pleased to have succeeded in receiving excuses from an officer, one who could not have taken part in the escapade; I wanted to extend what might be perhaps not an olive branch, but at least a shortbread of peace. Christmas was on the way.

A knock at my door. I opened. Two officers outside. One very handsome, a smart moustache, his cap at an angle. A gentleman. He clicked his heels and I held out a hand which he took and over which he bent his head. '*Oberleutnant* Alfred Klain at your service. Our sincerest apologies. I will ensure that such a thing will not happen again.'

I withdrew my hand. I hardly noticed the second man.

'Would you care for some coffee and biscuits?'

'We cannot stay, Madam,' Alfred Klain said, and turned to his accompanier, his eyebrows and a slight movement of the head indicating that the other man should be on his way. 'But just one cup. That would be very nice.'

Alfred Klain took off his cap and sat down at the table. His accompanier read the signal and disappeared into the hall.

I held out the tin of biscuits. Alfred grabbed a handful. I kicked him under the table. Alfred kept only two biscuits in his hand. He smiled. Ate. Swallowed. Sipped his coffee and I think he fell in love. He used to say it was love at first kick. And I had once again found my officer and the possibility of a new life.

'Interesting how these things start, is it not?'

Click.

We married in 1942 in Gorenzen, my hometown. It was a hurried event, just weeks before Alfred was to be sent to the Russian front. The mayor was dragged out of bed and had his shirt tails peeking out of his fly. I tried to ignore it. Alfred, staring straight ahead, did not appear to see.

A few days in the mountains, hiking, in the summer sun. Clothes discarded until we were just in our boots and knapsacks. An edelweiss. Don't break your neck, I said. Never, he answered, crawling back from the crevice (Edelweiss grows in the most dangerous places), his penis saluting. 'We will make babies for Hitler,' he said.

No! You're a liar!

'Do you have evidence to the contrary, Katrina?' This is painful for her. I may have a sadistic streak, but I am no sadist.

Click.

'Calm down, Katrina. They were in love.'

'My mother would never have wanted to make babies for Hitler. And she didn't!' *Who does the bastard think he is?*

'Who do you have in mind there, Katrina?'

She glares.

'Have a sip of something,' I say. 'And please refrain from casting aspersions.'

I think it is now a moment to distract her. New clothes?

She sips from the brandy and shudders.

'Too strong?'

She ignores me.

'Put on that red caftan. Yes, the one on the chair.'

She looks at the chair. She gets up and goes over. *Where the hell did that come from?* She holds up the caftan. She sways it back and forth. I think she likes it.

'Close your eyes,' she says.

I have to snort.

She stands naked, the green hospital scrubs around her ankles. Then, faster than I can catch my breath, she is in the caftan. She was not bad naked, but in the caftan she is splendid.

'Scarlet becomes you,' I say.

'Thank you.' She is almost demure.

'Shall we move on? Something else for a while?'

She nods, goes back to the couch and curls her legs up, covers her feet with the hem of the caftan. I find she is now curious as a child. Ah, the cinema.

There were no babies for Hitler. Alfred was shot down. Captured. He made it back to German lines and could have had a quiet time in the rear-echelon services after the hundreds of missions he had flown. But, no! Rear-echelon duties were not those of a hero, so he volunteered for last-ditch service to the Reich. He said he was with Otto Skorzeny, Hitler's top commando, SS Lt. Col. Otto 'Scarface' Skorzeny, which explains his capture by the Americans and his incarceration in Dachau. At least now he would be safe, I thought. He was cleared of war crimes and finally released in 1947. Then came Vienna.

Straight after the war, it was not good to be German in Vienna. Even standing in line at the butcher's to get Mama's favourite sausage, the local patrons would turn grim faces my way, almost physically pushing me aside, as if I, as a German, were at the root of all former evil and current distress.

Mama, as she liked to be called, always wore black, and she would bunch her long skirts in her fists whenever she lashed out at me, which was almost daily. I loved to go to the matinées and see *Tarzan* films. Mama disapproved but, whenever I could, I defied her, even enlisting the help of

Harald, Mama's favourite son. It helped the time pass while Alfred was attending to guests in the family restaurant. Most importantly, with Harald, I was able to get away from Mama more easily.

In 1949, the birth year of the German Democratic Republic, the child was born; so too was Mama's use of the word 'Democratic' as some sort of expletive as my Katrina burst into the world.

When the weather was fine I would put Katrina on reins, which most toddlers wore – those that were attached to a halter crossing the chest – and take her out to the Volksgarten, the large public park. We walked down the street, past the Rathaus, the Gothic town hall, over the broad Ring Straße where cars and red trams had to stop at the lights to let us cross. The Volksgarten was structured so that densely planted beech trees screened out the bustle and dust of the city. Red, pink and white roses were planted behind white metal chairs strung together with chains for the full length of the pebbled path that led to the playground.

One particular weekday afternoon, the air was cool and few people were about to catch the scent of roses that, in pockets, was as heavy as winter clouds thick with snow. As we reached the playground, Katrina strained at the halter until I unbuckled it and let her run to the swing. When she got there, she grabbed the swing's seat, a heavy wooden slab, and drew it back as far as she could. She held it still and as she let go she stepped forward to follow it. I ran forward as if in slow motion. The swing came back. The metal corner caught Katrina's right eyebrow. She fell down. The right side of her face was shiny red. I screamed. At the hospital, they gave her three stitches. At home, Mama screamed. 'Scarred for life', she screeched.

All that was over now and soon I would at last be on my way to Alfred, who, only six months before, had boarded a ship for Australia.

Chapter 9

In the large dining room of the *SS Neptunia* two of the stewards were clearing the noontime tables, their white jackets having lost the crisp feel of breakfast. Passengers, mostly women and children, filed through the glass swinging doors, queuing already on their way down the stairs and out to terra firma.

I still sat at a table by the first porthole, a pen poised in my hand above a postcard that had taken the place of the used dishes and cutlery. I smoothed my hair back from my forehead – tendrils curling as ever at my temples and nape – and dropped my free hand to caress my daughter's head on my lap. The three-year old was asleep on her back, her legs reaching halfway along the padded seat.

Someone watching me might have taken me for a young woman writing a card to her husband, like any of the other young migrant women had been doing before they crowded the deck of the ship, children in arms, to watch it berth in Colombo, Ceylon.

I shifted and eased Katrina fully onto the bench. Then I buckled the halter over her chest and tied the reins about one of the table legs. That should do it, I thought. It won't take long. Just time to drop the card in the box. '*Komme gleich,*' I whispered. Katrina hardly stirred as I rose.

The corridor and the gangway were clogged with passengers eager to try out their land legs, as if the voyage from Genoa through the Suez, the heat of Port Saïd, the seasickness, had begun to rob us of any firm sense of balance, so used were we now to rolling with the ground as it came up to meet us that the prospect of port almost had a carnival feeling to it. I pushed my way to the mailbox on the lower deck. Before the red slit I hesitated and then let the card slip into the dark, still in time for collection during our stay in port.

The card was a farewell to Vienna; although tinged with some sadness and bitterness, I also felt a blend of relief and liberation, for it was to bear the last words I thought I would ever address to my mother-in-law, and, as an ultimate irony, through her beloved son.

I made my way back to the dining room. As I approached the table, I saw the reins trailing the floor. Katrina! My heart thumped. I got down on my knees to look under the table. A sea of table legs. Where was she? I raced to the stairway. I could smell my own fear. I clutched the banister and let it go as a cramp locked my fingers. Passengers were still filing out. I pushed past them. Down the gangplank. I looked left and right. There! A flash of pale gold. White against black! The child in the arms of an old, bearded native dressed all in white. I stared, transfixed. I could hear my heart beating in my mouth. Wanted to scream. The man's feet were bare, his legs spindly. His hair hung in long twisted tresses. He smiled broadly, displaying an incomplete collection of long, stained teeth. He held a banana to Katrina's face, on which she munched.

'Katrina', I cried, and the man nodded. I grabbed my daughter. She flapped her hand anxiously towards the old man, who merely smiled. As I raced back to the ship and up the gangplank I could feel his eyes upon me, but I did not look back. I hugged Katrina to me. We were off to a new life in Australia and I was determined to become the best mother in the world, to watch over Katrina and never lose her again.

Click.

There were postcards, Katrina. This one and others to come. You cannot brush off the past. It will always come back in some way. You will have to deal with it, or it will haunt you forever. Do you want that? Have you really forgotten?

She stands up. Turns around. Her head turns to the left and then to the right. She is looking for me. I must occupy her. Place her in the moment.

'You cannot forget the unknown, Katrina, but you can remember what you have forgotten. Take a deep breath. It is your turn now.'

My turn?

She leans back and closes her eyes. Then she speaks.

Chapter 10
Katrina Klain

I'd heard different stories about my grandparents. My grandfather would send Christmas cards to important people in Vienna, even to the Chancellor, and of course he'd receive cards in return – he was, after all, a *Kommerzialrat* and served some of the best food in town. He would prominently display the cards he received from the various dignitaries of the city. He was what one might call *Emporkömmling*, nouveau riche, a self-made man.

My grandmother, Alberta, was very religious. She would pray several times a day and always had a rosary at hand. She always wore black. My earliest memories of her are very vague, if memories at all.

I was in my mother's womb. I must have been quite developed because I could feel colours and sounds. Sounds like my grandmother screeching: 'The child will become a monkey!'

I didn't hear the exact words, but I sensed them. Like I sensed that my grandmother wore black and bunched her long skirts in her fists when she lashed out at my mother. I disliked her for both. For the black and for the way she spat the word 'Democratic', although I couldn't have had an idea of its meaning.

My mother was from the eastern part of Germany. Later, when I was old enough, she told me that my father had brought her to Vienna, that in Vienna, straight after the war, it wasn't good to be German. She said I was born in the birth year of the German Democratic Republic. 1949. But I didn't become a monkey as my grandmother had predicted, although my mother did use to tease me and call me her little monkey.

My mother loved Tarzan films, you see. I could feel it even then. It must have been that feeling of flying through the air, like Cheetah. Imagine. I, Katrina Klain, knew what it was like to fly even before I was born.

Of course, my mother told me I couldn't have known what it was like, not from the inside, from inside her womb. But I did know. Somehow I felt it. It is such a struggle with memories.

Only much later did I find out why my grandmother disliked my mother. It was not just because she was a farm girl from Germany, and a protestant. My grandmother thought that my mother had discovered a secret, and had kept silent for most of her life. The silence must have been more excruciating for my grandmother than any divulgement.

To appease her, although we were already in Australia, my parents enrolled me in an expensive convent school. Loreto

Convent Kirribilli, and later Loreto Normanhurst. Heaven knows how they paid for it, but they did. My memories of that school are always linked to my grandmother, and to fear. My grandmother visited us once when I was about nine. The only nice thing I could remember about her was her bed. My father had bought a lovely springy mattress so that she would be comfortable during her three-month stay. Although the Christmas heatwaves were in full swing, my grandmother still would wear black and take a grey silk parasol against the sun for her daily walk up the hill to the church. She always had her rosary dangling from her left wrist like worry beads. She was a great worrier. I used to think she would dissolve in the heat and just leave a black puddle. All my friends' grandmothers wore bright blouses and Bermuda shorts in the summer. The black of my grandmother reminded me of my first days at Loreto Kirribilli.

'We do need to step back a little.'

How far back do you want me to go, Jaimie? To before I was twinkle in anyone's eye? Or maybe I was an accident?

'No. No. Just sit back. You have been through a lot. Just watch your life spool by.'

'There's a film of my memories?'

'Thinking of *Sundance*?'

'Ha. Ha.'

'It is all there. Just like today, Katrina. Though I must say that the methods here are far superior to any YouTube, and we do not have bandwidth problems, not here and not in the *Afterlife*. You will see that the film remains as true to your memories, truer perhaps than even you can remember in retrospect. So where were we? Ah, Loreto. A convent school for girls. Classy.'

She scowls at me.

Click.

I couldn't speak English when I started school at Loreto. It was run by nuns who didn't know that I never went straight home. They didn't know that I'd curl up in a sweatshop trunk full of dressmaking snippets until my mother was ready to take me home. I felt safe in that big trunk. At Loreto, big black birds fluttered about me in their robes and veils, cawing chants I couldn't understand. Some took me under a wing; others pecked at me, picked at me, scared me, their beads rattling like strings of seeds in a cage.

One rainy lunchtime I was in a large square room with benches stretching all around the walls. Little girls just like me sat in their blue pinafores, knees pressed together, their plastic lunch boxes on their laps. I nibbled my sandwich – salami on pumpernickel – stopped chewing. I shifted from one buttock to the other and froze. A wet warmth seeped down my legs and thawed me into action. Clutching my lunch box, the salami pumpernickel on its lid, I rose, looked straight ahead and crossed the room. I settled on the bench opposite, nibbled again at my sandwich and stared at the puddle on the other side of the room.

Click.

I look at Katrina. She is biting her lip and pulling at her right earlobe again. I must keep her in the moment.

Click.

I had to learn not to speak. Speaking in any language at the wrong time could be punished by the bamboo end of a duster that left welts on my legs. It was all very confusing, and it hurt.

By the time I was six, I'd long since adapted, and began asking questions. One day, when the sun had come out just after the rain, I asked my father, 'Why is the sky blue?'

'Reflection from the sea,' he said without looking up from his paper.

'You just cannot see the sea from here, *Liebchen*,' Mum said.

I climbed up on a chair and craned my head from the kitchen window.

'You cannot see it, can you?' Mum said.

I'd been puzzled, I'd shaken my head and come to Mum's arms.

'That does not mean it is not true,' she whispered and looked at my father, who nodded slowly.

The film spools fast forward.

I'm seven now.

'Why do they call the Blue Mountains blue?'

Mum glanced at Dad and said it was the haze of the eucalyptus that made them look blue from the valley.

Early one Sunday, as if to provide proof, we drove to Katoomba in the Blue Mountains. We stood at the lookout behind the Three Sisters, those crags peaking out of the bush that painted the landscape a greyish blue for miles and miles. And the crisp, fresh smell made the blue so true that it didn't matter that the Three Sisters were red.

It was only when I was nine and my parents took me to the Snowies that Mum told me that the Blue Mountains were not really mountains since they weren't as high as Mount Kosciusko, a blunt seven-thousand-footer, a real mountain covered in snow − almost like the Austrian peaks of my father's home, she'd said. The eucalyptus smell must have been frozen in the red resin the stunted snow gums wore like badges on their white bark.

I didn't ask further. But later I wondered if Mum thought I'd forgotten about mountains, the sea − about blue.

One Saturday we were racing to the beach over Tumble-Down-Dick Hill, on the road that dropped down and flew up, leaving my stomach almost plastered to the roof of the car. And on the crescent I screamed: 'I can see the water! It's blue, like the sky.'

Yes, my parents did try to have all the answers, even if some of my questions came too soon or were answered before I even asked. I'd sometimes grow impatient with the questions that remained unanswered, and also was puzzled when Mum told me more than I probably needed at the time. It had been Mum's way of satisfying my curiosity, I supposed, and coming to terms with my growing up. The way people sometimes say too much to avoid having to answer difficult questions.

Like the time when I was ten and Mum tried to explain a picture in my zoology book: I'd seen the shouldered monster of ovaries, and for years, even now so many years later, I could still hear my child-woman cry: 'I can't have that inside me!' Was that when I first started doubting my parents' answers?

At school I also adapted, although as a 'new Australian' I somehow felt that I didn't fit in, didn't belong, though longed to be...be Australian? 'The foreign girl is running rings around you,' Mother Carmel said to the other pupils as she handed me first prize, a holy card with golden edges. I was ten.

Click.

'Nine, eight, ten? Who knows? Even films are not always sure. The medium can become unreliable. But we shall continue.'

Click.

Even though Loreto was a private school, leaning then more towards elocution and deportment than to arithmetic and social studies, I knew that my parents weren't wealthy. But they weren't poor either, for Mum didn't use a saucepan to cut my hair. A girl in my class, Mary Prendegast, and her three sisters, they were poor; they all had that saucepan cut. Uniforms of royal blue pleated tunics, beige shirts and blue and gold ties were meant to be the great equaliser back then. The Prendegast girls wore faded blue tunics; their blouses had soft collars and their cuffs were frayed. Despite all that, though, they belonged.

One afternoon I was out by the school wall, hitting a tennis ball in even strokes back and forth. '...25, 26, 27...'

'Hey, Kat.' Mary Prendegast was right behind me, her two younger sisters bringing up the rear. I bit my lip and kept on hitting. Mary always seemed to spit my name.

'Kat,' Mary repeated.

'...28, 29, 30, 31...'

'You're a bloody Nazi,' she hissed.

I froze and turned as the balding ball dribbled into a corner. 'What do you mean?'

'Ask your Nazi parents,' Mary sneered and ran away laughing, her sisters giggling as they ran after her.

What did she mean? More questions. More questions.

Dad always said it was important to talk at the dinner table. But since his heart scare a bit earlier, he'd taken to eating his food in a more measured way and would chew and chew so that his answer to any questions became merely a shake of the head, a grunt or a nod. How old was I when he'd felt dizzy for the first time and had gone to lie down? It can't have been too long after I'd seen the disturbing ovary monster.

That evening I blurted: 'What's a Nazi?'

There was a loud silence as Dad slowly pulled his knife

and fork erect on either side of his half-finished plate. Then he swallowed his mouthful and said: 'Why do you ask that?'

'Mary called me a Nazi at school. It seemed nasty.' I looked from Dad to Mum and back.

'Why did she call you that?' Mum said.

'Because of the play we're doing,' I lied. '*Hansel and Gretel.* Mary asked how come I got the part of Gretel. If it was on account of my blonde hair. She said all the books have Gretel with blonde hair. And it's a German name.'

There wasn't really a play; I just didn't want to mention my beloved tennis. It was my first real lie and would probably cost me five Hail Marys. Or was it seven?

Click.

Seven.

'Excuse me?' I say.

'It cost me seven Hail Marys.'

Interesting detail to remember all these years. Ah, the power of ritual.

Click.

'What is so terrible about that?' Mum said.

For a moment I thought Mum meant my lie, but then caught myself. 'Mary said I was German and that all Germans were Nazis. What's a Nazi?'

'Nazis were Germans,' Mum said, and then paused. 'But not all Germans were Nazis.'

'Mary said the Nazis burnt all the Jews,' I said. Then in a

louder voice: 'So I told her I was Australian and had a paper to prove it and what was a Jew anyway? Mary didn't know. She just said the Germans burnt them all up. Said you and Dad did.' I turned to Mum. 'What's a Jew?'

Mum wiped her hands on her napkin and rose to lean over for my empty plate.

Dad aligned his knife and fork on his and stretched it out to Mum. Fatty scraps of pork clustered one edge. Then he cleared his throat. A tell-tale vein pulsed at his temple. 'That was the war,' he said. 'It is a long story. It is late. School tomorrow.'

I was in sixth class and 'school tomorrow' had become a daily catch phrase during the week.

The next day, Mum drove to the station to fetch Dad, something she'd been doing since his first heart scare. As usual he was tired after the peak-hour train-ride home. The streetlights were just coming on as they came in and Mum called out to me. But I stayed in my room and didn't answer. I was sobbing into my pillow.

'What is wrong?' Mum asked as my sobbing grew louder. She held me and rocked me gently without a word. No one talked at the table that evening, but just before bed, I asked Mum again: 'What's a Nazi, Mum? Is it true about the Jews?'

'Hush, go to sleep now. It is late,' she said. 'We shall talk about it another time.'

It was a Saturday about three months later, and Dad was out. The scarlet camellias were in full bloom as I came rushing into the house, clutching a postcard.

'It's from Austria, Mum!' I held out the card.

'Who is it from?' Mum asked softly.

Tall, white mountain peaks. No trees. All there was were the words: 'A short goodbye. A big kiss to Katrina.' Mum tried to keep her voice steady. 'It is from Harald, your papa's brother,' she said.

'Dad has a brother? I have an uncle?'

Mum went to the sideboard. Bruised camellia petals had fallen from their wiry stems. She swept them into her hand and propped the postcard against the empty vase. 'He is dead,' she said.

'But he can't be! He sent the card.'

'Perhaps your papa will tell you,' she said dully. I stared at her wiping her dry hands on her skirt and then went outside. She followed me, and then clipped three red camellias. Although I didn't say a word, the questions were clamouring in my mind.

That evening at dinner Mum pushed the card across the table.

'Katrina collected it,' she said.

Dad stiffened, then gazed at the card and said: 'Harald was my brother. He is dead.'

I swivelled from him to Bettina. 'Dead men don't send postcards,' I said.

Dad's lower lip began to quiver. 'For me, Katrina,' he said, 'he is dead.'

Mum placed her hand on Dad's forearm and looked sadly at me.

'Harald ran away,' she said.

Dad tensed and his face went the deep red of the resin on the snow gums. 'Ran away? A deserter! A coward!' he shouted.

I stared at him and pulled at my earlobe.

'Harald thought Hitler was wrong,' Mum said quietly.

'Sometimes it takes courage to run away.'

There was a smell in the air of moist mouldy moss. I was about to ask who Hitler was when Dad banged his fist on the table. 'What did he know about right and wrong?' he said. 'He laughed in the face of duty! Laughed at my medals! Laughed at me!'

'Perhaps he knew about the Jews,' Mum said almost inaudibly, so that I had to crane forward to hear.

'The Jews? What have the Jews got to do with it?' The pulse at Dad's temple was twitching madly. 'We didn't know about the Jews! We were not Nazis!'

'No, we were not, *Liebchen*. Nor was he. He took a great risk and he paid the price.'

Dad's face reddened a shade deeper. 'The price? Have I not paid the price, too? Even today?' His breath pumped out as the words came in a sudden rush.

'He helped one get away, Alfred,' Mum said.

'He helped a criminal! Do you think there were no criminals among the Jews?'

Dad stared at Mum, his mouth open wide. Then his head rolled back and he toppled to the floor.

Dad recovered. It had been just another scare, but I sensed even then that some questions could never be asked, at least not in his lifetime.

A few days later I tried again. 'What's a Nazi, Mum?'

Mum looked at me with surprise and then her gaze softened in a sad way. 'That's a name some people give to Germans here. They fought against them in the war. Since the Nazis were Germans, they think all Germans are Nazis.'

'Yes, but what is it? The way Mary said it, it sounded bad.

Are we Nazis, Mum?'

'No, dear. But they were the people in power under Hitler and he did dreadful things and everyone went along with him.'

'So Mary's right?'

Bettina sighed. 'Hitler promised a change. People were desperate, so they followed him. Then there was no going back.' She wiped her hands on her apron and fiddled with the plates.

Mum's words had not really explained what this man Hitler had to do with her and Dad; what he had to do with me. I didn't want to think about it any more. Years later, the incident had me wondering about Dad and his brother – who they were, where they'd come from.

The spectre of what my parents hoped had belonged to another world, another life, had followed them all the way to Australia, where it lived on, perhaps even quietly waiting. But I am Australian! I had to get away, be by myself. Go down the bush.

Click.

'Ah, the bush. I have always wanted to see what that is like. To be in the thick of it, as it were.' I can smell eucalyptus. If a voice can hear and see then it can also smell, and perhaps even touch.

I loved the bush. Thought I could never leave it.

'Not yet, Katrina.'

'I thought we had a deadline.'

'We had better be off, then.'

Click.

Chapter 11

The bush came right up to the back of the house. Banksia and bottlebrush filled the gaps between the sentries of eucalyptus gums, some with bark that would peel off paper-thin, others with blood-red resin glistening down white, insect-bitten trunks. Down by the creek, lush green frond stalks made the best whistles in the world.

I pulled a light-green stalk, inspected it quickly, slipped it between my lips and sucked in my breath in short bursts. A high metallic chirp shrilled back. I was as good as the boys. I'd always wanted to be one. Especially since the day Dad took me to a soccer game, and I fell over coming out of the stadium and my knee bled. He said: 'Be like a soldier, tall and straight. Don't cry like a girl.' I couldn't help thinking he would have liked me to have been a boy. When Mum took me for a haircut, I'd always ask for a short back and sides, but Mum shook her head, saying: 'Just a trim.' I was better than the boys in some things, but I wasn't one of them. I didn't belong. I wished I had a best friend, someone to talk to, someone to confide in, someone to be there at the times I felt so awfully alone.

Like just after my eleventh birthday, when the world was going to end. The younger nuns at Loreto fluttered about in their black robes, fingering their rosaries. In class on Friday, Sister John had told us how the Virgin Mary had appeared to three peasant children in Portugal. That had been way back in 1917, the year Mum was born.

Those children had said that the Virgin Mary appeared as 'a lady brighter than the sun'. While Sister John was telling us this I fingered the holy cards tucked in the corner of my desk. I'd swapped a good-conduct card of Saint Christopher for one of the Virgin Mary in a long pale-blue gown with a matching veil that reached down to her bare feet. The edges of the holy card were scalloped in gold. I knew just what she looked like.

'The Virgin Mary told the children three secrets. One of the children – she later became a nun – wrote the secrets down and sent them in a letter to the Pope. The meaning of the secrets, she'd said, would become clear in 1960.' Sister John crossed herself and continued: 'We know what two of them meant,' she said. 'Two of the secrets have already come to pass: the charred bodies in the oceans of fire of World War II...' – I shivered at that, and then Sister John's voice became louder – 'and the persecution caused by the errors of Russia.' Sister John paused and I turned the card of the Virgin Mary face down as if to silence any further words. The third secret could only mean the end of the world. The Fatima letter was to be opened the next day, a Saturday.

My parents were out shopping as one of those late summer winds tore through the State, ripping corrugated roofs off garages. I lay in my room, clutching my tennis racquet to stave off hidden monsters. I cried and cried. The end of the world. I wouldn't have time to go to mass. Just like that family the nuns had told us about, the one that went to the beach instead of to church and their train crashed down a black hole. Now I'd be sucked into what was to be the beginning of Hell...

The storm subsided and I knew Fatima had been a lie. Or the end of the world had just not come. I stopped going to mass altogether, but had nightmares about a house in the bush.

I was late for school. Took the short cut through the bush. A currawong cried out its name as I pushed through the ferns past Old Man Banksia. Dry bracken crackled underfoot. A lizard scuttled under a pile of rocks. The bush was alive. I breathed in and smelt eucalyptus.

Another deep breath and I caught a whiff of damp wood. On the path ahead of me. A brown snake. Watch out. And then I'm running home. Over the creek. Blackberry briars catching at my uniform. Slipping on the green sludge; holes in my stockings. On my toes, balancing across the rotten log to the other side, where a flat rock was half-covered by water.

On the rock, stick figures of a man and a woman, curves of a snake and a bounding kangaroo. The rock was alive. Aboriginal souls were trapped inside. Mustn't fall. I'd be sucked into an unknown Dreamtime.

Keep running. Run home. But the scrub thickened to a dead end and I saw a house next to a tall gum tree. Blood. Blood glistening down the tree's white trunk. My heart thumped. A butcherbird cawed. Go back. I pushed through the bracken and briars, arms flailing, tears streaming, nose running. Keep going. Don't stop. Don't stop. Don't stop.

I awoke sobbing, and groped for the corner of my sheet. My baby finger was bleeding from a fresh scratch. Scratched by a dream? I never mentioned it to Mum, and anyway she'd not really kept her promise.

Mum had told me about a promise she'd made. She'd told me a memory that I couldn't remember, but I don't think she told me the whole story. It was something about a postcard.

Click.

Ha! The postcard. 'Postcards play a big role in your life, Katrina.'

'Everyone sends postcards when they're away.'

'Away?'

He's putting me away. Thinks because he knows the facts he knows what's going on. Facts are broken things.

'Where is this going, Katrina?'

'I want to tell my story. I want to see my story up on the screen. Not your sterile documentaries!'

'Sterilely, verily. Very well. Back to you, then.' She was beginning to try my patience. But if it used up the time she still had? I must be fair. At least now. 'The deadline, Katrina.'

Fuck the deadline!

Chapter 12

Growing up, and boys, helped me forget, but tiny pricks would come back, working their way into the path I would take.

When I was twelve, the Fergusons moved in over the road. They had a daughter my age, Jane. When my breasts started to form I knew that I couldn't play at being a boy any more and so stopped wearing t-shirts and shorts and agreed to wear dresses Mum made for me. They had wide skirts that would spin out when I twirled. Jane also wore twirling skirts and when she spun her shiny black hair would spin out, too.

'That's because it's straight,' Jane said. 'I'd love to have blond curly hair like you.'

'But mine doesn't spin out like yours. It just curls even more.'

'It suits you,' Jane said in a grown-up voice as she gave me a smile.

We soon became close friends in the way children living next door to each other sometimes do. Jane would sit on the gas box by her front gate and I would run over, breathless, with the latest 'Guess what?' which would lead us to chat and giggle for hours, only stopping when from across the road Mum called out: '*Essen!*' As time passed we became one world and best friends.

Jane sometimes had trouble when I suddenly had an idea. Like the time I said, 'Let's go to town!' It was during the school holidays; we must have been thirteen going on fourteen. 'We can get dressed up.' Pillbox hats and gloves and low-heeled shoes with matching bags were the thing. We took the suburban train. It was a big outing. We were just going to do the shops, have a snack and take the train home again.

Mondo Cane was playing in an obscure little cinema down from Town Hall station.

'Let's go and see it,' I said.

'But, it's for over eighteen. *Peculiarities of man*, it says, *in various parts of the world.* Heaven knows what sort of film it could be.'

The strange, the unusual, the bizarre... I traced my finger under the words on the poster outside the cinema. 'Don't worry. It would have been banned if it were that bad.'

'But, it's such a small, dark cinema. You've heard those stories about girls getting jabbed in the arm and carried off.'

'Come on. They tell you those stories because they're foreign films. Anyway, how would they carry us off with no one noticing?' I said, trying to block out the picture of a needle coming at me in the dark.

'They'll never let us in,' Jane said.

'Do you want to see it? I know I do. It's worth a try.'

We got in and took our seats in the empty eighth row of the musty cinema.

I kept my eyes open through most of the film, squeezing them shut only once, during the part on self-flagellation in a southern European ritual on imitating Jesus. But I had no problem with the part that made Jane squirm where guests in a New York restaurant picked at glistening insects fried to a crisp and crunched them as if eating the greatest delicacy.

The film lasted longer than we expected. When we came out, night had crept in on the city.

'We're going to cop it,' I said.

At the station ramp, my father sat stony and stiff in the red sedan as we approached. 'Get in the car,' he said. 'You obviously can't be trusted to behave like adults yet.'

We kept our eyes downcast and said nothing. No one would know about our secret visit to the foreign cinema. But, like all secrets, the question somehow came up in the end and I was the one to admit the truth. It proved we weren't kids any more. It also grounded me.

You were getting a handle on secrets, Katrina. Or warming up for something?

She tugs at her earlobe.

I remember that day in 1962. It was the day a black-bordered letter arrived from Vienna to say that my grandmother had died. As if to prove the fact, a black-and-white photo of the old woman in her coffin was included. My parents buried the event in silence. It was also the day my mother told me about the eight East Germans who'd careered in their bus at top speed through the Berlin Wall.

Already then, at thirteen, I wanted to leave Australia. Was it just curiosity for the places in the snippets of news I was fed? Or was it the silence of the white snow on my dead uncle's postcard? I used to have weird dreams. My mother did, too. She told me how, during the war, she had lost her wedding ring and dreamt that Dad had been shot down. Three days later she was relieved to find the ring under the bed.

I had a weird dream about the postcard. There was another one, too, but I couldn't work out the connection.

My uncle was talking to someone invisible. 'You have our whole lives bottled up,' he said. 'I know the law. You can't do that.'

'The law? What law?' A voice echoed. 'Don't be a fool. You yourself were a listener, didn't you say?'

'That's different. It was war. It was the enemy.'

'The enemy? The enemy of the State, I suppose. Haven't you realised, you, the great lawyer, you who got way with so much, that the only enemy of the State is its people? Calm down now. It's all in the past.'

'What a flood of memories, Katrina. And dreams, too.' She ignores me.

Click.

Chapter 13

Many of the dreams I had I forgot the next day, but several came back to me years later. Maybe Mum was right. It had something to do with electricity. Dreams worked better out in the country than in built-up areas, she'd said when she'd told me about the dream she'd had just after she'd married Dad. This was one of the few things from that time that she shared with me.

Dad had been called to the Russian front. One day she lost her gold wedding band. For three days she looked everywhere. And then she found it slipped down behind her horsehair mattress in the 'girl camp'. Later she'd mentioned it to Dad. I don't know if this is true or just wishful thinking. Seems the day Mum lost her ring, Dad was shot down. Then there was Limbo for a day. On the third day, he said he saved his gunner and had swum with him across the Dnieper River. *In the middle of winter.* Hitler gave him a medal. Mum swore it all happened around the same time. But her story had more to do with electricity. Poles were going up everywhere. Even our dead-end road to the bush was bulldozed through. Our place was already changing and so was my world.

'Want to have a snack, a roll on the patio?' I said to Jane as I cradled the telephone to my ear one Saturday in my second year of university.

'Be over in a minute,' she said, and hung up.

Jane worked in an office in the city and was often out with one or other of a succession of boyfriends. I, too, had been caught up, if less wholeheartedly: mine was the tide of anti-Vietnam demonstrations that usually left me with a feeling of not being part of it. I was happiest when immersed in the German Romantics, and the *Sturm und Drang* movement spoke more to me than an anti-war one in the Antipodes. So it was only on the odd Saturday that we found time for one another.

I'd waited till I saw her parents' car drive out onto the street and disappear. Then I moistened three bread rolls and popped them in the oven. I set the small patio table out the back in the sunshine and placed butter, honey, two plates and two glasses on the cross-stitched tablecloth. In the middle I set a cooled bottle of Mateus Rosé. Dad won't notice if I pinch a bottle, I thought. He had a crateful. I was just bringing out the rolls when Jane came running down the drive.

'They're yummy with melting butter and honey,' Jane said. 'I just love your rolls on the patio.' We giggled and sat down in the deckchairs and toasted each other with the cool wine. There was something vaguely decadent about it all.

'As soon as I've finished uni I'm going to Europe,' I said, raising my glass.

'Me too,' Jane said, and raised hers. 'I'm going to London, on a working holiday. We have family there.'

'I've got no family, none that I know. Anyway, they're behind the Iron Curtain.'

'Wonder why they call it the 'iron curtain'.'

'Probably because of the barbed wire,' I said. 'A curtain of barbed wire.' I shuddered. 'What I really want to do is see Vienna and find out more about the place I was born.' And as an afterthought, I added, 'Maybe not just the place.'

'But you don't know anyone there.'

'Doesn't matter. You could come with me. Hey, we could go together. I'd go with you to London and you could go with me to Vienna.'

'But I don't speak German,' Jane said.

'I do. I'll speak for us both.' I sipped the rosé and laughed. 'Can you just see us? Waltzing around by the blue Danube.'

Jane began to laugh. 'What if you meet someone?'

'Meet someone? I'd love to,' I said, and emptied my glass.

'I mean before you go, silly.' Jane bit into the crusty roll. Butter and honey dribbled from her mouth and she wiped it away with her handkerchief.

'You forgot napkins.'

'Sorry. Don't dribble.'

'Bet you won't leave if you meet someone.'

'Bet I will. I won't let any bloke stop me from going.'

'We'll see,' Jane said, and bit into the last piece of roll.

'His name's Jake. Jake Saunders,' I said three months later. 'Electrical engineering, I think. Anyway, some sort of engineering.'

Jane listened. 'Where did you meet him?'

'A party last week.'

'Your uni crowd?'

I nodded. 'They're a great bunch.'

'But you all stick together.'

'Come on, Jane. They're pretty broadminded. Not snobby, anyway.'

Jane shook her head slowly. 'Tell me about Jake, then. Is he nice?'

'You know the thing I've got about red hair, well... And he's tanned under his freckles.'

'Bluey, eh?'

'Oh, no. He's more gorgeous that that. There we all were, horsing around to the Beach Boys when the music slowed down and the lights went low. He'd been watching me since I arrived. But, I didn't let on that I knew.'

I told Jane how Jake had moved closer, then how he had drawn me into his arms. I hadn't resisted. I'd tingled as he held me against his body, swaying, hardly moving in the dark. The music stopped and his lips lingered on my nose. 'Hi,' he'd said. 'I'm Jake.'

'They're only after one thing, you know,' Jane said.

'It wasn't like that. He was so gentle. I'm seeing him on Saturday. He's picking me up.'

'Ooo. Now we are getting close-up and personal.' Just my area of expertise, I must admit.

And that's why I want to tell the story and not leave it in your grubby hands.

'Now, now, Miss Holier Than Thou.'

'You have no idea. I bet you've never even been there.'

'Been there? I am there all the time, my dear Katrina.' Why does she think I was *in* this business? I have certainly had my own moments. And may yet have some more.

Chapter 14

'The People's car is red and black
It has the engine in the back;
It washes clothes and keeps them clean
For it is Hitler's noise machine.'

Jake opened the door of the old VW with a flourish and I laughed. 'I wish you wouldn't sing that silly song, though.'

Jake shrugged.

'No worries.' It probably had something to do with my parents being German, since Austria and Germany bundled up in people's minds. He thought 'New Australians' were funny – not funny ha-ha, but strange in some ways. I suppose he thought I was funny in other ways. I did try to make him feel that he was the only person in the world. But he said it was my eyes. They were brown; nothing funny about that.

He'd say I'd slip into his mind like a wisp, and next thing he knew I was really there. Who's funny?

One Saturday we headed for Bilgola, a beach nestled in the bush below the serpentine coast road. We surfed and swam and laughed and played. And then, exhausted, lying beside him on the sand, I slept. He told me later that it was while watching me sleep that he fell in love with me. My dark blonde hair screened my shoulders from the sun, cloaked my face; only the line of my cheek and my lashes peeped out. Even then he said he'd wondered how long it would take to really get to know me. I sometimes reminded him of a paper-bark tree, he said, with its fine membranes that peeled away to more of the same. Paper-barks were the first to flare when a bushfire raged, but they always survived.

All summer there'd be trips to the beach that at first would end with evening movies; later we'd miss them. The regularity of our outings eased us into a routine my parents either accepted or didn't notice, as long as Jake kept to my midnight curfew.

'They're scared I'll turn into a pumpkin.'

Jake laughed. 'You mean Cinderella?'

I shook my head and pulled at my ear lobe. He said I had a way of turning images on their heads, sometimes leaving him wondering what I really meant.

At lunchtime, whenever our lectures didn't clash, we'd meet outside the library at the end of the wall where the surfboards were propped. We held hands and sometimes kissed.

One day we were out by Pittwater where the water was still

protected by the peninsula. We'd had a picnic lunch and hiked through the bush. Back in the car, Jake said: 'Katrina, why don't we get married?'

'Jake,' was all I said as I grabbed his tousled head and kissed him firmly on the lips. He must have taken it for 'Yes'.

There were other times like the one at Pittwater. He hadn't thought about the future straightaway, he'd said. Only later had he started worrying about me getting pregnant.

'Don't worry, Jake. I'm on the pill.'

His eyes searched my face. 'Since when?'

'Since Pittwater.'

Relief on his face pushed away any twinges. We'd be all right.

We'd been talking about our future and would spend weekends looking at houses – split-level ones in the bush – but discussion soon moved to matters more serious than floor plans.

'The kids; we'll bring them up Catholic,' he said.

'I won't go to church.'

'But, Katrina, what will they think if their mother doesn't go to mass?'

'The convent did it to me. I won't go, Jake.'

Jake never missed Sunday mass, even if it meant popping in at the end in his Bermudas and thongs. His mother was a convert so the family took it seriously, more seriously than most, more seriously it seemed than my own parents.

'I'm finished with all that,' I said.

'What do you mean?'

'You've never had nightmares.'

He should have asked me about them, but my words

seemed to close that subject.

When he mentioned the pill, I just said it was my responsibility. 'Don't worry,' I said. He must have wondered if it was then that he'd started to lose me and he hadn't even noticed. Or was I just being stubborn? And then I'd nuzzle him.

In May when Jake graduated in mortarboard and gown I sat with his proud parents during the ceremony.

'I'd die if I have to get up there on that stage,' I said to him after the ceremony.

'Your graduation's next year.'

'I know I'll die,' I said. And somehow it was then Jake must have felt that I wouldn't be there. He couldn't explain it, he said later. It was just like a bobbing light on the water.

'I'm going when I'm twenty-one anyway,' I'd said. 'I'll just be marking time till then.'

'What do you mean, marking time? Don't you love me?' I didn't answer. Later he said that all he remembered was what I'd said that day out at Pittwater. We were sitting in his car, looking out onto the water. It was late afternoon and a fine rain was falling.

'I have to go, Jake. I've booked a ticket on the *Achille Lauro*. I won't be staying for my graduation.' I looked out of the car window across the water.

Jake turned in his seat. 'But what about us? Our future?'

'I'll come back. But I need to do this. How can I know where I'm going if I don't know where I'm coming from?'

'What's that supposed to mean?'

'I don't know anything about my family.'

'Do you think I do?'

'It's not the same, Jake. You're from here. You know what

your father did during the war.'

He took me in his arms. 'Oh, Katrina,' he whispered and rocked me gently. He hadn't understood, but when I said, 'Will you wait for me?' he'd said 'Yes'. He could get some of his training out of the way, save some money, get ready to settle down. I did love him, and he had faith and he had promised to wait.

Chapter 15

Promises. Promises. We all know where they lead. Jake was not unlike Bettina's Heinrich. A first love. Of course, there wasn't a war, and there was no broken neck. But a broken heart? They hurt, too. They've been known to finish some off.

Katrina is pensive. I will wait for her to resume.

Mum didn't like Jake. A Roman Catholic. An Australian. Oh, yes. It was only after it was all over that she came out and said it. She and Dad wanted me to marry an ambassador – wasn't that it? They were still impressed by titles and station, even in what they saw as egalitarian Australia. But I guess no nation is truly egalitarian, that there are always classes, some just out of reach. Dad's father had made it into Viennese society, and I suppose Dad had wanted to do the same in Sydney. And he did, in his way. He said he did it for Mum and for me. But it was his need. His need to succeed.

'Harald, too, made it in his own way in Spain, Katrina. But they all neglected to consider that when they had their pants down. Ha, the toilet bowl as the great equaliser, be it with a flush or a hose!'

She ignores me. She is full in her mind.

I don't think I ever asked what Jake had really been thinking.

I'd worked and saved for my trip. Before Christmas I did a three-week stint in the ladies' underwear department of David Jones in downtown Sydney.

'Jake, guess what? I can try on a bra for size without getting undressed.'

'Very useful,' he said. 'Specially in winter.' He began to laugh. 'I can just see you in your duffle coat...'

I tousled his head. 'Not me, silly. I try it on the clients.'

'In their coats?' Jake barely avoided my lunge and then caught me. I kissed him quickly.

'All my customers go off with smiles on their faces,' I said.

Had there been hints way back then that he'd never picked up? On weekends I worked in the nearby old folks' home, where I cleaned tables and washed bedpans and bottles.

'I can breathe through the mouth so I don't get the smells.'
I remember telling him that I'd overheard my parents one
day. I'd just come home and they were talking in the kitchen.

'We may as well let her go if she wants to fly so badly,'
Mum said. 'We can't hold her back. Remember you were on
your own two feet much earlier, and so was I. We have to
learn to let go, dear.'

'A whole year before I see my baby again,' Dad said. 'Why
does she rush like this? I won't let her go.'

'Hush, Alfred. She'll hear you. Hush. We rushed to leave.'

'But that was after the war. We wanted to start a new life.'

'Was it just because of the war? We were young.'

I'd left Mum's sentence hanging between us. It was as much
use trying to hold me back as it was holding down a brumby.
I'd have to find my own way. I guess Jake thought it would
be back to him.

'You knew differently, though. Didn't you, Katrina?'

They do say you should let go of those you love. I am
beginning to like this woman. But she seems to have little
respect for Rule 2.

'Rule 2, Katrina. The deadline.'

Don't rush me!

Jake wasn't the only thing on my mind. I still had to wind up
some paperwork at uni, which took me back to my first year
again.

I remember my first day studying German at uni. First of March 1966, the day the German Democratic Republic formally applied for membership of the United Nations. It was raining that day – the day Mum changed.

'What's up, Mum?' I'd said when I came home. Mum was sitting in her rocking chair by the window. Rivulets spread on the pane, holding her gaze in their downward course. She didn't turn to greet me.

'It is official. Now they, the East and the West, will never be one again,' she said. 'I just heard it on the news.'

'Does it matter, Mum?'

'They are one people, Katrina. We have family in the East, in Sibigrode. We may never see them again.'

'I don't know them anyway,' I said.

Mum pressed the back of her hand against her cheek and stared at me.

'I mean, what's family if you don't know them? Why do we have to have countries anyway?' I said.

'It's a part of belonging,' she said. 'We all have a country... somehow.'

'But why can't we just take the Earth and shake it about and sprinkle people all over the place? Then there'd be no problems about who you are and where you come from.'

She sighed. 'Katrina...'

'That way, everyone would be the same.'

'It is not as simple as that.' Her voice was tired. 'You will find that out one day. You will soon be living your own life, you might even leave us, and your father and I will be left alone here.' Mum had always encouraged me to be independent, preparing me for the day she knew I would leave in the same way that she herself had left home. Dad, too, had left home, but that was after the war and his choice had not been altogether free. But his brother, Harald, Harald had stayed. 'You have no other family,' Mum said. 'You will be on your own.'

'What about my uncle?'

'He is dead.'

'So a dead man sent you off on your quest.'

Not just that. I had to go. It was time.

Chapter 16

Standing on deck, straining through a thicket of pink and turquoise streamers and gripping the ship's railing with one hand, I waved to a place in the crowd at the international terminal of Sydney's Circular Quay. The crowd was moving like a massive amoeba that seemed to have swallowed the figures I sought: my parents, my best friend, and the man I had promised to marry, to return to within a year. Tears welled in my eyes, but did not fall. They would surely see me in my shocking-pink top. Mum always told me to wear bright colours. 'They'll help you get noticed.'

I let go of the railing and waved with both arms. I'd never had much trouble being noticed. I was petite with blonde hair that was much longer than it looked, hair that refused to be tamed even when I tried ironing it, which I soon gave up; I never would look like Marianne Faithfull. My first name wasn't as common as Mary or Marianne; Katrina was an uncommon name in Australia back then, and my surname always drew interest. Klain with an 'a'. Yes, that's how you spell it. No, it doesn't mean 'small'. But that was soon to be behind me. I was nineteen, I was leaving Australia, my name was my name, and...*basta!*

As the ship pulled away from Circular Quay, the streamers breaking the last link between passengers and loved ones, I wiped my eyes and let out a long breath. At sixteen I'd already wanted to go to Austria. For a holiday. Promises. Promises. So I worked for it, saved for it. And I paid for it, so now I was the one to decide. I couldn't have waited another year for Jane to be twenty-one and go with me. At midnight I still stood at the railing in the flood of the moon. For a moment I thought that the man living there had winked at me. I winked back. It was 17th February 1969 and I was on my way at last.

A year away was all I wanted, but standing on the deck with the wind in my hair, smelling the salty taste of freedom, I knew that a year wouldn't be enough. For what, though, I didn't know. I took out a cigarette and backed into a sheltered alcove by the door. A hand suddenly appeared. Click. A flame. I turned around and with a cupped hand shielded the flame with just the most cursory of glances at the hand's owner. I drew on the Dunhill. I remember saying 'thank you' and the gist of the first conversation with a stranger who was to anchor this voyage in my mind.

'*Prego.* You going to England?'

I shook my head. 'Genoa.'

'Ah. Where is your cabin?'

I laughed. I had the perfect protection. 'Lower deck. Third class.'

'You are sharing with other ladies?'

'I guess you could call them that.'

I thought of how I had stood at the cabin door with my three new white suitcases. 'It gets very cold in Vienna,' Mum had said. 'And it's an elegant city.' I'd packed the three formals Mum had made for a twenty-first birthday and two university balls.

Two of the 'ladies' were already in the cabin. One sat all in black on a lower bunk, feeding the beads of her rosary through her fingers and rocking to and fro. The other sat upright on the other bunk. She wore a black scarf over her head, knotted under her chin. She hummed in a keening sort of way. Just as I began stowing my suitcases under the bunks, the third woman entered the cabin.

'Let me know if anything is in the way,' I said.

The woman wore a black woollen hat pulled deep onto her face. She blinked slowly and then pursed her lips. All three reminded me of my grandmother.

That night I woke to the sound of dry retching. My hair was damp from perspiration and the ragged remnants of a dream. *My grandmother. Dressed in black. Poking at me through my mothers' belly.* Then an old woman groaned. She was retching. I jumped up, grabbed the plastic white bucket from its holder on the wall. Just in time. The woman raised heavy lids and wiped her mouth with a large cotton handkerchief. She nodded and slumped back, leaving me holding the bucket.

Shit! I thought. This is only the first night. Six weeks of this will drive me crazy.

This was to be the last voyage of the *Achille Lauro* as a transcontinental liner and a migrant ship. The grandmothers spoke separate languages and did not understand me, nor, I suspected, did they understand each other. Southern. Eastern European. Like my own grandmother, born in Trieste? It didn't matter. There were enough other things to do on a six-week sea voyage.

The crew was giving Italian lessons and I signed up. I also signed up to be in a dance troupe for the musical *Can-Can*. Not that I was such a good dancer; it was more the purser, Pietro, who was very persuasive with his passion for choreography. He strutted on deck and pointed a finger at each one of us in turn.

'You. You. You and you! You shall do the wheel.' We looked at each other and raised our eyebrows. 'The cartwheel. Can-Can! *Avanti!*'

I'd never done a cartwheel before and the prospect of doing it out there on deck and seeing myself fly overboard was daunting, but since it wasn't as if I were going anywhere else, I said: 'I'll give it a go.'

'Go!' Pietro said and leaned back with his large tanned hands on his hips.

I stretched my arms out before me and did a little hop. Then I closed my eyes and careened through the air, landing almost with both feet at once, feeling a warm firm hand in the small of my back, steadying me, a voice saying '*Brava!*'

I had done my first cartwheel. I had done the impossible. Pietro grinned at me and kissed me on each cheek. I met him later at the bar, and drank Blue Horizons. The iced water was free and kept my head steady. Anyway, I couldn't afford to spend money on drinks and didn't want to have them paid. There was no such thing as that clichéd free lunch.

'I hope I didn't scare you the other night,' he said.

'It was a bit spooky the way you just disappeared.'

Pietro laughed. 'There's a service door in the alcove. I thought I was coming on a bit too...'

'Italian?'

'Ah. Reputations. They are, how do you say, killers? But you looked so lost, so alone.'

'I wasn't alone. I had the grandmothers,' I said.

Pietro rolled his eyes. 'Depressing,' he said, and pushed a tumbler of ice cubes and water towards me.

I looked round the bar. Three or four seats were taken. Through the swing doors men and women lounged on settees. 'The mood's a bit, too. Will it go on like this for the whole trip?'

'That's why we try and arrange things to occupy the passengers, at least the young ones. If they're doing something, the older ones can watch.' Pietro leaned back and stretched out his legs. 'On the way out, we hardly have to do anything to get things moving.'

'You mean out to Australia?'

Pietro nodded. 'Outbound was towards a new life. Dreams. Hopes.'

'That's how I feel. I feel as if I'm about to start a new life.'

'You and a few others feel that way. But the rest of the passengers on this trip are going back to Europe. They've either left family behind or been disappointed. Some are torn between continents. Others have failed.'

It must be hard going home as a failure, I thought. I swore that was something I'd never do. 'Where is your home?'

'Italia, of course,' Pietro said, and snapped his fingers. 'Trieste, Italia. And you?'

Trieste? I stared at him. Then shook my head. It was not a question I had ever asked myself. 'Does it matter?'

'I think it does,' he said. 'Where were you born?'

'Vienna.'

'Ah, Austria. We are from the same Empire if not the same country.'

Crikey, I thought. My grandmother was from Trieste, the last port of the Austro-Hungarian Empire. 'That was ages ago.'

'That you should know this? *Brava!* His eyes mocked me.

'I studied German,' I said. 'Mostly literature, but I do know something about the countries I'm going to see.'

'*Scusi.* So when did you come to Australia?'

'I was a child. Maybe 1950 or 51.'

'So, after the war.'

'Yes. Why?'

Pietro shook his head. 'You lived in Vienna?'

'I think so. What is this? What are you trying to say? I'm not German, if that's what you mean. I'm Australian. We didn't speak German at home.'

'Calm down. I'm Italian. Everything was either German or not during the war, and even a bit after. What was Germany then? What is it now?'

I felt suddenly hot. I grabbed my glass and drank some of the ice water. 'I'd like something stronger,' I said.

'Of course. Gin and tonic?'

I nodded.

'Have I touched a nerve?'

I shook my head.

'I told you the trip back to Europe was depressing.'

'It's not that,' I said. 'It's that when people hear where I was born and when we left Austria, they always clam up. It's as if they're doing some mental arithmetic. All immigrants before the end of the war were Jews; all those straight after must therefore be...'

'Nazis?'

'Well, it's not true.'

'Probably not,' Pietro said. '*Chin chin.*' He raised his glass and looked me in the eye. 'So why do you care?'

Between Fremantle and Cape Town there was nothing but water. Ten days of it. On the last three nights of those ten days, Pietro's troupe performed the Can-Can in First Class and I graduated from a Blue Horizon in the tourist bar to Grappa in the purser's cabin. But his words kept ringing in my head. *Why do you care?*

'Is not this the crux of the matter, Katrina? Why do you care?'

She purses her lips and interlocks her fingers, a residue of her convent-day prayers.

I turned twenty in Cape Town. Pietro had to stay on board ship so I went on land with three of the other passengers, all in their twenties: two Italians who'd been crocodile-hunting up north and an English girl, Jessica, getting off at Southampton. The buses were marked Whites up front, Non-Whites behind, so we sat at the back of the bus and headed for Bantry Bay. I don't know why any more. Perhaps it was to see Lion's Head, or the Darwin plaque, but all I still remember is a middle-aged woman with diamonds sparkling at her throat strolling the beach promenade. The way she looked at us gave me a distinct feeling of apartheid.

My German professor back in Sydney had come to Australia from South Africa shortly after one of his students had committed suicide. A few years later, a friend from Vienna was arrested for embracing a black African woman. He fled the country before his trial, but his hair went prematurely grey. The Australian surfers with their board bumps stayed on in Cape Town for the good waves.

Why do you care?

We farewelled Jessica in Southampton, and in Genoa the Italians and I went our separate ways. I took a slow train to Vienna via the snow peaks on that postcard that had seduced me when I was sixteen, when I first wanted to go to Austria and my parents said I was still far too young.

PART TWO

INFLIGHT PANOPTICON

II

Chapter 17

Katrina Klain

I arrived in Vienna in the early European spring of recently melted snow still clinging in muddy clumps to city gutters. I took up lodgings in Pension Czernik.

'We are a small hotel with five simple rooms, and the toilets and bathroom are at the end of the corridor,' the woman at the reception desk said. She was well past middle age, with a sad horsey face and her grey hair pulled back in a bun. She wore pale-blue sleeve protectors and a loose floral pinafore that revealed a white *dirndl* blouse caught at the neck by a deep blood-red brooch.

'Each room is named after a composer; yours will be the Beethoven room. You may leave your luggage here until the room is ready,' she said.

'Frau Czernik?' I said.

'Brauer,' she answered. 'Czernik was my maiden name.

You have your own key. That will be one month in advance. You also have to fill out these papers for the police.'

'The police?' I said. No one registered with the police in Australia.

'It is the law. Within three days you must do it. At every place you stay.'

I took the beige forms and walked the two floors to my room. It was small with a sink in the corner, opposite a bed and an old-fashioned cupboard. A small wooden table and two chairs were by the window. There were square white cushions between the double windowpanes as extra insulation. It would do, I thought as I sat down on the bed and unfolded my map of Vienna.

I couldn't afford more, but I'd also picked Pension Czernik because of its location in the Josefstädterstraße, just round the corner from the town hall, the Rathaus. (I'd wondered about the rats for a moment, but then remembered that *rat* meant counsel or advice, so it figured.) The pension was also three blocks down from the address my mother had given me – the address where our family had lived before going to Australia. I imagined that the flat had long since been sold, at least since the death of my grandmother several years earlier. I didn't know if I wanted to find out who lived there, or if they remembered my grandmother. Now that I was in Vienna at last, there didn't seem to be the same hurry. There were other things to do. Things like getting my details ready for police registration. That had to be done within three days.

With a finger I traced the road to the city, down to the Ring by the Parliament building, on to the State Opera House and down to the Graben. At Saint Stephen's Cathedral I stopped and knew it couldn't be far to Elisabethstraße and the

Gösserhof. I folded the map, wondering if I would recognise the sketched buildings.

I'd never been all by myself before. Once the papers were done I could do what I wanted, go where I wanted. I fell in love with Kärtnerstraße with its stylish boutiques and cosy cafés, the elegance of the Graben in the shadows of St. Stephen's spires, reaching down to cloak the city centre. I'd spend hours in the Volksgarten, sipping coffee and scribbling in my notebook.

Every day I'd pass 20 Josefstädterstraße and look up at the first floor. There was never a light on, and the windows were always closed and looked as if they hadn't been cleaned for years. There's still plenty of time before I go up there, I thought. And so I pushed the practicalities of my quest aside, preferring to meander about in the city.

On rainy days, I'd sit in the underground Kärtner Café, where escalators converged, and drink strong coffee with thick cream. I'd write in my notebook, playing with words, trying to paint poems.

It's not that it matters
if there's a pot at all
to hold the earth.

I'd drink glass after glass of the water they served with the coffee. It was the best in the world, they said. It came straight and pure from the mountains.

Is it the clump that counts?
the water? for the roots?

And the tumbleweed?

I'd watch commuters bustle to and from the heart along the city's buried arteries. Something was missing in the poem. A tumbleweed had no roots. And what about the wind?

'*Gestatten?*

I looked up.

'May I?' said the man. He was in his thirties, I thought, clean-shaven and wore a dark-blue suit. His eyes were strangely intense, his hair was short and spiky and not unlike the porcupine dolls sold in the tourist shops.

I closed my notebook and nodded that he might sit.

'*Ein grosser Brauner*,' he said to the waitress in toe-peepers laced to the ankle, the shoes I'd seen all the waitresses wear.

'What are you writing? *Entschuldigen*, sorry. My name is Fritz. Fritz Brauer.'

'My name's Katrina...Klain.' I lowered my eyes and fiddled with my notebook. Why did I say that? Habit? The waitress arrived with a steaming cup of coffee and I stole another look at the man as he glanced to the waitress rummaging in the money pouch at her waist, half-hidden by a tiny white cotton apron. He looked pleasant enough, very sure of himself.

'You are English?'

'Australian.' I could say that so easily. 'Are you Viennese?' I said quickly, and brushed imaginary fluff from my red pleated skirt and uncrossed my legs.

'Yes. The real thing.' A smile creased his mouth. 'I have noticed you when I pass through here.'

'Oh?' I'd always been so deep in my scribbles, trying to form them into poems. I crossed my legs and looked him straight in the eye.

'Are you writing a diary?'

'No. Poems.' I brushed a wisp of hair from my forehead and tucked it behind my left ear with my little finger. No one before had been interested in my poetry. Well, I had never written out in the open. I tugged at my earlobe.

'What about?' His gaze held mine, and as he smiled, the corners of his eyes crinkled.

I looked down to my notebook. I uncrossed my legs to find a more comfortable position. 'My impressions of Vienna.'

He finished his coffee and interlocked his long slim fingers on the table before me. I was about to say how the city appealed to me when he looked at his watch: 'Katrina, I am sorry. I must leave now. May I drop by again, to speak about your poetry? Give you some impressions of Vienna, from the, – how do you say? – the horse's mouth?'

'With pleasure,' I said, and almost stood as he got up to leave.

Fritz held out his hand and I shook it. His hand was warm and firm.

It did not linger. I resisted turning my head to watch him walk away.

Then I called the waitress.

'*Ein grosser Brauner, bitte.*'

I went to the Kärtner Café every afternoon of the next week. It hadn't rained for days. On Friday, I sat in my usual place, opened my notebook and stared at passers-by. When the waitress brought me coffee, I had only written the date. My words had dried up as if my eyes had sapped my energy searching for Fritz.

'How quickly you have forgotten your Jake,' I say.

'Oh, shut up. I was young. On another plane.'

It was getting dark as I left the café for my room. As usual, I shunned the red trams on the Ringstraße to walk by the Opern Kino. It was the only one playing English films, with German subtitles, a far cry from *Mondo Cane* with Jane. I glanced at the posters for *Easy Rider*, thought for a minute of going in, but kept on walking. I didn't want to sit alone in the dark seats. Maybe I'll bump into him, I thought. I rounded the Parliament with its Greek columns and statues pointing down at me with their gilt fingers, and strode past the Renaissance Natural History Museum on to the Gothic Rathaus. I didn't realise that in fifteen minutes I had passed through three ages of architecture. When I got to the Town Hall, I crossed narrow streets until I arrived at the door of Pension Czernik.

The wooden hall floor smelled of wax scoured with ammonia. I entered the Beethoven room. It was musty and I opened the double single-paned windows between which I kept some fruit and mineral water. It was still cold on the ledge between the outer and inner windows. I kicked off my shoes and flopped onto the bed.

'On Monday I'm looking for a job,' I said to Beethoven's bust on the dresser. 'You're right,' I said to the deaf head. 'I am hungry.' I washed my hands, rinsed my face and patted it dry, then grimaced at myself in the mirror above the white enamel washbasin in the corner of the room. 'They could have put a loo and a shower in,' I said aloud as I turned on the two-row square of tiles beneath the basin.

I nodded goodbye to Beethoven and pulled the door shut. I took the staircase, ignoring the wrought-iron lift, and slipped through the smaller door inlaid in the massive house portal.

Half a block down the road, lamps glowed through the glass-blown windows of the Hirtenwirt. The Gasthaus door held a menu in German and English. Wiener Schnitzel, that's what I'll have. I pushed aside the heavy curtain still hanging over the door against the draught. I saw an empty table for two at the far end of the room and made my way to the seat that would put my back against the wall. The wood panelling, with its ledges of country-patterned plates just above my head, felt comforting.

'*Sie wünschen, Fräulein?*' the waiter said.

'*Wiener Schnitzel und Wein, bitte.*'

'*Weiß?*'

'Yes, white.' I didn't touch the sliced black bread in the basket on the table. Every slice would add a *schilling* to my bill. And the bread would spoil my appetite. Apart from breakfast, I realised that I'd only had coffee all day.

The waiter brought breaded veal and I squeezed lemon over it, flicking the decorative anchovy roll aside with my knife.

'Try it with a mixed salad, Katrina.'

I jerked my head up and my eyes met Fritz's.

'I am sorry if I startled you. I looked for you this afternoon.'

'Hallo Fritz.' I concentrated on cutting the meat.

He eased his long body into the chair opposite me. His hair stood on end as if electrified. His eyes widened, drawing my gaze to his. 'I have been caught up in a number of things, with the agency. I think I told you I dealt in art photos, aesthetics – that sort of thing.'

I looked up. 'How did you know I was here?'

Fritz stared at me. 'You do not like riding trams, do you?'

A tiny shiver ran through me.

'I followed you,' Fritz said, a smile cruising his lips. 'And now that I have found you...would you be free on Sunday? I would like to take you to an exhibition.'

Silently I sipped my wine and steadied my gaze. 'Of your photos? I mean, the ones for the agency?' I hesitated on the word 'agency' and imagined a CIA agent, hat at an angle, collar turned up.

'No. Schiele. Egon Schiele.'

'A photographer?'

'An Austrian painter. He died in 1918.'

'I've never heard of him. So he's not modern?'

'He is, in a way. Shocking even; then and now.' Fritz smiled. 'So, will you come?'

'Shocking?' Something worse than the CIA?

'You shall see. I shall pick you up at eleven, we can have a bite to eat and then go to the Belvedere.'

'The Belvedere?' The palace art gallery. 'But you don't know where I live,' I said.

'So are you going to tell me?'

I hesitated. 'Pension Czernik,' I said. 'Josefstädterstraße. You can ask for me in the reception. I'm in the Beethoven room.' I wondered what Beethoven would say. I smiled at the thought. I'd have to shout.

As Fritz rose I thought he was about to wink, but his eyelid did not move. 'Sunday then. Enjoy the mixed salad.'

I stared after him as he left the restaurant, turning once more to wave before he passed through the heavy curtain. What had I got myself into this time? Sunday. Fritz. Egon Schiele. Suddenly my mother's words flashed across my mind. 'Never trust your own countryman abroad.' Was Fritz a countryman? Was this abroad?

I finished my Schnitzel and called the waiter. *'Bezahlen bitte, Herr Ober.* I'll just wait and see what happens. Why did I leave home anyway? 'Home' was becoming a word I was finding harder and harder to define.

On my way back to the pension, I saw a light glowing in one of the rooms of 20 Josefstädterstraße.

'The CIA, Katrina? You seem to like watching old films. The next ones will be starring you, methinks.'

Ha ha.

'And what an idea. Shouting at Beethoven.'

No worse than shouting at a disembodied voice.

'Now, now.'

Chapter 18

Harald Klain

20 Josefstädterstraße. We had certainly come down in the world, I must say. A long way down since the Gösserhof when my father was still alive. That was before the war. My brother, Alfred, was away in London on a hotel exchange. The other half of the exchange was Kenneth Browning, tall, lanky, a Jew who became the closest friend I ever had. It was a friendship of no strings and just being. Only later did I find out that Alfred had fallen in love with Kenneth's older sister, Agnes. We Klain boys certainly had a thing for older women it seems.

It may have had to do with our old governess – we called her *Fräulein*; she looked after us while Mama attended to her many tasks by Father's side, and later, replaced him.

Mama was a good mother in that she loved us. We knew because each night on returning home from her patronly duties in the various restaurants and the hotel, and before going to bed, she would take Alfred and me in her arms and tell us she loved us. It always broke our sleep, but at least she had been there. Even after Father's death, when we moved to the 8th district and our last flat in the Josefstädterstraße, she was there for us. Well, for me, since Alfred had gone to Australia and baby Fritz never returned from Russia.

Yes, I promised to find him and did all I could with the Red Cross. To no avail, despite the fact that I had become an influential lawyer with access to information and ways of subverting the *Amtsweg*, that farce of Austrian bureaucracy. Fritz is either dead or has lived happily ever after with a new identity. Priests were not safe anywhere, so he probably went into marketing. Father wanted him to look after that side of the business, but Mama had promised him to the Church, God knows why. I sometimes wondered what deals she had made with Him in her incessant and secretive praying.

Yes, I loved my mother. I think she was one of the first women whom I admired and at the same time saw through. I learned a great deal from observing her. The way she dressed. Her demeanour as the wife of a *Kommerzialrat. Frau Kommerzialrat.* Ah, Austria and her titles. The only thing I could never work out about her, at least not until I received Bettina's postcard from the ship, was her secretive praying. Not the prayers on show in St Stephen's Cathedral, but the ones in the dark corners of our rooms, the pretence of having dropped something and looking for it on hands and knees. But apart from that I learned to watch women.

Even after I was exiled and that horrible court case dragged her with me through the local press, I loved to observe women. I was rarely wrong. Ha. Just the one time

when I was sneaking back into Austria to tie up some loose
ends.

***

I was sitting in the first-class compartment of the Wiener
Waltzer, the fast train from Zurich to Vienna. I adjusted my
rimless monocle in my left eye and inserted a Du Maurier
cigarette into my short ivory cigarette holder. I enjoyed
being aware of my actions in slow motion. I did not look up
as a young woman sat down opposite me, but continued to
turn my cigarette slowly until it was firmly clenched in the
holder. I had caught sight of her on the platform just before
she boarded the train.

She was in her late twenties, I thought, and let my senses be
guided by sounds and the scent of her. Fruity, but with a hint
of musk. A woman with a sense of humour perhaps, a sense
of life, even seduction. I heard an almost imperceptible swish
as she smoothed the skirt of her dress towards her knees. It
was as if I were sensing the movement of long legs crossing.
Silk, I thought. Raw silk. It did not slither like satin. I would
ignore her. Bide my time. Wait for the moment when she
rummaged in her leather handbag. Without looking I sensed
the bag as a shadow beyond my vision. Crocodile. She was
a thoroughbred, of that I was sure. But I could wait a little
excruciating while longer. I had tested it often. She would
soon begin wondering if something were wrong. Take out a
compact. Survey her face. Perhaps even put on some lipstick.
And just when she was at her most doubting, just when she
felt vulnerable, that was when... It never failed.

I placed my unlit cigarette on the tablet attached to the

window and looked out at the water of Lake Constance glittering in the late afternoon sun. My indirect vision took in dark hair. There was something in the air. I could smell it. Not a scent, but a movement. How often had I felt what must have been the animal trepidation of a helpless prey. But neither this woman, nor any of those I had loved, or tried to, had ever been helpless.

The woman slipped a hand into her bag and pulled out a compact. I could feel her eyes surveying me above the mirror. Snap. She put it away.

I reached for my cigarette and brought the mouthpiece to my lips. Then I hesitated and looked straight at the young woman. Her eyes were dark brown. Wide. Open. Their velvet depth, I imagined, was due to her dilated pupils. 'Cigarette?' I said and held out the pack of Du Maurier.

'Thank you,' she said and drew the cigarette to her lips.

The flame of my lighter arced from the woman back to my own cigarette. The woman exhaled and looked out of the window.

'Are you travelling far?' I asked.

'No,' she said. 'Just to Buchs.'

I nodded. Too bad. No point going further.

When the woman alighted, I sat back in my seat. Yes, for the most part women were strong. Never the prey. At least never the women to whom I had been – and was still – attracted. The helpless prey I had seen from another angle. I felt a sudden cramp in my right leg. Had to stretch it. Ah. Ah. Yes. My brother.

My brother had been helpless. Helpless, despite his bravado. I drew on my cigarette and let my mind wander. Back. Back to the war years. Back to a scene etched in my mind as one of the forks in the road of my life. Back to when my brother Alfred had struck me. Fight the cramp. Watch the films of my life.

Fade out.
Fade in.

The brothers, both in uniform. We stand in the small alcove leading into the Gösserhof. Alfred wears the uniform of the *Luftwaffe*, I, that of a simple soldier. Neither has a cap on. The lights are low so that we appear to be alone in a fuzz of grey and gold.

'He can't win,' I say, staring at my brother's Iron Cross pinned above his breast pocket. The dull metal glows against the grey of his uniform. I lean forward slightly as if to inspect the medal just as the back of Alfred's hand crushes my cheek. 'That's treason!'

My feet are anchored to the wooden floor of the alcove as I sway like the reeds in the Neusiedel Lake, pliable enough to survive any onslaught, any storm. Even my brother's. My face boils from the proud heat that glows back at me from Alfred's medal. Then, as if timed to finish with the end of the film clip, Alfred Klain marches out the door.

Fade out.

And I? I just stopped marching.

The train screeched to a halt and I sat up straight. Although the woman was gone, a vague scent still lingered. I had seen many like her. Thoroughbreds. Elegant. Just like the ones the other evening at the Duke of Avaron's. Skorzeny had been there. I had heard much about him. A likely candidate, I thought. I always marvelled at how many likely candidates there were in Madrid. Not just exiles like myself, like Stanko and Monique. Displaced royalty. Ex-Nazis. I had to laugh. It was a short, rasping cough of a laugh. The realisation worries me just a moment. The irony of it all. I found that most appealing. The ultimate revenge in a way, and so simple. How we forget how much preparation there is for things that seem so simple, so artless. And then there was timing, and luck. I stubbed out my cigarette and pulled the butt from the ivory holder. One made one's own luck, I had learned. If one were vigilant, flexible.

As the train approached the border I pulled out my passport and flicked it open. *Republik Österreich.* I looked at the photo of a blond man with high cheekbones. I had gone so far with this face. No need to change now. When the uniformed border policeman came through the carriage and stopped by my side, I held out my passport. Done.

The drone of the train's wheels had a hypnotic effect as I thought back over the life that was now once again bringing me to Vienna. It had been ten years since the embezzlement scandal had been in the news and had made me flee Austria. Ten years of lying low in Spain. Not that the lifestyle with Stanko and Monique could be considered anything remotely like low. The penthouse flat in the Avenida de America also had my name on the door. Just like it had been in Vienna when I joined the legal offices of Monika Zorko; she was Monika then, when I first met her. Only later, when she and Stanko fled Austria, did she call herself Monique. But that was later.

When I finished my studies I swore I would not work for a man. Men with power had always disappointed me. What had my father done before the war? My brother? Alfred had bet on the wrong horse, but how many had he taken with him in that belief? No. If I had to work for anyone, then it would be for a woman. I knew all about women. There had been the ones running after me, asking whether they pleased me. I thought back to one of my answers, back in the Fifties, before I, too, had to leave so precipitously.

'Do you love me?' the woman had said. She was the wife of a big Viennese businessman I had wanted to approach for the deal of a lifetime. But I had already made the first contacts and no longer needed the wife as a way to her husband. I had the man in the palm of my hand. Amazing how easily greed can make things work out.

'Your breasts are too small,' I said. When the woman came back three months later after having begged her husband to pay for plastic surgery in a clinic in Switzerland and said, 'Do you love me now? I've had my breasts enlarged,' I answered that I hadn't told her she should do anything about her breasts and that love had not been the question. The woman was mortified. I just shrugged and then whispered, 'You know you can't afford a scandal, my dear.' With that I knew the woman would content herself with my lips on her forehead and a caress of her newly plump breasts.

Monika Zorko, however, was a very different matter. Her breasts were naturally well-formed. I smiled as I thought of the way her crêpe de chine crossover blouse would afford the glimpse of a perfectly peaked nipple when she chose to lean forward. Monika had a brain and a body. She was also safely married to a bull of a man who kept in the background. It was Stanko who financed her legal offices even then. I suspected that certain deals had been struck, but that did not deter me. Had I not myself achieved recognition as the brilliant young lawyer who was able to get a murderer sprung free? Yes. The mind games. That's what I loved. And Monika Zorko certainly loved to play.

I'd met her when I'd finished my first year of law studies at Vienna University. She'd been hunting for prospects and had sat in on some of the lectures. I couldn't help staring at the petite woman with the dainty black-veiled hat. A red fur was flung about her and the fox heads resting over her shoulders gave me the feeling that this woman had eyes in the back of her head. She sat to my right a few rows ahead, her shapely legs crossed and reaching out into the aisle. Once or twice she turned and surveyed me. Then slowly looked back, leaving the eyes of the foxes upon me.

Then she was gone. I continued my studies. War was declared. War. The hell of it. The hell of it breaking my life, my career. I had already lost my first and only real friend. Kenneth Browning, thank God, had got back to England before things got hot. I had felt it coming. So had Papa. He had known.

Many had known and had kept silent, safe in their privileged delusion of not being targeted. But they were, in the end, were they not? We were caught in our complicity.

Oh, you might say, it was war and there was no choice. But there is always a choice. One just had to be clever about it.

My brother thought I had deserted. I am not a coward! Not then. Not now. I had always worked the system to be in the right place at the right time, or to avoid being in the wrong one. A last-ditch effort on French soil was perfect for being unable to keep up and thus falling into 'enemy' hands. How could I think the British the enemy when my dearest, my only real friend, was an English Jew?

I was brought to Ganger Camp in Romsey, and at the end of the war I wrote to Kenneth Browning from there, hoping for a visit from him. I had sent him a map of where we might meet. But I received no answer. It was understandable, of course. But the ongoing silence until my release in late 1946 was worse than his having fallen in the war at German hands. His silence broke my faith in friendship, and yes, perhaps even in love.

It was only when I came back to Vienna from the prison camp in England and started to pick up the pieces, and met my brother's wife, Bettina – ah, Bettina – that life seemed to hold the glimmer of some future for me. But what kind of future? The women I wanted always belonged to someone else. Was that what made me hunger for them? The unattainable? Or was it trying to succeed in the impossible, prove that the rules were wrong? Prove I could win against all odds? Just like now.

It was dangerous to come back to Vienna under my real name, with my own passport. But with luck nobody would be on the lookout for me just yet. Mama was dying. They would expect me later, at her funeral. Not now. No one would expect me now. I could also use the visit to secure any papers that were still left at my lawyer's office. I, who had been the brilliant young lawyer, then defrocked like an errant priest, thrown out of the guild, I, Dr Harald Klain, now still needed my own lawyer. Well, this probably would be the last visit to Vienna. But one never knew. There was the thrill of it, like working without a net; I still craved that thrill.

As the train pulled into the Westbahnhof, I slipped into my brown trench coat and swung my leather overnight bag down from the rack. On the platform I lit a cigarette and then strode in the direction of Mariahilferstraße, where I took a tram to the Ring. It was risky, but I would push my luck further and take a room near our old family flat in the Josefstädterstraße.

***

'Do you have a room for a week or so?' I said to the woman at the reception of the Pension Czernik. She was in her early forties, the best age for a woman, a bit stiff for her age, perhaps. Neglected by her husband, if she had one, or perhaps an old maid.

'Yes,' she said as she opened a large exercise book. 'Until the middle of next month. But it is the only one left,' she added quickly.

I surveyed her. I noticed how her eyes dropped to the book and then flickered back up to my face. 'Is there a Herr...?'

'Brauer,' she said. 'Not any more.' As an afterthought she added, 'Only my....' And stopped.

'I'm sorry,' Harald said. Another victim of the war, I thought. Not the dead, not the maimed in body and mind, but those who lived on by the sides of returned and broken shells, of ghosts from the past; whether the return of long absent husbands, lovers, friends was welcome or not, those who lived on were the real victims. These victims carried with them the real nightmares that could surface any time, any place – for it was they who would never truly understand what it was like to come back, or not, what it was like to be sent out to kill, to live a feeling of righteous power that was all-engulfing with the pull of a trigger, a gun aimed at the heart, or the pumping of a spray of bullets into a bloody garden of bodies. The real victims would never understand, and their suffering would reside in the doubt of not knowing, their hearts seeing, yet their minds incapable of understanding.

My eyes flashed. I knew they flashed, I could feel the heat burning from inside. And I knew Frau Brauer had seen. 'I will take it,' I said.

'Don't you want to know how much?' she said.

'I know how much.' I know how much this has cost you, I thought and stared past her into another world.

'Herr...'

'Herr Doktor. Herr Doktor Klain. Harald Klain,' I said, and took her limp hand and let my lips hover above it. I withdrew my hand. Frau Brauer was trembling. Without a word she turned and took down a key and handed it to me.

'Here are the papers. Please fill them out. At your leisure,' she added. 'At your leisure, Herr Doktor.'

I nodded. 'Will you show me my room?'

The next time in Vienna, should there be one, I would go back to the flat. Not hide in a pension. Go back to 20 Josefstädterstraße.

Chapter 19

Katrina Klain

It was not yet nine in the evening when all the heavy main doors of the old apartment houses were locked. I pushed open the smaller in-laid entrance door, a door within a door within a portal frame and stepped into a large stone-walled foyer. Letterboxes were suspended in rows – three for each floor – all had names in copperplate against the numerals: on the first floor, No 4, Hrdlicka; No 6 was Trautmann. There was no name against No 5. I looked up the curving staircase and went up. On the landing no light came through the panes of Nos 4 and 6. A yellow glow came from the third flat at No 5. I looked from one door to the other and then knocked firmly on the pane of No 5. No answer.

I was about to turn away and go back down the stairs when I heard keys jangling and the sound of a bolt being pulled back. I stood waiting. The door opened slowly and a small dark figure blocked any further view.

'*Ja? Was wollen Sie?*

The old woman was shorter than I was and her head was slightly bowed. Her grey hair was pulled back from her face. A chain prevented the door being opened further. A long grey apron covered long dark skirts, but she was not quite thin enough to be taken for a wicked witch.

'*Entschuldigen,*' I said. 'I saw the light. Is this where the Klains used to live?'

The woman closed the door. A rattling. Then she opened it again.

Wider. The chain dangled from the doorway.

'*Wer bist Du?*

'My name is Katrina Klain. I think my grandmother used to live here.'

'There is no Klain here,' the old woman said and began to close the door.

'*Bitte.* I know that. I just wanted...'

'*Morgen. Drei Uhr,*' the woman said and closed the door. Then the light in No 5 went out.

Tomorrow? Three pm? Tomorrow was Saturday. I skipped down the stairs and ran back to the pension. How would I ever get to sleep? Tomorrow at three.

Shops in Vienna closed at noon on Saturday. I tried to focus my thoughts and made a list of the things I needed. Teabags. Milk. Butter. Cheese. Apples. The fresh goods I put in an enamel bowl on the floor by the window. At night I would put them on the windowsill.

The afternoon sun shone as I meandered down

Josefstädterstraße, stopping to look into every shop window. Groceries. Plastic bathroom goods. Children's wear. *Tabak-Trafik*. I laughed. Tobacco traffic. That was where they sold cigarettes, newspapers, and bus and tram tickets.

I still arrived five minutes early.

I pressed the brass button on door No. 5. There was no answer. The doorbell was stuck. Bloody hell. Might've known this wouldn't be straightforward. I knocked on the frosted glass. No answer. As my knuckles again struck the pane, the door clicked open. Strange. Is everyone who lives in the heart of Vienna that trusting? It certainly wasn't the case yesterday. There must be somebody there. 'Hallo?' I said. No answer. Great. I pushed gently, entered a hallway and sniffed. It was dark and smelt of damp bundled clothes trying to dry. A corridor hinted at light. Here goes. I followed. More light. Keep going, Katrina. I entered a large empty room. Dust motes jumbling in a shaft of light from an open window. The clanking of a tram bell. The ceiling was high and decorated with white stucco. In a corner a man was standing on his head.

He was upside-down still and the cuffs of his trousers dipped forward. A narrow black tie hung over his nose and chin and his head rested on what looked like a folded jacket. His eyes were closed but his eyelids flickered. What...? Was he meditating? Can you meditate standing on your head? And what was I supposed to do now? I waited in the doorway and stared at him. It felt like ages but I'm sure I saw his eyelids flicker and then clamp shut again. Was he checking me out? He stood stiff like aluminium tubing and his breath whined like a faint wind through hollow scaffolding. Then his legs wavered and his feet dropped to the floor. He straightened himself up, adjusted his belt, and as he passed a palm over his ash-blond hair, I could've sworn that I heard the faint click of heels.

He shook out his jacket and took something out of his pocket. Then he scrunched his face up. A blue eye fixed me through the rimless glass of a monocle.

'*Grüß Gott,*' he said, and I gulped. I'm not sure what I was expecting, but the man had knocked me well and truly off-balance.

My hand slowly went out to his. '*Grüß Gott.*'

'I am told you are Katrina Klain.'

I nodded.

'And that you would like to see where your grandmother lived.'

I watched the man's lips. They moved slowly, precisely. His cheekbones were high, his eyes wide and blue, yet slightly hooded.

'You knew your grandmother.'

A black crow flitted across my mind. 'Who are you?' I said.

'Ha! Attack is always the best defence,' he said, and turned to the window. Then he spun round. 'I am your grandmother's son. Harald Klain.'

'That's impossible,' I said, but as I uttered the words I knew I was wrong. 'Harald Klain was my uncle. My father said you were dead.'

The man came towards me and stretched out his hand and just as I was sure that his finger would touch my cheek, he withdrew.

'I imagine Alfred would have said that and, in a way, I am dead. But I swear I am Harald Klain. Although the Doktor is long gone.'

'*Doktor?*' I said.

'No longer of consequence,' he said, and then cleared his throat and pulled a packet from his breast pocket. He took out a cigarette, tapped it against the pack and slipped it into his mouth. Then he pulled a lighter from the pocket of his trousers, flicked, lit a flame and inhaled. 'I do not have much time in Vienna and I realise that it must be a shock for you to suddenly discover that across the world you have...an uncle. Indeed, for me it is not devoid of a certain, shall we say, thrill, to have my own kin stand before me; and most attractive she has turned out to be.'

I found myself blushing.

Harald Klain exhaled luxuriously. 'We shall have dinner together. Let us say, Tuesday evening?'

I held out my right hand. *'Mit Vergnügen,'* I said, trying to keep my voice steady.

Harald took my hand and raised my fingers to his lips. 'The pleasure, I am sure will also be mine.'

I tried to suppress a grin, yet at the same time my heart was pounding. 'Till Tuesday, then, Uncle. Shall I pick you up?'

'You may 'pick me up' as you say, at 7pm. But please call me Harald. I am not used to being an uncle.'

I bet, I thought, as I left the room. Play it cool. Play it cool. On the way back to the pension I stopped at my reflection in a shop window. I was old enough to be his daughter – or young enough. I was old enough to be his...date. I wondered if he would have liked a woman like me, with my blonde shoulder-length hair, almond-shaped eyes, high cheekbones – they ran in the family – just those freckles on my nose; I would powder them. No! I looked fine. Slim. Not too tall. Good legs. He'd looked at my legs. Maybe it had been my red tights. Oh, cripes. Dinner with my uncle. I stopped.

He was meant to be dead. How could I even have let myself become excited about meeting my uncle as if he were a date, an attractive man, even alive. But he was my uncle. And he was meant to be dead. Dead. Death in Vienna. I shivered. Tomorrow was Sunday. Sunday lunch with Fritz and then some painter called Egon Schiele. *But what about that Doktor?*

'Ah, Doktor. Not all doctors save lives. Some even have been known to sell souls.'

What's he going on about?

'Think about it, Katrína. You are the one who studied German literature, did you not?'

'What's that got to do with the price of eggs?'

'She has a strange sense of things, I must say. Eggs, indeed. But she is close.' I laugh. I too can be funny ha ha.

Chapter 20

Lunch with Fritz had been a simple affair of *Spezialtoast* and beer in the same underground café where we'd first met. We alighted from the red tram at the Südbahnhof and crossed the broad Wiedner Gürtel to the top entrance of the Belvedere Palace.

'We must go for the visuals, now.' I nearly said 'jugular' but that would be getting ahead of ourselves. 'Camera. Roll! Technicolor!'

Click.

The pebbles caught in my slingbacks. I had to keep bending down to flick them out. The broad grey avenue leading up to the stairs of the palace was flanked by lime trees, and punctuated by wooden benches and columns. I waded through the small stones, some smooth, some sharp. Fritz adjusted his gait to mine, smiling. Was he smiling at my discomfort?

The posters for the exhibition had been plastered on the columns the length of the avenue to the entrance. Always the same sketch: self-portrait of the artist with his mouth open.

'That one was done with black crayon in 1910,' Fritz said.

'His hair's almost like yours,' I said. I'm glad you have more clothes on, I thought as a tinge of heat warmed the base of my throat. The drawing stopped just below a hand over the artist's stomach, but it was obvious he had modelled for himself in the nude.

We went up the broad marble staircase to the first floor. Fritz paid two entry tickets and with a sweep of his arm ushered me to the left.

'The exhibition starts here. His early works.'

The shiny wooden floors caught the click and clatter of shoes. Not many people. Five-metre-high ceilings. Pictures spread out. The early works were portraits: men in their stiff white stand-up collars, women with hats, and lace choking their throats. Then followed interiors, landscapes. Just like any old paintings, I thought.

'Schiele studied at the Academy of Fine Arts in Vienna,' Fritz said. 'It was hard to get in. Someone now famous tried a few months before him, but did not make it. Guess who?'

'I don't know.'

'Adolf Hitler.'

A waft of a smile touched Fritz's lips as he steered me into the next room. The style had changed. There were still portraits and interiors and outdoor scenes, mostly of houses. But the style had become more angular, and the women's clothes were highlighted with rings of gold and red.

'Egon's teacher at the Academy said the devil had sent him,' Fritz said.

'Doesn't look too devilish to me,' I said, and wondered why Fritz used Schiele's first name. No one called Picasso "Pablo".

'Wait. Here you see Gustav Klimt's influence. You know that famous picture, *The Kiss*?'

I'd seen prints of the opulent gold and colourful spirals enfolding the lovers in a cloak. It was flaunted on calendars and postcards in the tourist shops. 'Did Klimt say that to him about the devil?'

'No, Klimt was not his teacher. In fact, he told Schiele that he was the better one.'

'Klimt does have more gold. I don't understand,' I said.

'You will.

As we moved into the next room, the style had changed yet again.

'Egon and Wally – she was his favourite model – had moved to Krumau in Bohemia when he did these,' Fritz said.

A watercolour and crayon picture of a little girl sleeping on her stomach was the first thing Katrina saw. The blues, greens, reds and whites of her checked blouse and striped skirt contrasted with the black coverlet on the bed and with the flesh of her naked buttocks and legs. Another showed two teenage girls locked in each other's arms, the black of their garb offsetting the white of their faces and the flesh above their stocking tops.

'They banished him from Krumau for 'public immorality'.'

I said nothing. We moved towards the next chamber.

'Ah, these ones are special,' Fritz said. 'Many people did not understand poor Egon. He shocked them, of course, but he lived for his art. These are all of Wally, his lover.'

My face grew warm. The pictures had become fine, angular line drawings on a gouache background. Embracing women, almost nudes but for red or black stockings, or a hitched-up bodice. Most half-clothed. An orange mouth to match taut orange nipples worn above blatant pubic hair. Two crayon drawings of reclining nudes with fingers darting into nether parts. One nude wore boots.

I turned to Fritz, my cheeks hot. 'Is that all?' I tried to keep my voice steady as if it was something I did every day – look at Egon Schiele's works.

'I hope you are not shocked, Katrina,' Fritz said, his thumb gently rubbing my nape.

'No,' I said, and shook his hand off.

Fritz dropped his arm. 'How about some fresh air? A coffee on the terrace perhaps?'

'That would be nice.'

The flush on my cheeks cooled as we traced our paces back to the entrance. I'd seen nudes before, been to galleries, but Schiele disturbed me. Touched something in me.

We sat at a small, round wrought-iron table on the terrace overlooking the Schwarzenberg Platz, the spires of St Stephen's in the distance. The Viennese coffee steamed through the lashings of cream and the sprinkle of chocolate dust.

'He was grossly misunderstood, you know,' Fritz said. 'One of the greatest artists of our time.'

'He's awfully erotic,' I said. 'And tortured.'

'You have understood, Katrina. He was tortured, by his art. He left Wally soon after the incident in Krumau, married and lived happily ever after until...'

'Until?'

'He died in 1918, three days after his wife, Edith. Spanish flu. An epidemic. He was twenty-eight.'

'How old are you, Fritz?' I said as Fritz's features washed in with those of Schiele that I'd seen on the photos at the entrance.

'Twenty-eight.' Fritz's laugh was shot with surprise.

That night, I had a dream. In the morning I could only remember snippets: *a man with Jake's eyes, with Egon Schiele's hair, with Fritz's voice, standing on his head and then following me in a maze not unlike the gardens in which the aristocracy of bygone days played hide and seek. Then I was alone, huddled in a dark forest glade, feverishly gnawing at some raw meat.*

Then it was Monday and the nozzle of my hot morning shower in the communal bathroom washed the last remnants of the dream away.

'So you were starting to get a feel for Vienna. Interesting.'

'I need to go on. I have a deadline,' she says.

Chapter 21

When I arrived at 20 Josefstädterstraße on the following Tuesday, Harald Klain was already standing on the footpath in front of the grocer's shop next door. As I came abreast he took me by the elbow and hailed a black taxi coming down the cobbled street. Inside the taxi, Harald Klain spoke for the first time: 'Elisabethstraße, Gösserhof.'

'Where are we going?'

'Did my brother not tell you about the Gösserhof?'

I shook my head. It wasn't a lie. I'd never been inside and my father had told me little about his life before mine. There had been a brother. He was dead. That same brother was with me now, ushering me into a large dining hall towards a small room set out with damask napkins and heavy silver cutlery. Over the fireplace in which unlit logs were neatly stacked hung a painting: four draught horses pulled a cart with dozens of wooden beer barrels. Seated aloft with a whip in his hand was a stout man in shirtsleeves, a green waistcoat and a black tie. He was urging the team forward from an entrance crowned by a green sign on which large white letters were painted: *Otto Klains Gösserhof Restaurant.*

'Your grandfather,' Harald Klain said.

I was silent as Harald Klain pulled out my chair and helped me settle at a table for two in the corner of the room.

'So he never mentioned...before?'

I stiffened. I felt a sudden need to defend my father. His absence demanded it. 'He was shot down over Russia,' I said. 'It's normal he doesn't want to talk of the time...before.'

'Normal? Silence is normal?' Harald Klain's hand pulled out a red-and-white packet of Du Maurier from his pocket. He tapped a cigarette, lit it, inhaled deeply then exhaled. 'I recommend the *Tafelspitz*,' he said, snapping his fingers for the waiter to approach.

I said nothing. The waiter had not seemed perturbed at being summoned in such a way. In his place, I would have ignored Harald Klain.

'*Tafelspitz. Zweimal. Weißwein. Trocken,*' Harald Klain said. The waiter nodded and left.

'What is *Tafelspitz*?' I said.

'Of course. You cannot know. Please forgive me.' Harald Klain put out his hand, palm up. '*Tafelspitz* is the most tender cut of beef boiled so that it melts like butter in your mouth. Served with a chive sauce and a horseradish and apple mix. To titillate the senses.' Then he smiled.

Suddenly I felt like I was dining with a Fred Astaire look-alike in an old black-and-white film.

'How old are you now, Katrina?'

I stared blankly. Being with my uncle was like having hot

138

and cold showers. As the waiter approached with a laden tray, Harald Klain stubbed out his second cigarette. The meat steamed before us as the waiter poured the wine.

'*Prost*,' Harald Klain said, and smiled at me over his glass. Then he raised his glass to the painting over the fireplace. 'To the family,' he said, and we drank. 'How old?' he said again.

'Twenty.'

'Pity.'

'Why?'

'If you were twenty-one you could let me adopt you.'

'Why would I want to do that?' I felt my face get hot. Harald Klain had a way of getting under my skin.

'You could be my heiress.' He laughed. 'The flat you came to still has a low rent. It can only be passed from parent to child for that low rent to go on. As it is, I have lost the facility.'

I raised my eyebrows and tasted a morsel of the boiled beef.

'I must leave Vienna,' he said. Then, fixing me with a piercing look, he added: 'You could ask permission.'

'It would kill my father if I asked him to let you adopt me. It would kill him if he knew you were alive. You have never given a sign.'

'No sign? *He* gave no sign! When our mother was dying, did he come? I had to risk my life. Yes! Risk my life! My brother. He ran. He ran like so many did. He became a hero and then ran to a new life. The true heroes – ha! – theirs was the stigma of years.' He gulped from his glass and took a few breaths. Then quietly he said: 'So you want to know about me?'

I nodded. But for an instant, I didn't want to. I wanted to run. Run home. Run to Dad. The Dad I'd known before the postcard. The father who'd cuddled me, stroked me, made me laugh, showed me how to be tough, be a soldier. Yes. I wanted to know.

'Then I shall tell you,' Harald Klain said as he pushed his half-eaten *Tafelspitz* aside and lit another cigarette. 'But not straightaway. I still suffer from my last trip to Vienna. My mother's death. Death seems to eat into the most important pieces of one's memories. Death dresses them up. Death becomes one.'

I remembered the photo of my grandmother in her open coffin. I shuddered. But he'd been all alone. I was suddenly sorry for him. He was still all alone. And he was not dead.

'One cannot tell a life's story in a day,' he continued. 'This is just a beginning. We have to get to know one another. But that will have to be for another time.' Harald Klain waved to the waiter. 'I told you Katrina that I must soon leave Vienna. In fact, I must leave with the last train tonight.'

'Tonight?'

'One day all will become clear. Trust me for now. For the sake of, shall we say, *Wienerblut*, Viennese blood.'

I blinked then smiled as Harald Klain patted my hand. I watched as he paid the waiter and then he passed me a green note.

'One hundred *schillings*. Please take a taxi back to your pension. I shall have to leave you here.'

He told me no more, but that night I glimpsed in a dreamtime what must have been a clip from his past or my mother's future.

My mother is in a mid-station, a purgatory, or limbo of sorts, what did Luther call it? Damn! Weren't we meant to be with God, but where is she really? In a lounge room with TV and a loose end she has yet to tie up.

'Don't you want to join us?' Harald says, and raises his glass of cognac.

'I am looking for your brother. Where is Alfred?' Bettina says.

Harald lounges back, his legs crossed, one elbow propped on the next chair back, his cognac glass cupped between fingers just by the ear of his neighbour with a plunging neckline. 'Alfred?' He turns to the woman at his side and says: 'My brother runs this place. This is his wife. She's German.' He winks. 'But we were all German, n'est-ce pas, chérie?' The woman at his side reddens. 'Herr Doktor, but not any more,' she says, and adds, 'Surely?'

The blood rushes to Bettina's temples. She stares at Harald. Early fifties. Dapper as always in his what they now call 'bespoke' suit. That was the last time.

And then the dream ended. I was unable to sleep. I took out some paper and wrote a letter to my mother. To tell her that I'd met Uncle Harald. I didn't mention the word 'adoption'.

'Aha. So you had your silences. And your reasons, I take it.'

'I didn't want to hurt her,' she says. 'But I had to tell her I met him.'

'So you did hurt her, Katrina,' I say. Do we not all?

Chapter 22

There was no telephone in my room at the Pension Czernik. I'd been thinking about Harald, wondering when I would see him again, when I remembered I still had to post the letter to Mum. Tomorrow. I took out a collection of poems I had brought with me from Australia. Rilke. Flipping through the pages I stopped at the lines: *On what instrument are we strung? What musician is playing us?* There was a knock at the door.

I slipped the thin ribbon to mark the place and put the brown suede book on my night table next to the travelling clock and transistor radio.

'Fräulein, there is a gentleman to see you,' Frau Brauer said.

'Who is it?'

She cocked an eyebrow and said: 'A certain Herr Fritz Brauer.' I kept my face free of emotion as she added: 'We do not allow visitors after 10pm.'

'It's only six, Frau Brauer. I hardly think he will stay that long,' I said. I had to smile. Six in German sounded like sex. 'Might he be a relation?' I couldn't resist saying.

Frau Brauer did not answer. She wiped her hands on her skirt and went down the staircase.

I closed the door and took a step to the mirror, fluffed my hair.

'Katrina?' A knock underscored the call of my name.

'Coming,' I said and opened the door.

'I have brought some canapés from Trzesniewski's, a bottle of Gumpoldskirchner.' Fritz held a cardboard box, the red tape ribbon hooked on one finger, in the other hand, a bottle of white wine.

'Fritz.'

'I have Liptauer and tuna spread. They are the best in Vienna. Black bread.'

I cleared the round Biedermeier table in the corner of the room and rinsed the glass that held my toothbrush.

'I don't have any glasses. Will this do?'

'We shall have to share it, then.' He smiled, his hair reminding me of Schiele's.

He cut the red ribbon and folded the edges of the cardboard box down like a plate. Slivers of black bread were topped with different spreads. I tried two. The pinkish one tasted of garlic and cheese, the creamy one of tuna and onion.

'Sip some wine with it. It heightens the taste.' Fritz poured the pale liquid.

I felt the wine soothe the tang of the garlic. 'My breath will smell.'

'Mine and yours,' he said. 'So we will not notice.'

We ate and drank. I watched Fritz's eyes roam the room.

'Is that your prayer book?' He pointed to the brown suede book.

'No. I don't have a prayer book. My Rilke. I picked it up in a second-hand book shop in Sydney.'

'Poetry...', Fritz murmured. He reached out his hand and stroked my cheek.

I rose to take the book. 'It's a lovely edition. Compact, too.'

Fritz nodded. 'Existential.'

I hadn't been expecting him to say that. 'There are love poems,' I said. The nape of my neck prickled. 'I think I drank too quickly, Fritz.'

'One must never drink Gumpoldskirchner quickly, Katrina. One must sip it.'

I settled onto the bed, yet sat as if it were a hard-backed armchair.

Fritz seated himself by my side and slipped an arm about me.

'Katrina....'

Now it'll come, I thought. He'll try and kiss me. I wasn't sure if I wanted him to. Yes, I did want him to. Why doesn't he kiss me?

'Katrina...' Fritz slipped an envelope from his breast pocket. 'Have you ever seen anything like this?'

Half in relief, I said, 'What?'

Fritz stroked my right shoulder with his right hand as his left dislodged a sheet of folded paper that he opened like a fan. He held it dangling before my eyes.

I saw many small squares, little pictures. 'What is it?'

'Look closer,' he said and kept stroking my shoulder.

A sickening feeling crept up from my stomach. I stared at the tiny photos. Blood raced to my temples. Women. Women with their fingers in their crotches. Women spreading their buttocks. I jerked. His grip tightened on my shoulder.

'It is all right, Katrina,' Fritz keened. 'They are art photos. Miniatures.'

I sprang up. 'Get out!' I screamed. 'Get out of here.'

Fritz shrugged, folded the paper and put it back in his pocket. 'If you ever need money, Katrina Klain,' he said my name slowly, 'I'm always on the lookout for new, fresh, talent.'

'Get out! Get out!'

Fritz closed the door. I stood transfixed. Then, sure he was gone, I rushed out to the toilet at the end of the corridor and threw the remaining canapés into the enamel bowl. They didn't flush, but swam about until the spiral of water had eased away. Back in my room I downed the last of the wine and dumped the empty bottle in the wastepaper basket.

He had wanted me to pose for him. I rushed back to the toilet and vomited.

I was still shaking when I got back to my room. I'm finished with men. Pietro. Fritz. Schiele. Harald. Hitler. Words. Words. Words to cover the silence. My father. My uncle. I grabbed the book of Rilke and flung it across the room. It fell with a rip in its spine.

I squatted on my haunches like I used to in the bush. I picked up the book and stroked its smooth leather. Jake. I couldn't be finished with him. But all the others, I thought, as I rocked back and forth.

Oh, look at her now. Katrina loose in the big bad world. And now she is shaking.

'Perhaps a cup of tea?' I say.

'You and your bloody, tea. I'm dead. I don't need tea!'

'But you liked the brandy,' I say.

Bastard!

What can I do but smile? 'Did Beethoven give you a dirty look? Or should I say *Arbeit Macht Frei?*

'You have a twisted mind.'

'Well, you did say that you needed to get a job. Wash all these men out of your hair. Well, not all, perhaps.' Is she really making that rude sign with her arm? Well, well, well.

I was finished with men, or so I thought, and I had to get a job. The latter, I hoped, would clear my mind. But as I walked the two blocks to the United Nations Industrial Development Organisation located behind the Rathaus I couldn't help thinking about my uncle. He had left suddenly, in a way proving that I was on my own. I wondered how my mother would react to my letter. I slipped the pale blue envelope into the letterbox outside the UNIDO building and went to the entrance. The glass doors pulled away before I touched them. I went to the reception desk and asked if any jobs were available.

'Clerical or professional?' the woman said.

I wondered what was 'unprofessional' about clerical work. 'Both, please.'

The woman passed a pink form and a blue one across the counter.

'Blue is professional,' she said.

I sat in a large modern armchair in the corner of the foyer, filled out the forms and then handed them back to the woman. In the box asking when I could begin, I wrote 'immediately'.

'How long before I hear from you?' I asked.

'Forms are kept for two years; anything between tomorrow and then,' the woman said. 'But if you don't hear within a week or two, you may forget it.'

On seeing the disappointment in my eyes, she added: 'Why not try the Atomic Energy? It is down the Ring just past the Opera House.'

I thanked her and left. One lot of filling out forms was enough for that May day. The sun was shining. I'd go to the Volksgarten, sit among the rose bushes. Maybe even treat myself to some apple strudel.

In a café with coffee and hot strudel melting the dollop of vanilla ice-cream on its crown, I thought of Harald Klain and the little he had told me. I tried to think clearly. The form-filling no doubt had cleared my mind. A sort of meditation, focusing on something minimal. One little block after the other. And what about Fritz? He was twenty-eight. Older than Jake. I tried to imagine Jake at the Schiele exhibition. I couldn't. I knew I was being unfair. Visits to art galleries were not things we'd done together. Apart from one or two visits with Mum to Sydney's NSW Art Gallery, I'd never been to galleries either.

If we'd gone to art galleries, maybe I wouldn't have needed to leave so badly. There was no Schiele in Sydney. Sure, there'd been the big speeches at uni that said culture with a capital C only lived in the old world. Now I was here. But unlike a tourist exploring landmarks I teetered as if on a diving board, somehow unable to plunge into the secret waters of my past that were linked to things that may have been terrible. Vienna had already shown me two sides of art, and two sides of death.

I slept late. As I came down to the reception desk, Frau Brauer said, 'There was a call for you at nine. Someone from UNIDO. You are to call back this morning, a Frau Schwarb.'

The only telephone in the pension was on the reception desk in front of Frau Brauer. 'I'll go straight there, it's only two blocks. *Danke*, Frau Brauer.' I rushed back up to my room. Slow down, girl. Breathe deep. Get changed. This may be a job.

'May I speak to Frau Schwarb?' I asked at the desk.

'Frau Schwarb? Personnel?'

'Yes, she asked me to call. My name is Katrina Klain.'

Peering over her glasses, the woman dialled a number. The glasses pinched her nose the way her tight black bun pinched her face.

'503, fifth floor.' The woman's hand swept in the direction of a dumb waiter contraption between two marbled lifts. I'd seen the open-faced lift in some of the older buildings. The only thing modern about the building I was now in was the heavy glass door at the entrance. I waited in front of the paternoster, readying my step to hop onto the platform moving slowly in its never-ending up-and-down loop; too risky, I thought, and took the lift.

I gave myself a last quick look in the mirror of the lift as a muted ring announced floor 5. I had pulled my hair back at the nape. A flat navy grosgrain bow covered the elastic band. The neat white cotton blouse tucked into my navy pleated skirt gave me a freshness, and I hoped made me look 'professional'.

The name on the door of office 503 said N. Schwarb – Recruitment. I knocked on the half-open door. 'Frau Schwarb?' The woman in 503 rose. She was tall and angular with blonde hair pulled back in a chignon.

'Miss Klain? Come in and sit down, won't you?'

I lowered myself into a chair at Frau Schwarb's desk, on which forms were piled high. The woman swept a hand in the air. 'So much backlog,' she said. I smiled wanly.

'I have looked at your application. It is interesting, but I am afraid you are overqualified.'

'I have to eat,' I said, and gave the woman a steady look. Hold her gaze. Don't blink.

Frau Schwarb opened a card file on her desk. She flicked through the cards then looked up at me. 'We may have something to start in June, for the summer,' she said. 'It is only filing, but it is a start.'

'I'll take it,' I said, and relaxed my shoulders, quietly breathing out. Dad had always said that a good education would open all doors, so how could a Bachelor of Arts be a handicap? Just get in, I thought.

Twenty minutes later, I was back in the foyer, in my bag a three-month contract and a slip of paper reminding me that I should report back to Frau Schwarb on Monday, 5th June at 8:30 am. That was three weeks away.

Three weeks. Somehow the roller coaster rides of the last few days had left me feeling lost. I had to get away from Vienna for a while. Go home. How? I thought of the letter I'd written my mother. What if Dad saw it? I couldn't ring home. Home was so far away. The closest thing was Mum's family in the GDR, the German Democratic Republic. It was my family too. I'd send Mum and Dad a postcard from East Germany. I'd send Jake one as well. Maybe I'd have a reply when I got back.

'Ah, might the postcard girl be homesick?'

'Shut up,' she says. 'I bet you've never been far away from home.'

What could she know? There had been London, of course. But there had also been wars. Not world ones of course, just a skirmish here and there. I must admit that I did have a liver not unlike a lily. Nevertheless. I should perhaps try and appeal to her. Just a little. I shall let her talk. Women do so love talking, although I have met my share of male chatterboxes in my other life. Fear does that. Panic, too. But this will be different. We shall see.

Chapter 23

When I'd left Australia I'd winked up at the man in the moon, not knowing that before the year was out another would take a small step that might change the world. That was more than six months ago. I thought of Jake. He'd sent me a postcard from Noumea. He said he'd be there for a few months for work. I missed him. It wasn't that his absence left a hole; it was just that there was so much more when he was there, and there wouldn't have been Fritz if he had been. But I'd wanted this time. I stared out of the train window as the countryside chugged by.

'Another postcard? You should string them up, Katrina.'

I should string you up.

'Is that a threat?' I laugh out loud.

I'd come in from the east, from Vienna via Prague. After the awful experience with Fritz, my need to run had suddenly been strong; a need to get out. I'd been tough when I left Sydney. I hadn't thought twice then either. I'd been tough like Dad had taught me to be. I saw us walking hand-in-hand down the bush and felt a sudden tenderness for my father. But it was interrupted as the train screeched to a halt on the Czech-GDR border.

Two puffed-up, grey-uniformed men entered the compartment. Each took an aisle.

'Passport,' one said, then took the navy booklet I handed him and flipped through to the Czech visa to make sure I could really leave Czechoslovakia. When the other passengers had shown their papers the officials swung down on to the platform as if they had run out of air. The train lurched into motion over an expanse of grey, barren terrain and then screeched to another halt.

A dour-faced official in a grey uniform filled the doorway of the compartment. 'Passport,' he snapped. '*Koffer aufmachen!*'

I didn't know whether I was expected to first show my papers or open my suitcase. I held out my passport.

'*Koffer aufmachen!*'

I took down the suitcase with the stickers, CABIN - ACHILLE LAURO, plastered on the lid. I opened it.

'*Was ist das?*'

'A koala,' I said, 'a koala bear,' as if the word 'bear' would ensure its innocence. They weren't bears of course, but he wouldn't know. What did he care, anyway? He took out a knife from the instep of his boot. I froze. I shifted on the seat and reached out a hand, as if it might speak for me. What was he doing? Is he crazy? I was about to yell, but held my tongue, and just watched as he slashed the stuffed creature in one clean rip right down the belly. Stop! But the word never left me. He put the knife away and glanced at me. Then he dug his fingers into the synthetic entrails. I felt sick. My palms were wet. Then with a flick of his wrist, he threw the fur carcass into my suitcase. I shivered. 'Books?' he said.

'No,' I whispered.

'Books?'

'No!'

I trembled and stared straight ahead as he went on to the next passenger. 'Passport!'

I was glad to alight. The physical exercise of changing platforms in Halle and boarding the local train had calmed me as I took a seat in the almost-full compartment.

A teenage girl sat opposite me. She was struggling to open a bottle of – the label said – 'Malz Kola'. The deformed word drew my hand down to my suitcase. The koala gift was inside. What had they been looking for? I swallowed. So cute, the only gift I had had for my family, and they had to ruin it.

The blonde girl in her knee socks, white blouse and dark-blue skirt started worrying the bottle cap on the side of the metal armrest.

I rummaged in my bag. '*Bitte*,' I said and held my hand out for the bottle. The girl gave it to me with a look of surprise. The bottle was warm. Their Coca-Cola, I thought. Warm coke. I plucked off the top with my pocketknife opener and handed the bottle back.

'*Danke*,' the girl said and began to sip and then, as an afterthought, offered the bottle to me. Had she done it spontaneously, I might not have noticed her hand.

'*Nein, danke*,' I said, and continued in German. 'How many stops is it to Sibigrode?'

'Just one more,' the girl said, and switched the bottle to her left hand and tucked her right hand in the pocket of her pleated skirt.

Six fingers. '*Danke schön*,' I said.

The girl must have noticed the difference in accents. My German wasn't fluent, but it was clear I would get by, as a stranger would, and the girl with the ice-blue eyes had seen that. Yet I found her accent and words more familiar, more innately known than the speech and dialect of Vienna. German was many things.

The girl must have felt a certain ease as well. 'Where are you going?' she asked.

'To the Friedrichs. Do you know them?' I said. Of course she doesn't. I remembered how I'd laugh when asked if I knew someone so-and-so in Sydney. Now I was doing the same thing.

'No. But the town is small. They will know at the station,' the girl said.

The train pulled in to a simple grey platform with a low one-room building and outhouse. With a wave of '*Auf Wiedersehen*', my suitcase in hand and my carry bag over my shoulder, I got off, realising I would probably never see the girl with the strange hand again. But one never knew. Who was it, I wondered. Oh, yes. Anne Boleyn. They'd taken her for a witch. Well, she could always have it removed. Plastic surgery here, at the end of the world? I smiled to myself, now where was Down Under? I shrugged and walked towards the small, squat building.

'The Friedrichs' house is the last one on the road to Gorenzen, about twenty minutes on foot,' a man said in a low, flat voice. He must have been the stationmaster. He was the only person there; the building would not have had room for anyone else and his grey uniform and cap gave him an official look.

It took me thirty minutes to walk down the dusty road that had been tarmacked, but never repaired. There was no footpath, just rubble and sand seeping into rough grass. The houses stood aligned, grey after beige after grey. Any garden they had must have been in the back. I remembered seeing a garden in an old photo my mother once showed me. Behind the houses were fields, flatness, and in the distance, copses of trees. Further off the low hills rolled, and even further I could see peaking forests: the Harz, I thought. I remembered Mum speaking of the Harz Mountains. The last house had trees – tall elms, two of them – and there was a tiny garden in the front. Just a few bushes, hydrangeas behind a peeling picket fence. All the houses had peeling picket fences, but this one peeled more.

I opened the gate and walked up to the front door. I looked about, placed my case on the ground and hit the knocker.

The door opened and a stout old woman in long skirts and apron, her grey-white hair pulled back in a bun, stood before me. She had a round, flat face with high cheekbones, just like Mum's. Her wrinkles bore witness to smiles and sorrow.

'Tante Klara? It's Katrina, Katrina from Australia. Bettina's daughter.'

'Bettina? Katrina?' With each word the old woman's face softened and her smile seemed as if it would envelop me as her arms opened in greeting. 'Katrina. How did you get here? All the way from Australia! Heinz, come look, it is Bettina's

Katrina.'

An old man a head shorter than Tante Klara shuffled to the entrance. He had a full head of sparkling white hair and a bushy moustache clipped short. He wore a grey hand-knit jumper that was neatly darned in a spot past his stomach. His gaze was strong from steel-grey eyes as he smiled and said: 'Yes, it is Bettina's Katrina.'

I stepped forward to his tentative embrace then pulled back. I didn't know what to say.

'So will you stay with us? You can have the room your mother had before she left,' Klara said.

I nodded and followed my aunt up the narrow, creaking stairs. The room was small with an attic window and scrubbed wooden floorboards. A bed stood pressed against one wall. Its dark wooden headboard was decorated with a rose and two symmetric swirls that opened upwards, like curling vines. A small dresser stood opposite. It had the same carved pattern around the mirror fixed on top of it so that it looked like a dressing table. In the corners the mirror was blotched brown with age, and on the dresser stood a large white china jug in a china basin.

As I opened my suitcase on the linen bedspread, I heard my aunt's footsteps creaking up the stairs.

'It is simple, but clean,' she said. 'The toilet is outside, *Liebchen*.'

'That's OK, Tante Klara,' I said. It was like being sent back in time, with fragile yet durable things. But running water would have been nice.

As if reading my thoughts, the old woman said: 'A lot of people have very modern things these days. I cannot see the use of it all myself. But there is Irmgard, my daughter, your cousin, you know. Well, she and her husband, they are up in the Harz, they mind the deer, and even up there, Irmgard has running water and shiny taps, even an enamel toilet inside the house. And she has a refrigerator. Here we put everything in the cool cellar. Oh, I remember...'

I smiled. 'What, Tante Klara?'

Tante Klara puffed and sat down on the bed. 'Oh, it was when your mother started school....'

It was hard to imagine Mum having started school. 'Yes?' I sat down on the bed next to my aunt.

'It did cause some talk in the village.' The old woman's skirts began to jiggle as a belly laugh stifled into a chuckle. 'You know, here in Germany, the children on their first day of school, well, they receive an enormous cone filled with sweets, bonbons...'

I'd heard of the tradition. I'd even seen photos in the West German *Burda* magazines Mum got months late and used for her dressmaking patterns. There'd be photos of children in street clothes, not uniforms like I had to wear. The children held bright-coloured cones almost as big as themselves. No doubt, mothers would make bright skirts and shirts and jackets for the first school day. So it went that far back.

'What happened?'

'Well, the teacher – all the classes were together in one room – he told the children that the tree with the cones grew in his cellar.'

'And?'

'Well, your mother, oh, that Bettina...' Tante Klara started to chuckle again and held her hand on her stomach. 'Bettina and one of the boys from the village thought the tree would grow bigger and have bigger cones if they fertilised it. So they poured a bucket of...cow piss...' Tante Klara's skirts jiggled more and more, '...into the cellar window of the teacher's house.'

She wiped tears from her eyes with the corner of her apron. '...He kept the freshly baked bread just under the window on a stone ledge....'

I burst out laughing. 'And he couldn't get mad at the children?'

'No, he could not get mad with them. He should never have told them such a lie.'

We smiled at each other. Then, as if it had all gone on too long, Tante Klara said: 'I will let you unpack now. Then you come down.'

I unpacked and thought of my mother. She must have been fun to know back then. I remembered evenings of mad giggling about nothing when Mum and I would roll about on her bed. I suddenly missed her.

That afternoon I took an old bike from the shed.

'It still works. I take it now and then when the sun shines,' Onkel Heinz said.

I biked to the next village along a deserted country road to fetch fresh bread rolls for supper. They were firm and brown and smelled of malt. A gingerbread world of malt: malt bread, malt coke; everything malt.

The countryside, with its grey houses in huddles, its copses of trees peppered through tilled fields, bore no scars of war and no greasepaint of modernity. It was not the regime, I thought, but time that held it suspended, as if in aspic.

The following day, my cousin Irmgard and her two young sons came to visit Tante Klara. I knew the word had spread fast that Bettina's daughter from Australia had dropped in on the village. It was Sunday. Onkel Heinz donned a white shirt with a stiff stand-up collar. He wasn't going to church. There were no churches, or they weren't used as such. He just went out to the gate. It must have still been an occasion, a memory of bygone times, for he even had on his black Homburg hat.

Irmgard was a tall woman, well into middle age. She had gone to great pains with her clothes. She wore a white blouse nipped a notch too tightly by a dark-blue skirt that spilled over thickening hips. She tweaked at her waistband as she approached the gate with a large paper carry-bag and two boys in tow.

'Katrina, my dear, you are just like your mother, Aunt Bettina. This is Rolf and this is Helmut,' she said, pushing a sullen twelve-year-old and a friendlier looking eight-year-old before her.

The photos I'd seen of Mum in her youth had shown a slim, dark-haired woman. I was blonde; Mum used to call my hair California blonde since it darkened in the winter and lightened in the sun. I had Mum's cheekbones and her dusting of freckles, but my face was not flat and round like these people.

Helmut thrust out with both hands a large box-like contraption.

'This is for you. A gift. I made it myself,' he said.

'*Danke.*' I took the object. I had nothing in return. I couldn't give him the ripped koala. 'I'm afraid they took away the gifts I brought; they took them away at the border,' I lied. 'Your gift is lovely. What is it?'

'Take off the paper. It's a windmill. Made of matchsticks.' The boy blushed. His older brother, the first sprigs of acne peppering his cheeks, watched impassively.

'Thank you, Helmut,' I said. 'I'll put it inside, it looks fragile.' Turning to Irmgard, I said with a smile: 'It must have taken him ages.' Then I carried my prize up to my room. What am I going to do with it, I thought as I placed it on the dresser.

When I came out again Tante Klara and Irmgard were busy setting a wooden table under the shade of the elm trees behind the house. There was coffee, malt coffee, and baked cheesecake. I recalled the waft of sour sweet that had tickled my nose that morning.

'I do not believe it,' Onkel Heinz said.

'But it is true, Onkel Heinz.' Rolf slammed his fist in the air.

'Yes, they did,' chirruped Helmut.

'A man cannot walk on the moon. That is impossible. They are telling us stories again,' the old man said.

I placed a hand on my uncle's elbow. He was sitting on the bench, upright and proud, his Homburg straight on his head. I imagined that he must surely look like that at a funeral, only there he would stand to bid farewell to an old friend. 'It's true, Onkel Heinz,' I said quietly. 'A man, an American, has walked on the moon.'

The old man shook his head: 'I do not believe it,' he muttered over and over again. How hard it was for him to accept things others took for granted. But I was that way, too. Jake, he had taken it for granted that I loved him. I did, of course – or did I? And the gifts? I'd been so sure I could breeze in with a strange antipodal stuffed animal. Who would mistrust a koala?

'Katrina,' Irmgard said, in a voice that snapped me back to them. 'I was wondering if you needed something like this? They are the best in the GDR,' she said proudly. 'My brother-in-law sells them in his, well it is not his...' Her lips tinged with bitterness as her voice softened. '...his *Kaufhaus*. We are known for good quality.'

I didn't know where to look as my cousin held out a floor-length red flannel horror of a dressing gown. 'You will need this in Europe,' Irmgard added. 'It is colder here than in Australia.'

I stretched out my hands. Irmgard had made a show of her gift. I couldn't refuse it, but no way was I going to wear it. I hated dressing gowns. But it was a gift, a gift from my family, here on the other side of the world. I could always give it to the Caritas, or another one of those charity places, when I got back to Vienna. 'Thank you, Irmgard. I'll make good use of it.' I turned to fold and place the gown on the bench.

'And I...' Irmgard glanced sideways as if to block out Heinz, who was still nodding sadly to himself. 'These, too, they are of superior quality. You can always fill them with handkerchiefs, but I think they should fit.'

I stared and tried not to laugh out loud. Irmgard held out a pale, dusty pink bra, polyester, sewn in concentric circles and ending in a point where a nub should be. They were burning their bras back home and I would place a pencil under my breast once a week, the pencil always fell. My breasts needed no support, not for a long while yet.

'I have a white one too,' Irmgard said.

God, I'd never wear those, I thought as I said *'Danke'*. My reward was Irmgard's proud glow. These people were the closest I would get to a family. Yet they were strangers, as distant as the man in the moon, but I didn't want to walk on their round faces.

The next day we went up to the Barbarossa caves to see the king whose beard grew into the ground through a massive table as a sign of his sorrow. 'Did your mother ever tell you the story of Barbarossa, Kaiser Friedrich?' Irmgard said.

'Something about him trying to unite all the German dukes, bring peace? Didn't he fall in the crusades?' I said.

'Legend has it that he did not die. He hid in the caves with his flaxen-haired daughter and members of his court.' Irmgard's voice dropped to a whisper. 'And there he stays sleeping until Germany becomes one.' Her whisper hoarsened. 'Hitler imagined uniting all German people.'

'And look what that led to,' I said. 'It looks like Barbarossa will go on sleeping forever.'

Irmgard's eyes caught mine. For a long second her gaze was straight.

'We never thought they would really put up a wall. We had our chance. We should have left then,' she said. I watched the tears glisten in my cousin's eyes. 'But this is our home, Katrina. Do you understand?'

I shifted from one foot to the other and then walked off a few paces in that height of the Harz. I wasn't the one Irmgard should be telling such things. How could a tumbleweed understand? I had no roots; well, I knew they weren't in the GDR, despite the comfort of the accent in the area where my family lived.

'There's something else, though,' Irmgard added. 'I shall always hate the British.'

I heard myself asking, 'Why? Didn't they help to give you your country? Your German Democratic Republic?'

Irmgard turned away from me. 'It is more complicated than that,' she said. 'Or perhaps it is simpler.' Her voice wavered.

'Tell me,' I said, holding out my hand to Irmgard, yet not daring to touch her.

'It was near Dresden. Flyers we got in the munitions

factory where I was working towards the end of the war said 200,000 died in the bombing of that great city! They massacred our people. Our culture. Criminals! The war was nearly over, or we thought it was. We were making our way home on foot. Civilians. Young. Old. Home from the war effort. Suddenly leaflets fell from the sky and the road ripped open at our feet in a battering of gunfire. The girl walking beside me – coming home from the Labour Service – they helped farmers whose farm hands were at the front – the girl – Nina – Nina was hit. I held her bleeding, ripped body in my arms as she died and the leaflets floated down upon us from the British planes. The leaflets were in German. They said: *'Wir sind die lustigen Acht, Wir kommen bei Tag und bei Nacht.'* Suddenly Irmgard screamed and swung round to face me. 'The jolly eight. By day and night. There was no need to do that. The war was over. I can never forgive that. Despite all, this is my country, my home.'

Despite all? Did she mean the Jews? I had to ask. 'What about the Jews?' I said softly.

Irmgard drew her shoulders up so that I thought they would swallow her neck. Then she relaxed. 'Who really understands?' she said sadly. 'It was a difficult time. But we had no problem with the Jews.' She paused and then looked into the distance as if expecting old King Barbarossa to awaken. 'Our grandfather – yours and mine – a Jew had helped him. Had lent him money at decent rates to pay off what he owed on his land. This was after the first war. A Jew helped our family.' She smiled at me, then her eyes clouded over. 'When it all started, when we were told stories, that we must ignore, yes ostracise them; could you tell from the outside? We were all neighbours; our grandfather hid two of the daughters of the man who had helped him. We all knew in the village, but we kept quiet. Bettina, though, never knew. She came home one weekend from the *Arbeitsdienst*, in her uniform, so proud of herself. No one dared tell her. We could not take the risk.'

'The risk? My mother a Nazi? Is that what the *Arbeitsdienst* did to her?'

'We couldn't take the risk, Katrina.' Then she continued: 'I was still quite young then. It's just what I heard. The daughters got away. But the British. I saw that.'

I stared at her. Then her voice suddenly broke into a cracked laugh.

'We can be naughty, too,' she said, seemingly desperate to change the subject. 'There is a joke, you know. Ulbricht, our leader, loses his wallet one day. He offers a reward – any wish – to the finder. A pretty eighteen-year-old girl finds the wallet and he asks her what she wants. She says: 'Open the wall for twenty-four hours.' Ulbricht laughs and says: 'You naughty girl, you just want to be alone with me.'

I smiled weakly. There was more to my cousin than her too-tight waistband. And what about the running water and the shiny taps? Shiny taps in a country without the latest domestic equipment, in a secluded home up in the hills, a home on the country's border where rangers, ostensibly, keep a lookout for deer?

On the train back to Vienna via Prague, I soon forgot the shiny taps to which only the Stasi and their informants could have had access. As the countryside pulled by and I drew further away from people I had always been told were my family, I pondered on the meaning of the word. Blood coursed in my veins. It was mine. Not theirs.

On Monday I would report for duty: my first job.

'Before you go there, Katrina. Just a quick question.'
  What does he want now?
'The shiny taps made you wonder.'
  Yes.
'I am wondering, too. About you.'
  Me?
'Even back then you suspected something.'
  What is he going on about?
'Think about it, Katrina. Shiny taps in a country without the latest domestic equipment, in a secluded home up in the hills, a home on the country's border where rangers ostensibly keep a lookout for deer.'

She clenches her fists. She is not as naive now as she was then. I shall not mention Bettina and the *Arbeitsdienst*. It was just a precaution, and one never knew.

'Back to work then,' I say. I will soon have to take over and run things my way in this place. She is turning this into her own *plaidoyer*. But it helps her forget the deadline, which, of course can be of advantage for me. I am enjoying our small interchanges, even though some do sadden me.

Chapter 24

'I have to report to the Personnel Office,' I said to the woman at the desk.

The woman nodded and I moved towards the paternoster. I'd take it this time and not wait for the lift. I had to judge my timing before stepping on to the floor of the open-faced platform.

Frau Schwarb was waiting. She ushered me into a large office with three desks. 'The other two colleagues are on holidays,' she said. 'But here is Frau Poncet. She will tell you what to do.'

A dark-haired woman in a beige Chanel suit rose from her desk and offered her hand. She had that thoroughbred look of young women I'd seen on the covers of society tabloids, so I was surprised when she said: 'My name is Madeleine.' No title. No surname. Not even a neigh.

'Katrina Klain,' I said as I shook Madeleine Poncet's hand, the gesture already a reflex.

'Take the far desk over there by the window. There is a lot of filing,' she said, and pointed to two heaps of pink and blue papers piled on the desk I was to occupy. 'They are for our roster. That is where we keep all the details on people we come back to when we need them.'

I placed my handbag in one of the drawers, settled in my padded chair and moved the two piles to the middle of the desk before me. Madeleine explained that the forms had to be sorted by colour.

'Blue for the boys, and...' I said.

Madeleine suppressed a smile. 'You learn fast.'

I spent the first three days separating professional from clerical and manual applications. When I found only three women's names on the blue forms, I thought of what I'd heard: there was no discrimination in the UN. Did fewer women apply for professional jobs, or were they culled along the way?

I separated blues from pinks for an hour and then Madeleine said, 'Let us go and have a coffee.' She was a professional, but the way she dressed, the pale Chanel suit, the silk blouse with a soft bow at her throat, the signature Chanel shoes with the black patent toes, made me feel that she didn't have to work for a living. We took the paternoster up four floors and got into line to the quiet clatter of cups at the entrance of the cafeteria. Here and there someone in the line turned around and smiled at Madeleine and looked at me. She smiled or gave a small wave. In the cafeteria, bright tapestries and posters covered white walls that matched Formica tables and plastic chairs. The tables and chairs were arranged in groups of four, close enough not to waste space, far enough away from each other for some degree of privacy. We collected our cups. A waitress in a seersucker uniform served the different coffees: black, milk, Viennese. There were ashtrays, small plastic-like bowls in white with UN marked in blue.

'How do you like it?' Madeleine said.

I nodded. 'It's a big place.' I felt I should show some interest in the work I had to do. After all, I was having coffee with my boss. 'I do have some questions. What about those that are older than two years?'

'The files? They go to the "deads",' Madeleine replied and winked.

'Forever?' I asked, itching to wink back and surprised at her darkish sense of humour.

'It is rare that they are resuscitated,' she said, lighting a cigarette. 'Sometimes it happens. They are better off in the "deads" than in the waste bin.'

'And when are they resuscitated?' This was beginning to sound like a funeral parlour, or at least intensive care.

'When we cannot find the right profile.' Madeleine caught the beginning of a grin on my face. 'I know all the profiles don't stick, but there are other...considerations.'

'Like?'

Madeleine drew on her cigarette and then blew a perfect ring. 'Like geographical distribution. Maybe one day, hiring women will become a priority.'

'But wouldn't that be begging the issue? Surely the most important thing is job competence?' I leaned forward across the table then drew back and stirred my coffee. 'I'd want to be hired because people thought I was good, not because I was a woman.'

Madeleine stubbed out her half-smoked cigarette. 'Katrina, take what you can get. To get on, you need friends. You need connections. Vitamin C, I call it. Once you are in, that is where your work comes in. That is how it was for me,' she said, and laughed. 'I only started here at UNIDO after Easter. Got moved from the Atomic Energy.' She rose and placed the two empty cups and the ashtray on a tray by the door. 'We had better get back.'

As we walked in silence down the four flights of stairs and the long corridor back to the office, I wondered about Madeleine, her connections, her vitamin C.

'If you need anything, just ask,' she said as she stood by my desk while I once again took up her pastel files.

The weeks passed and Madeleine and I took coffee together in the afternoons. At lunchtime, I'd go out in the sun and eat a packed lunch in the Rathaus park with a book, *Exodus* by Leon Uris. My contract would end in just over a month and I thought I had a good chance at something else, typing in the pool or punching numbers in the Finance Department. But what did I want?

'Madeleine, I don't know what to do. I like it here but I feel I'm just marking time. I feel I should be doing something else.'

'Doing what? How about improving your German? The university has intensive German courses,' she said. 'With your degree, you might even try some translation work; but it is a hard area to break into if you do not have...'

'I know. Vitamin C,' I said as Madeleine gave me a long look.

'But I'd have to get some sort of part-time job. I wouldn't be able to afford the room at the pension,' I said.

'It is funny how we try and find reasons to keep ourselves back, when our feelings try to make us go forward.' Her voice had a sad ring to it, but her face remained impassive.

I brushed some imaginary crumbs off the table with the back of my hand. 'I could give English lessons.' I could pose, I thought. And a shiver of Fritz rode my spine.

'What is wrong?' Madeleine said.

'Oh, nothing.' I could hardly tell my boss, yes, my new friend, about Fritz. Not yet anyway. He could go to hell. There were other ways to earn money.

'You could do some waitressing,' Madeleine said. 'You are attractive. If you put on a *dirndl*...'

We laughed as if sharing a private joke, imagining me in a *dirndl*, my breasts nestling in the white low-cut blouse and my waist nipped by a decorative apron of the traditional garb surprisingly acceptable as office-wear. Fritz was hovering at the corners of my mind. I shook my head. 'No, not waitressing. I'll find something. Term starts mid-September?'

'Yes,' Madeleine said. 'I think I know someone who might need an English-speaking coach for schoolchildren.'

Two days later she gave me a list of five names and telephone numbers of people looking for English coaching.

I took to jotting notes in my journal. I had neglected even opening it since my poems and Fritz. But Vienna was sucking me in, and my friendship with Madeleine was making me want to react in some way. Writing things down helped. But things came out unexpectedly.

It's something about feeling at home in a place where everyone's parents have been in the same war, on the same side. But the silence. Was it shame? Had those soldiers known? Or is it Vienna itself? My mixed-up heritage. Irmgard in the GDR. The *Arbeitsdienst* of my mother. There were no sides for the individual. Everyone lived their own

170

hell. Dammit! I want to live! I don't want to carry forward the sins of my father. Has he sinned? Would I ever know? Could I ever ask? Why should I feel guilt? I miss the bush, I want to go home.

Tears welled in my eyes as I put down my pen and closed the book.

Why doesn't Mum write?

Chapter 25

Bettina Klain

Why did I not write? What was there to write? That Alfred blamed me every day for having let his daughter go? She wasn't even twenty-one. I, too, had sworn never to let her go. Let them fly and they will come back, people said. I never went back. But she will be here in a few months, the time for letters to go back and forth. Also the time to forget. Alfred will need to forget, too.

That Dutchman who came to our home. Pretended his father knew Alfred from his time in England. Alfred was always one to fall for compliments. Yes, he was good at the Rembrandt Hotel. Yes, he could help the Dutchman brush up his German. But the Dutchman was a journalist on the hunt for Nazis. I thought Alfred would have a seizure. I had to calm him down. Alfred rummaged madly through some papers.

'There!' he said to the Dutchman. 'There is the proof! Now get out of my house!'

I could not write that.

I could not write that two days later he had a stroke. That he was in hospital, and that one night in the same week all the lights went out.

I could not write that.

She will be home soon. She will have so much to tell me.

It was right to have let her go. Jane, too, now has gone. Jane was twenty-one. It comes to the same. Jane will see her. Remind her. Remind her to come home.

Perhaps one day, I shall return to Gorenzen. Perhaps.

Chapter 26

Katrina Klain

The year pulled into autumn and I started a translation course at the University of Vienna and gave English lessons to well-off children. I negotiated a lower fee at the pension with the promise that I'd renew by semester. Madeleine had been offered a job in Geneva organising conferences and was soon due to leave. She promised to stay in touch. 'I'm your Vitamin C,' she said with a laugh.

Early October a letter came. It was from Jane. By the time it arrived, she'd written, she'd already be in Europe. She'd arrive by train on 10th October. Could I meet her at the station?

I ran up the steps of the station, glancing at the arrivals board. The grey train was drawing in. I stepped back and surveyed each passing doorway. There she is. Her hair's grown. Suits her. Come on, Jane. Jane waved. We tumbled into each other's arms.

'We'd better get out of the way or we'll be trampled by the army,' I said as the crocodile of grey-clad soldier boys crawled off to military duty. 'Is that all you've got?' I asked as Jane dropped her rucksack to the ground.

'I left two suitcases in London. Thought this would do for a short visit.'

We caught the red tram and sat silently staring at each other with huge smiley faces.

'Thought you were in a hotel. That's what you wrote on your postcard,' Jane said.

'A pension they call it. I've got a small room but I've asked for an extra mattress. '

'Anyway, I'll just stay the one night,' Jane said. 'I want to get to Milan, too, before I go back to London.'

'Who's in Milan?' I said.

'A man I met on the train. I said I'd pop by on the...'

'Way back?'

We laughed. 'Way back when,' we said together and hugged.

'Speaking of,' I said. 'Let's dump your stuff and we can get some food and then we can talk.'

I was hungry for news from home. It *was* still home.

We sat in Café Eiles with frankfurters and beer.

'Saw your parents before I left,' Jane said. 'They keep to themselves. Didn't have much to say, but...'

'Probably too busy with the business. Mum wanted to start her own reception place and concentrate on wedding cakes. She doesn't write.'

'Do you?'

'I did. It's her turn.'

'They're looking forward to you coming home,' she said. 'Only another couple of months and the year will be up.'

'Four months,' I said, biting into my second frankfurter. 'Try it with horseradish,' I said.

Jane did. 'It's making me cry,' she said. 'Too hot!'

'Take some bread. It'll calm down.' I wanted to ask about Jake, but couldn't.

She wiped her eyes. 'Wooo,' she said.

'I need more time,' I said.

'For what?'

'I don't think I want to go back. Not yet. I've started studying translation at uni here.'

'But what about Jake?'

'Have you seen Jake?'

Jane nodded.

'And?'

'He asked me out. After he got back from Noumea. Old time's sake and all that.'

I had a strange feeling of annoyance. I knew nothing about his time in Noumea. Just the postcard he'd sent. And Jane wasn't really in his group. Our uni group.

'Nothing happened,' Jane said quickly. 'Although he did ask to come up, but I was glad I was batching and could say no.'

'If you hadn't been, you would have let him?'

'No!' She turned her flushed face away from me.

So in a way we were quits, Jake and I. Nothing had happened. Funny how that worried me. My own slip-ups didn't seem in the same league. I started to laugh and raised my glass. 'Don't worry about it, Jane. Here's to us.'

She smiled and we clinked glasses.

'I'll come to the station with you tomorrow,' I said. 'No time to see Vienna this time.'

Jane shrugged. 'Next time,' she said. 'We've got all the time in the world.'

At the Westbahnhof, we sat on a platform bench with twenty minutes to kill before the train. We'd talked all night about silly things we'd done in our childhood, our dreams of leaving. And now we had both left. I told her that I'd had good and bad experiences, but didn't go into any details about my sea voyage or Fritz. I told her that I'd met my uncle. I wanted extra time to talk some things out, but words were tired and had lost their power. And something was changed.

'Forget anything?'

Jane shook her head. 'You?'

'Jane. I don't want it to be like this. But things have happened and I can't seem to go back.'

'It's OK. Guess that's what happens when you always expect things to stay the same. We'll get over it.'

The train pulled in and out, with me giving her one last hug and a long wave. Then I went back down the stairs to the bus stop. It had begun to rain. I ran.

I arrived soaked back at the pension. I licked a mixture of tears and raindrops from the side of my mouth.

PART THREE

INFLIGHT PANOPTICON

III

Chapter 27

Christmas came and there'd been a letter from Madeleine.

Geneva, Christmas 1971

Dear Katrina,

Geneva is lovely at Christmas time. No snow this year, but all the lights are on in the city. A fairyland. I am doing well at work. I am helping the man in charge of secretariat recruitment for the Conference. They are even saying I may fill his shoes. I might even throw them out and get away with going barefoot.

I have met someone special. He is East German, of all things. Peter Held is his name. I know it means 'hero'; I can see you smile at the name. Peter is an interpreter from the GDR. He is different. Not like the clichés. Wears jeans all the time. Has a keyring with a Ferrari medal and does not even drive.

I had best stop now. I am off to Paris for some days with the family.

Merry Christmas.

Love, Madeleine

Geneva. My mind raced. I'd love to go there. I imagined the city by the lake. There were photos in one of my textbooks. I pushed the dictionary away and grabbed the book on international organisations and turned to the chapter on the United Nations. The stark, beige UN building in its lush green grounds. Was that a real peacock in the gardens, walking around free? I closed the book and stared at the letter on my desk, chewing on a pencil. This Peter Held. Was Madeleine serious? Why should he need a keyring? His flat. Madeleine's been up to his flat. Wouldn't they be in hotels? It's going on? Longer?

I'd write to Madeleine. Tell her I was interested in work, say, as a trainee translator. I could brush up my school French in Geneva. I thought Madeleine had said they had a translation course at the University of Geneva. I'd check with her. Maybe this was what it meant to have vitamin C. This was ridiculous. I still had another three years in Vienna if I wanted to finish the course and become an interpreter.

But three years were too long. Maybe things would go faster in Geneva. Trainee interpreter. But what about my uncle? The family? I couldn't leave Vienna just like that.

Between Christmas and New Year, I swotted for my January exams. A German-English dictionary sat on top of a pile of textbooks. Folders were open on the floor. Loose sheets of paper filled the wastepaper basket. Screwed-up balls of paper that had missed the basket lay at its base. It had been five months since I'd started the course. The university, luckily, had given me credit for my studies in Sydney. Time was becoming increasingly important. I had to pass my exams. Especially since Madeleine's letter.

'So your quest was on hold?' I say.

Bloody hell! I was young. 'A lot was going on. I was starting a new life.' *And I had found a friend.*

And some things were too painful to pursue. Always dangerous. They always raise their ugly heads again one day. But she will learn.

It was thanks to Neil Armstrong and his walk on the moon that I'd decided to become an interpreter, not just a translator. *Traduttore, trattore*: to translate is to betray, or some such. To interpret went further – translation without a net – consecutive or simultaneous; once the words were spoken, it was all over. When I saw the tape of my professor at the Dolmetschinstitut interpreting the words of an American journalist covering the moon landing, I knew that was what I wanted to do.

To give a foretaste for the job, my professor had given me exercises to see if I'd be able to handle the strain. The exercises hurt.

'Count aloud backwards in English while listening to the speaker in German. Then tell me in your own words in English what the speaker said.'

I stumbled on – 19, 18, 17 – as I heard: '*Heute um 17 Uhr 10, ein Amerikaner*, Neil Armstrong...' ...16, 15, 14... I was doing it. It was like riding a bike. Don't fall off. Don't get the pedals stuck. 'Today at 17:10, an American, Neil Armstrong...' I stopped. The numbers. The regularity ...13, 12, 11... I couldn't put my finger on it. My mind kept counting. Now forwards. 7, 8, 9. I heard the thud of a tennis ball hitting against a wall ...10, 11, 12. Mary Prendegast's voice. Nazi parents. My heart was beating so loud I thought it must drown out the numbers. Backwards. Count. 6, 5, 4... 'The first human being...' 3, 2, 1, 'to walk on the moon.'

The exercise was over. I held firm except for a slight trembling of the fingers of my right hand. It was the way my fingers used to tremble after I'd won a game of tennis. I had to beat this thing. If the worst came to the worst, though, I could still do translations. But there was no way to avoid the exams.

'Must hit the books,' I said aloud. But I couldn't concentrate on my work and began rummaging around on my desk until I found the card Mum had sent. It was a bush scene in ochres and browns; three men were sitting about a campfire. *Dusk at the Camp*. I propped my head in my hands, my elbows on the desk. Mum hadn't written much. But what she had written was so final it numbed me. *Alfred has left us.* What more could she have written? Why hadn't she phoned? She couldn't have. I hadn't given her a number. When had it been? Pain welled up in my stomach and a deep, hollow sound roared wordlessly from my mouth. Through my sobs, my lips could only form the words: *Merry Christmas*.

I had to go on. But where was I to go?

Jake had sent a card, too. So had Jane. There'd been no sign of life from Harald Klain.

Harald Klain. No word from him since he left so quickly after our meal at the Gösserhof. So much had happened since then, but now that I was all alone I wondered where he was and why he'd not kept in touch, not left a clue to contacting him. And what if he was trying to find me? Where would he look? The Gösserhof?

English lessons and the odd translation stints would bring in a bit of money. And I could do my own research. Go to the archives. I was on my own now. Had some time. I had to use it.

'Yes, you had to use it. And you have to use your time now. The deadline. Remember?'

'So, what's this deadline?' she says and pulls at her earlobe.

I wish she would stop doing that. 'You will know when it is there,' I say.

'That's a rook! Bet there is no deadline.'

'There is always a deadline, Katrina. And what is this "rook"?'

'Cheat!' she screams.

Chapter 28

I walked through the Volksgarten in its untouched blanket of snow on the other side of the gravel-bespeckled path and through to the Graben. There before me was Saint Stephen's cathedral, its slender Gothic spires reaching for the sky. Elisabethstraße could not be far now. I looked once again at my map and turned into a side street off Kärtnerstraße. Halfway along I saw a green sign marked *Gösser* hanging over the narrow street. My heart started pounding. The door of the restaurant was painted in ornate Gothic script like that in one or two old German books Mum had had. It wasn't easy to read at first. I hadn't needed to when I'd been there with my uncle. *Gösser. Gösserbräu. Gösserhof.* Maybe it had changed names over the years, I thought, as I pushed open the glass door of the restaurant and went inside.

A waiter nodded at me as I passed. Lunch guests had

already left so I walked from room to room, until I found the painting over the fireplace.

My hands trembled as I stared at my grandfather.

'Can I help you?' a man's voice said behind me.

I spun round. 'No,' I said. 'I mean, yes. That is my grandfather. Do you know anything about him?'

The man rolled down his sleeves, then pulled at his black bow-tie. 'Your grandfather? That was before my time,' he said. 'That picture must have been painted before the war.'

I shook my head slowly. 'Of course. Before the war,' I said dully.

'Do you think there is anyone here who remembers?'

The man shook his head and began peaking a stiff napkin into a hat.

'You might ask someone in one of the houses next door. There are a lot of old people still in the flats around here.'

'Thank you,' I said. 'Do you mind if I stop here a while?'

'Take your time. It is still early,' he said, placing the napkin on the table and taking another to form into the same shape.

I didn't notice him leave the room as I stared once again at the painting. Maybe I'd even find a neighbour who could tell me more. Anything was possible on the eve of a new year.

'Which did not mean it was New Year's Eve.'

'Who's being pedantic now?' she says.

I smile.

The next day was New Year's Eve and I didn't want to be

alone when the New Year rang in. Not alone in the cold. I wanted to start my new year with some semblance of warmth. I'd never felt comfortable in the year-end heatwaves in Sydney, but what I was going through in Vienna, now, was too much to bear; all the snow, and the loneliness of my dreary room in what had once been my family's city.

'The best place to go is the square by Saint Stephen's, the *Steffl*,' Frau Brauer said.

Frau Brauer became almost wistful and added: 'The place is alive with revellers. I used to go there before...the war.'

'The war?' I said and then, on seeing Frau Brauer leaf through some papers on the reception desk, realised that a distant reverie had escaped her tight lips.

'It is good to revel,' she said curtly.

I wasn't sure I wanted to revel; I just didn't want to sit in my room. I didn't want to be alone.

At about ten that evening I dressed in layers, pulling on two thin lambs-wool jumpers and adding woollen tights under my slacks. My Drizabone would keep the warmth in, I hoped, as I put on my gloves and tartan scarf and left the pension. I crossed the Ringstraße to the Heldenplatz, heroes' square. One man's hero, another man's... I stopped. This was no time to think of heroes; they just made me think of soldiers and war. Tonight I'd lose myself in the crowd and just see what happened. And so I became part of the swell of bodies moving as one down Kärntnerstraße towards the Graben and Saint Stephen's Cathedral.

Floodlights fell from the spires of the Gothic cathedral onto the crowd below. People stood and swayed in threes and fours, some with bottles of *Sekt*, the cheaper Austrian champers, in their hands, others with plastic glasses of mulled red wine from one of the stands speckling the square. The cold, crisp air was filled with the smell of sausage and *langos* – deep fried pastry – and garlic.

Bang! The first firecracker. Bang! Bang! Then another. A champagne cork flew through the air as the sky lit up pink and green with fireworks from a nearby balcony. Flash! A light blinded me. I swung round to face a camera lens.

A young, dark-haired man grinned at me and then handed his camera to another man by his side. Before I could react the first man had swept me up in his arms and was twirling me around in the one-two-three beat of a Viennese waltz. Then the man stopped, let me go and stepped back with a mock bow almost down to the ground. For a moment I hesitated, then laughed.

'*Hübsch wenn sie lacht,*' the man said, turning to his friend.

I raised my eyebrows. 'I don't...'

'Speak German?' the young man said and took me in his arms again. 'Then let us dance.' And he twirled me around while people moved back to make room. 'I said how pretty you are when you laugh.'

'Stop,' I said and pulled back. 'You're mad.'

'Mad in Austria,' the young man said, and suddenly came to a halt. 'May I introduce myself?'

I caught my breath and nodded.

'Rudi Figl,' he said, and with a wave of his hand towards the man standing with the camera, he added, 'My friend, Carl Sokorny.'

'Katrina Klain,' I said, as I pulled off one glove and held out my hand. I was too dizzy to focus on Rudi's friend. Rudi raised my fingers to his lips and then quickly turned his head to kiss the back of his own hand. 'It is not very healthy all this kissing of hands, you know.'

I reddened and quickly drew back my hand.

'Only teasing,' Rudi said. 'And you do not speak German with a name like, what was it...Katrina?'

'Klain. With an 'a'. I'm Australian,' I said, then all of a sudden felt foolish.

Just then, Rudi grabbed his camera from Carl and flashed about him. The countdown was starting. Five. Four. Three. Two. One. *Prosit!* Happy New Year! Kiss her! Rudi was clicking wildly and Carl Sokorny planted a kiss on my cheek. I stepped back, but everyone about me was saying *Prosit! Prosit Neu Jahr*, and kissing each other.

Caught up in the excitement I kissed Carl back and said, 'Happy New Year!'

Rudi clicked. 'Now me,' he said, and kissed me on the mouth. I pulled back. 'Hey,' I said, then saw Carl smiling and slowly shaking his head behind Rudi's shoulder. But then I laughed again and the three of us hugged. Then the moment was gone and we disengaged our arms, a movement that left us hanging together on an invisible thread.

'Why all the photos?' I said quickly. 'Are you a photographer?'

'A lion reporter,' Rudi said.

'He means cub,' Carl said.

'Aren't you too old?'

Rudi gave a mock scowl and said seriously, 'I am an eternal student of journalism. Just started late in the work force.'

'Rudi does not have to work,' Carl said, putting his arm about his friend's shoulder.

'Not like Carl,' Rudi said. 'If you want to taste *Zeitgeist* then come with me.'

'Oh, no,' I said, putting my hands up to shield myself in a

parody of a damsel in distress. *The spirit of the times.* Spooky.

'My father's older brother was a great statesman,' Rudi said.

'Do not believe him,' Carl said. 'He is no relation to the famous Figl.'

My eyebrows shot up. 'What famous Figl?'

'Leopold Figl started the new Republic after the war. Said Austria was free,' Carl said. 'Rudi is not related to him.'

'Got me!' Rudi laughed, and clapped Carl on the back. 'Carl knows all about history. He'd have to, being in with all those dry old papers all day. But I shall tell you a secret. Do you want to hear it?'

My mouth formed a yes.

'He has a drop of blue blood.'

I looked at Carl. He did not look too aristocratic with his sandy blond hair. His green loden coat was open over a polo-neck jumper and dark-blue cord trousers. He could be from anywhere, even Australia, I thought. Just the coat was like ones I'd seen often in Vienna. What was he supposed to look like? It wasn't as if he had to wear a badge to prove it.

'We all have blue blood, but it is really red,' Carl said, and held out his hand, palm up. 'See that vein?'

I nodded.

'Look at yours. What colour is it?'

I held out my hand and looked at the vein at my wrist. 'Blue,' I said.

'And now look at Rudi's.'

Rudi was trying not to laugh as he stretched out his wrist.

'What colour is his?' Carl said.

'The same,' I said.

'So, my theory is correct,' Carl said. 'We all have blue veins, but when we cut through them...'

I stepped back. What was he getting at? This talk was getting scary.

'The blood is red.'

'We are all the same?' I said.

'Full marks!' Rudi said and clapped his hands.

'You're making fun of me,' I said.

'No,' said Carl.

'Just mad,' Rudi cut in. 'Now tell me how long you will be staying in Vienna.'

I felt confused, as if caught between a zany black humour and an outright flirt, almost a proposition. 'I don't know,' I said.

'What he means,' said Carl, 'is can we take you home?'

'Or do you want to stay and party with us,' Rudi said with a grin.

Fireworks lit up the skies and bangers were making it difficult to hear. I shook my head. 'I'll find my own way home,' I said. 'And the party, well, it has been...delightful,' I added, and curtsied. Then I held out my hand primly and shook Rudi's then Carl's. 'I'll be staying a while though.'

'Then we shall meet you again,' Rudi said, and blew me a kiss.

'*Prosit Neujar*, Katrina Klain!'

Just before turning to walk back to the Opera, I glimpsed Carl wave his hand in farewell.

'Free with your kisses, Katrina.'

'For Heaven's sake.'

'I just say.'

She puffs. But it sounds like a snort.

Chapter 29

Life was in sleep mode on New Year's Day as the city recharged its batteries beneath a blanket of light snow.

I had slept late after the previous night's throngs welcoming in the New Year. The crisp cold had made my cheeks smart on my walk back to the pension, giving me the feeling I was really starting the year in a new place. It had been so unlike New Year's Eve in Australia, with dancing and hugging on the beach and Eskies overflowing with ice-cooled beer.

When I came down from my room at eleven that morning Frau Brauer was at the desk.

'So,' she said, 'did you revel?'

I nodded. 'There were so many people. Is it always like that?'

'There are more tourists now,' Frau Brauer said. 'Before,

when I was younger, there were only Austrians, or at least only German was spoken. Later there was the war and we only celebrated indoors, if you could call that celebration.'

'And what was it like just after the war?'

Frau Brauer's eyes gazed beyond me back into a distant time. 'There was great revelling,' she said quietly.

I tried to imagine Hedwig Brauer dancing beneath the Steffl, twirling a waltz, laughing and kissing. Perhaps she had been in the arms of a man she loved, or perhaps she had just been flirting.

Suddenly Frau Brauer said: 'My fiancé had just come back from the front. We had lost the war, but he had come back whole. For a while we thought it a good time.'

I was puzzled. The other day Frau Brauer had clammed up, yet now she was telling me things from her youth, even seemed happy in some of her memories. I didn't know whether I should prompt her for more or just wait till she'd told her story.

As I was just about to speak, my stomach rumbled so loudly that I thought Frau Brauer would hear.

'The Gasthaus next door is open for lunch,' she said, 'and there are others further down the street that would also be open today.' Then she turned to tidy some sightseeing brochures on the shelf behind her.

'*Danke*,' I said, wondering if the woman would come back to her story and puzzling at why she had even started it.

Outside, the street was coming to life as people in twos and threes headed towards the *Gasthäuser* open for the holiday. It was as if the city had awoken, if only slowly. People relaxed differently here, I thought. In Sydney they stayed home on New Year's Day, nursing hangovers and the realisation that resolutions made the night before would not be kept. In Vienna, they chased their hangovers with hearty food and beer. Perhaps they did not make resolutions. I had made one resolution when the chimes of *Prosit!* sounded: I resolved to discover the story behind the mystery of Harald Klain.

A quick lunch in the Hirtenwirt and then a walk over to Elisabethstraße. I could explore Elisabethstraße and look at the names on the letterboxes of the nearby apartment houses. I didn't know what I was looking for – perhaps a Klain.

If it had been after the Three Kings I could have gone to the archives. Didn't the blond chap from last night, Carl, say he worked there? Why hadn't I paid more attention?

I sat down at a table at the back of the restaurant. The walls were covered with plate mirrors, and candles flickered on the tables with their long damask tablecloths that reached down like petticoats to the chairs and the seats of the leather benches clinging to the walls. A waiter in a long green apron came to take my order.

'*Bier. Schinkenrolle, Bitte,*' I said. It was too early for a big meal but the Russian salad rolled in a piece of ham would be light enough. On the next table a magazine was furled about its long wooden holder. Others hung from hooks on the wall. No dailies today, just weekly tabloids. I flicked through the pages then turned the magazine to its cover. *Wiener Wochenblatt.* I remembered the magazine Frau Brauer had been browsing at the desk of the pension the other day – *WieWo* –, but couldn't imagine what could have caught her interest. *WieWo*, I thought. Not just a snappy name for the magazine. *Wie* – how? *Wo* – where? A bit weird. I finished my beer and made my way back to the pension. I didn't have to go further. I could ask Frau Brauer if I could borrow her magazine so that I could study it again. Or perhaps Frau Brauer could tell me what the article was about, but something told me I had to be careful around her.

When I came back to the pension, Frau Brauer had gone and a sign was up that she would not be back until later.

I walked back into town to look at the houses in Elisabethstraße. The grey facades were all alike, although some had been renovated more recently. Not all the houses had chipped windowsills and some even had large modern windows. The first house was locked. Many of the houses had a main door now, with an intercom system. I couldn't just press one of the buttons, and anyway, what would I say? I felt as if I were bumping into a dead end in a maze. I knew that the lead I was looking for was out there, but I didn't know where it was and when I would find it. And I didn't have forever. Geneva was calling.

I'd written to Jake to ask him to write to me c/o American Express in Vienna. Even though my first year away was almost over, I wasn't ready to go back yet.

When I arrived back at the pension, Frau Brauer was at the desk, the tabloid open at a page with the photo of a man's face.

'*Guten Abend*,' I said.

Frau Brauer looked up, her eyes narrowing. 'You were born in Vienna?' she asked.

I nodded. 'How did you know?'

'It was marked on your papers for the police.' She closed the tabloid.

Everything is controlled. Catalogued. Archived.

'I knew a Klain once,' Frau Brauer said.

I stared at the woman.

'He used to stay here from time to time. Years ago. He was quite a charmer.'

My heart started racing. 'Do you remember his first name?' I said into what seemed like an endless silence.

'No. We called him Herr Doktor. Herr Doktor Klain. He was wearing a brown trench coat that day. I remember because it was summer and he had his coat buttoned and belted,' Frau Brauer said. 'He didn't speak much and just filled out the papers, but he had a way of looking at you.' Frau Brauer paused and stroked her cheek with one finger. 'It was as if he were undressing you, except he kept his pale blue eyes on my face.' Then she cleared her throat. 'He stayed for about a week. Always wore the coat. Just nodded and smiled with that look of his when I greeted him as Herr Doktor.'

I stared at Frau Brauer. The woman was opening and closing like a clam, one moment the flesh exposed, the next the shell tight. 'Did he say why he had come?'

'I said, he did not talk much,' Frau Brauer said. Then she stroked her cheek again. 'He asked if there was a Herr Brauer. When I said not any more he asked no more questions. But all this is going back about ten years. I just remember that he was charming.'

When I went up to my room I wondered about the charm of Harald Klain. After all these years, he had obviously made a lasting impact on Frau Brauer. And Herr Brauer? Wasn't Fritz a Herr Brauer? I tasted something bitter and wiped a hand over my mouth.

'The bitter taste of paranoia? Or were you seeing ghosts?'

196

She tosses her head.

'Brauer is such a common name. There must be dozens of them in Vienna. Not as many as Hrdlicka or Posbicil, but dozens, nevertheless...'

'Who are...?'

'Never mind,' I say.

Monday. The archives would be open. I tied my scarf over my head to protect my ears from the piercing cold and slipped a map of Vienna into my bag. *Nationalarchiv*. Behind the Heldenplatz. The main entrance facing the Ring. I strode briskly down Mariahilferstraße. Twenty minutes later I arrived at the State Archives. A brass sign said that opening hours were from 9h30 am to 4h30 pm. I looked at my watch. 9 am. Behind the Ballhausplatz I saw a café. Breakfast. Coffee.

'See that balcony?'

She looks.

'That is where the famous balcony is. Look.'

She is confused, I can see.

'The balcony where Hitler stood to the cheers of the city. The balcony where Figl proclaimed Austria to be free. And, soon, where Bruno Kreisky in 1971 would welcome home the banned ski star, Karl Schranz, who now, so many years later, plays with Russian Czars.'

'What are you going on about?'

'Forgive me. I became a little carried away. Lies have a way of doing that. Back to your coffee.'

From the window I could see the balcony.

I sipped my *mélange* and bit into a round crust of raisin bread. Hitler had greeted the people of Vienna from that balcony. What was his name, Rudi Figl? His grandfather or uncle, or no one at all related to him, had cried out *Freiheit*. Something about another Karl? And now I would search for my own history. If I were lucky I might even bump into Rudi's friend, Carl Sokorny. My head was spinning.

Wide stone stairs led to the entrance of the *Staatsarchiv*. Heavy glass doors barred my way. I pushed. They gave. At a desk in the foyer a man in uniform sat behind a cardboard sign: INFORMATION.

'I'm looking for information on my family. My uncle. Could you please tell me where to go?'

'This is the archive. Part of the State Library,' the man said.

'Yes, but what floor do I go to?'

'This is the archive.'

'I know that.'

'Historical archives.'

'Yes.'

'No family information here. Unless we are talking more than one hundred years ago. Famous people,' the man said, and sniffed.

'Please. Then where should I go?'

'Rathaus,' the man said. 'Town Hall.'

'Thank you,' I said. 'You have been most helpful.' How rude can you get?

The man shrugged.

I pushed out through the glass doors and stood on the steps. The air was crisp and the sky was laden with snow clouds. The Rathaus. I could see its Gothic spire through the park on the other side of the Ringstraße.

'You will now let me have a go,' I say.

She shrugs.

'You have no choice. If you do not, we will get stuck in your story, and you will miss the deadline.'

'So you are helping me?'

'Indeed.'

Chapter 30
Carl Sokorny

I like my job in the personal archives section of the Town Hall. I am in charge of birth and death certificates for the inhabitants of Stadt and Land Wien, which includes areas lying around Vienna and not just the sprawling twenty-three districts that spin out from the city centre like a cartwheel.

My job allows me access to data that did not make the history books, necessarily, but constitutes the fabric of a population, a country. It also enables me to meet people from all over the world, all looking for the same thing: where they came from.

I am used to having people come all the way from America, North and South, even New Zealand, South Africa. I myself am on a similar search, in a way. What holds me back, holds us all back, is perhaps the fear of what we might find.

I was mulling over this when there was a knock on the door

to my office. I glanced at my watch and then straightened the papers on my desk.

'*Herein*,' I said.

Katrina Klain walked in. She stopped. 'Hallo.'

I rose to my feet. 'We meet again.'

Katrina looked round the small room with its old wooden furniture. She glanced at the tall wooden cupboards with roller fronts before one wall, and over to the window giving onto the inside quadrangle with its solitary tree. I straightened before her. I was glad I had worn my jacquard sweater in tones of mustard and dark green. It livened things up, although I did still wear a tie. I stretched out my hand and she came over to my desk. 'Nice to see you again,' she said, as she sat down in the seat facing me.

'I'm looking for information on my family. My father, my grandfather, my uncle.' Then she added with a smile, 'I'm so glad you speak English. When I saw the word on your door, I got a bit worried.'

I wondered if she'd been trying to translate *Parteienverkehr*. Party traffic. Party sex. I cleared my throat. Best not to go there. 'English, French, Spanish, and this is where I landed.' I smoothed a hand over the neat pile of papers on my desk. 'The name is Klain, isn't it?'

Katrina nodded. 'Yes, Klain. Herr Sokorny,' she said, and grinned.

'Carl, no?'

'Even here?'

'Why not?'

'So, can you help me?'

'I think so. But it will take some time. Tell me all you know. Names. Dates.'

Katrina leaned back in the wooden chair. 'Klain. Alfred.

Harald. Then there's Gösserhof. I was there the other day. Belonged to my grandfather. Elisabethstraße. Birth dates. Let me see. 1918. 1920? I don't know.

'*Luftwaffe*? Air force.' Her voice became hushed. 'Dachau.'

'And you?'

'What do you mean, me?'

'Weren't you born here in Vienna?'

Katrina stopped. 'Yes. But it's not about me.'

'But there are papers on you if you were born here and there'll be papers on your parents. Marriage certificate, for example.'

'Oh. Yes, of course. Born 1949.'

I scribbled on a pad of paper. 'It will take a couple of weeks. Are you free for lunch?'

Katrina's eyes widened. 'That long?' she said.

'I thought I was being quite fast,' I said.

Katrina laughed nervously. 'I didn't mean that. Yes. I'll meet you for lunch.'

'Downstairs at 12h30 then? We'll go to the Ratskeller next door.'

Katrina nodded and stood up. 'Till then.'

'*Wiedersehen*,' I said.

Chapter 31

Katrina Klain

Out on the street soft flakes had begun falling. But it was not as cold as I expected. I covered my head with my scarf and walked through the small park to the university. As I crossed the street between the Rathaus and the university, I thought about Carl. I'd hoped to find him at the Staatsarchiv, but had not thought I'd find him in the Rathaus.

A squealing of tires. I looked towards where the noise was coming from. A black-clothed figure in a helmet was bearing straight down upon me. The motorbike came close. I flung myself to the side of the road. Burning rubber. I picked myself up and heard another squeal as the bike careered round behind the square of the Rathaus. I was shaking. My knees and elbows were smarting. I looked down and my tights were bloody holes at my knees. I turned to look back to where I'd come from. The street was narrow. There was no traffic. Then I realised the shock of an almost hit-and-run. Why?

I looked down again. What a mess. I couldn't meet Carl like this.

There was a drugstore over the road on the street that went into the centre. I'd try and gets some new tights, and some iodine for my knees. Had the bike tried to hit me, or scare me to death? Why would anyone want to do that? It must have been some kind of mistake. Maybe someone had confused me with somebody else. Or the rider had lost control. Swerved onto me in the curve. He was going fast. I trembled again. Shit. It was hell being alone.

When I met Carl I told him what had happened. 'I'm still shaking,' I said.

'I can see that.'

'What does it mean?'

Carl looked at me gently and put down his glass of wine. 'I don't know. He must have been too scared to stop.'

'Well he certainly scared me,' I said. 'I could have been killed.'

'I don't think it was intentional. How long is your visa?'

'What visa?'

'As a tourist you can stay three months. After that, you need a visa.'

'I didn't need one when I was working at UNIDO.'

'No, but once you left you lost your international status and became a tourist again. If someone wanted to scare you, get you to leave, that someone would have to know that you only have three months to do what you've come for.'

'What I've come for? Come on, Carl. You're making it

sound as if someone really is after me. I only want to find out about my family. Anyway, apart from you, now, who knows that I can only stay three months?'

'Listen, Katrina. I'm trying to be logical. You're registered at the police aren't you?'

'Yes. But not the police.'

'Where did you fill in the papers then?'

I stared at Carl. 'Pension Czernik.' My cheeks felt hot. 'Not Frau Brauer?'

'Who is Frau Brauer?'

'The woman at the pension. Carl, do you think it could have something to do with my uncle?'

'Your uncle?'

'She said she knew him. That he stayed at the pension.'

'What's his full name?'

'Dr Harald Klain.'

Carl's face lost colour. Then he said gently: 'I think you should move out of there.'

'But where should I go?'

Carl was silent. Then he looked at me seriously. 'Now don't take this the wrong way, but I think you should move out of the Pension Czernik. I think you should come and stay at my place.'

'Your place? I hardly know you.'

'I said not to take it the wrong way. I have a spare room. You can stay there for a while until we find out what is going on.'

What is going on, I wondered as we left the Ratskeller.

'Is your rent paid up?'

'Till tomorrow.'

'Is Frau Brauer there in the evenings?'

'Not after seven.'

'Go back later and get your things, then take a taxi to this address. I'll be waiting.' And he slipped me a folded piece of paper and a one-hundred-*schilling* note.

'I can't,' I said.

Carl shook his head. 'See you tonight.'

'So quick to move out and move in with someone you hardly knew. But that's…'

'That's how it happened. I trusted him; I…' she says.

'You needed to trust someone. A bit of a gamble.' I cannot say she is brave.

'I didn't think, back then.'

'Would you do it today?'

Today? I'm here today. Not much choice.

True.

Chapter 32

At 9 pm I left Pension Czernik with my suitcase. I took a taxi at the rank three hundred metres away and stared out of the window at a moving Vienna on a winter night. The taxi drove round the Ring, out past the curved façade of the Urania building before crossing the Danube Canal to the second district. The Riesenrad, its enormous wheel lit up, glowed from the end of a broad avenue. Taborstraße.

Number 23 was one of many turn-of-the-century apartment houses. Light glowed through each of the long double windows. As I got out of the taxi and paid, a window on the third floor opened and a head leaned out. 'Catch,' Carl said, and let drop a small pouch. It landed with a thud and a jingle at my feet. 'For the house door.'

I picked up the pouch, pulled out the key, opened the massive door and pushed hard. Inside the dim foyer a lamp lit a panel on the wall. It had names and numbers. Sokorny. Third floor. I pushed the button of an old wrought-iron lift and waited as it creaked its way down. With one foot I held open the door and dragged my suitcase into the cubicle. The door snapped closed behind me and I was face-to-face with a large square mirror. Its corners had small brown spots like those on the blisters of the wrought-iron lift cage. I pushed back my scarf and wiped a smudge from under my eye. I bit my lips to give them some colour and then moistened them with my tongue. Then I caught myself. This wasn't a date. This was a move to safety.

But how do you know you're going to be safe? a small voice said in my mind. You have to trust, another voice said. Then the lift stopped with a jolt.

Carl stood on the landing, the door behind him hanging wide open.

He stepped towards me to pick up my suitcase. '*Willkommen*,' he said.

Trust, I thought. 'It's so good of you,' I said.

'It's very simple,' he said, leading the way down a dimly lit corridor into a high-ceilinged room. He set my case down and helped me take off my coat. 'Make yourself comfortable.'

The ceiling had white stucco plaster like a rose. From the centre hung an old-fashioned chandelier. The prisms gleamed against the light. Dark-green velvet curtains were drawn back with thickly coiled tassels from long windows. The floor gleamed a rich brown between muted-blue Persian carpets. Two leather couches angled a corner. In the other a tiled oven reached to the ceiling.

'It's like a palace.'

'It is my palace,' Carl said, and laughed. 'Would you like a drink? Some white wine?'

I was about to nod yes, but quickly said: 'Water will do.'

'So, water it is. The best in the world. Straight from the mountains to my tap.'

Now it was my turn to laugh. 'To your tap?'

'Viennese water should be bottled,' Carl said. 'But why should we bottle it?'

Why should we? I looked at the man who was now leaving the room. There was still the question about the other man who had knocked me over.

'Did you manage to find anything in your archives?' I said, trying to keep my voice even.

Carl came back with a tall tumbler of water in one hand and two glasses of white wine cradled in the other.

'Yes,' he said as he placed the wine glasses on the floor between us and held the tumbler out to me. 'Your father's name was Alfred. He was born in 1918. He had a brother, Harald, born in 1920. Their mother, Alberta, died in 1962.'

I stared at him as he said the names of the members of my family. There was something strangely cold and clinical about it. Perhaps it was normal. They were just names and dates on papers for him.

'My grandfather? Otto Klain?'

'He died just before war broke out. 1939.'

'And the Gösserhof?'

'It wasn't his. It was leased. From the Gösser Brewery in Sols. Styria.'

I sat silent and placed my tumbler on the floor untouched. 'Do you think Frau Brauer has something to do with all this?'

Carl sipped his wine. 'Katrina,' he said, 'I don't know.

Maybe that motorbike scare was an accident. But I think there is something about the name, Klain – your father or your uncle.'

'What do you mean?'

'In the Fifties, records show that your uncle was excluded from the bar.'

'But he was a *Doktor*, Frau Brauer said. She said she'd met a Dr Harald Klain.'

'She knew that? Dr is a title many people in Austria wear, and they wear it proudly. It's not like in England, or in Australia, I suppose, when it's only a doctor of medicine who calls himself Dr. Here, it is anyone with a doctorate, a PhD, even honorary ones.' Then he laughed. 'I guess it's to make up for the titles lost. But they do the same thing in Germany, where they can keep the titles.'

'So he was a Doctor of Law?' My mind opened to memories of the past. 'I have vague memories.' Then I stopped. Here I was talking to a complete stranger about things that my father or mother might have said. It was all going too fast. I had hardly touched the water, not to mention the clear blond wine in the glass on the floor. 'Carl,' I said. 'I'm so terribly tired. Didn't you say you had a place for me to sleep?'

'I'm sorry.' Carl got up. 'Come. I have a bed in my study. You'll be perfectly safe,' he added with a smile.

'Edgy, Katrina?'

'Wouldn't you be? Crikey!'

'So let us see what this Carl Sokorny is about.'

Click.

Chapter 33

Carl Sokorny

I lay in the broad double bed in my room, my hands tucked under my head. Katrina Klain was a mystery yet. At least her family was. But the name Klain had brought forth so many leads. I had been unable to follow them all that afternoon. My godfather had just written his diaries. There was mention of Dachau. Trials. A last-ditch attempt by Hitler. *Operation Greif.* Alfred Klain had been involved. The incident with the motorbike had attuned me, perhaps. Yet it was improbable for there to have been a link between the incident and anything related to the war years. The few facts I had found were only those cold objective ones linked to certificates of birth and death, or other official papers, like the one about Harald Klain being excluded from the bar. I'd often had to do research on papers belonging to *Auswanderer* who had migrated to the US or Canada, even Australia. But this was the first time that those dry facts began to relate to real, living people. A real living person who was sleeping in my study.

My mind turned to Katrina Klain. What had made me offer her a sanctuary – if it was that? She'd been no different from many of the girls Rudi had managed to accost on our evenings out together. Or maybe she had. She hadn't ended up with Rudi. I turned my head to wipe the thought away on my pillow. Then I turned back. Rudi! Rudi worked with the papers. He was a journalist. Not quite. An eternal cub. But Rudi could check out Frau Brauer. Yet Rudi was so unreliable. Better not ask him. I turned on my side and curled up. With hazy visions of a black-leather garbed man, the face of a woman not unlike my mother's, and a face that was Rudi's, I drifted into an uneasy sleep.

The water came up to my armpits; that's how deep it was. I could have walked all the way to Hungary had I a mind to. That was the thing about the Neusiedler See; you could walk in it, swim in it, even drown in it. My mother had taken me there on Sundays, in a bus. She never talked about dangers, only about what was lost, what was owed. People, she said, were drowned during storms because they'd gone out beyond their depth. It had been their own fault. She never spoke of those who had been crushed, sucked in by the force of the waves, those who had clumped themselves at the edges, swaying and bending like reeds, those who had walked away, and those who had had to keep walking, running and hiding.

Waves began lapping at my chin as the sun hid behind pale clouds, thick like the langos *fried at the Vienna food markets. It was as though the breezes were pulling the warm water upwards just* as my feet sank into the lake bed. I swam a few strokes and then walked a few steps. I could feel the silt holding me back. A wind turned the sky into dripping grey oil.

I parted the reeds and at last reached the shore, my toes squelching in the brown silt. I stumbled onto the spiky grass on dry land and stared out over the brown-grey water, trying to piece the bits together, trying to see where I fitted in.

Chapter 34

Katrina Klain

'Carl, do you think you could help me find somewhere cheap to stay? It won't be for long. I have to go to Geneva. I have a friend there and I think I can get a job with the UN.'

Carl drank slowly from his coffee mug. 'I have to show you something.' He got up and went to his desk. 'Here it is. Read this,' he said, stretching out a magazine. 'It's not the sort of magazine I usually buy, but I saw it in a *gasthaus* when I was having brunch, so I bought the issue this morning, while you were sleeping,' he added.

He was so nice. I smiled. Then I saw the words *WieWo*. It was the magazine Frau Brauer had been reading. 'How? Where?' I said.

Carl gave me a funny look and shook his head. 'Look at the photo. No, not the man. The little one of the front-door plate. What does it say?'

I stared and read aloud:

'*Dr Stanko Zorko, Dr Monique Zorko, Dr Harald Klain*', as my finger traced the lines of the story below the half-page photograph of an old man. The face stared proudly, almost taunting the photographer who had taken the photo. I read the legend: *In a penthouse flat in Madrid our reporter met the fugitive...*

'Stop,' Katrina cries.

Click.

'What is the matter?' I ask. 'We must move on.'

'Zoom,' she says. She barks the word.

I know what is coming. In a way, I have been expecting this.

'Our reporter! Look at the byline. Jaimie Stadler.'

I shall have to do this with style. 'At your service, Katrina.'

'You! You knew all the time.'

'I have the facts.'

'You bend them and twist them.'

'I did introduce myself when you came in.'

What sort of place have I landed in?

'Let us move on, Katrina.'

'Move on? Is that what you say when you want to avoid an explanation?'

How could I explain? She would not believe me. I waited. She says nothing. What is she doing?

She is taking the box from which my voice emanates. She breaks off the funnel, throws it all on the ground. My gods. She is stamping on it. My voice wheezes. I was not expecting this. She looks at the box smashed to the ground, hears my voice, looks around. The screen. The door. She sees me. She sees my hologram. She laughs. She laughs?

'You are the biggest liar,' she says. 'Look at you. In flares. Give me a break!'

I could not resist using a much younger me for my hologram. Beatles hair, flared jeans. Very well.

'You're sick,' she says.

So there I am. But nothing can hold me back. Not wars, not scandals, not even talk shows. I think of that rapper and how he made a laughing stock out of me. Told me to get out. It was a shock. A shock that led to this place not so very long ago. 'Shall we move on?' I say.

Click.

I scanned the article:

The penthouse apartment is elegantly furnished with modern furniture, old icons and statues of the saints. An old and extremely robust man presses a microphone to his throat. An operation two years earlier has left his voice almost non-existent. He presses the microphone harder, almost burying it in the folds of his neck. His voice is truncated almost, droning like snores, the voice of a robot. And now he wants amnesty to be able to die in peace.

For three decades the Austrian authorities have been looking for this man. His name is Stanko Zorko and it has appeared in hundreds of headlines that call him the 'King of the Export Swindlers'. With forged export papers he is meant to have reclaimed 50 million schillings in taxes. That would be almost half a billion schilling today.

'And today, Katrina. More than thirty-five million euros and entry in the list of Best of Austrian Finance Scandals. What a claim to fame!'

My eyes raced through the article:

'I was a crook. Like so many others. But they were all corrupt: businesspeople, politicians, government offices, political parties. But I never embezzled tax money. Others did that. And in roundabout ways they financed the parties...

...plastic ties for an African tribe...goods that were never produced and were only exported from Austria on paper.'

I passed Carl the magazine. 'What does it mean? Not the language. The implications.'

'You mean right and wrong? Black and white?'

'I guess.' When your own flesh and blood is involved, where do you stand?

'There's something else, Katrina,' Carl said.

I sipped from my cup. Waited.

'The Zorko story is an old one. It was meant to have died long ago. Last I heard was that Zorko wanted amnesty to be able to die in peace. At least that's what my father said when that reporter rang to ask him about Spain. I wonder if it's the same reporter... Katrina, my godfather, my father's cousin, is a certain Count von Sokorny. His real name was Otto Skorzeny. The most dangerous man in Europe, they said. He's dead for all I know. But there's a link. He and this Zorko and possibly your uncle, Harald Klain, were linked in some way.'

A skeleton in his grave, or in the closet of the Sokorny

family in Vienna? 'And me asking questions is dangerous?'

Carl shrugged. 'Maybe not. I was in Madrid about ten years ago. I wonder if there's a link with what's going on now. The strange thing is, why should it matter after all this time?'

'What happened in Madrid?'

'I'll just get some fresh coffee to help me remember.'

Katrina looks at my hologram. 'Well, do your job. That's what you're here for.'

I say nothing. I try to keep my face impassive. She can see me now. I must watch my reactions. One always has to when something is at stake.

Click.

Chapter 35

Carl Sokorny

1962. In my sixteenth summer I spent the school holidays in Madrid. I had taken the train, a two-day trip.

'There'll be your godfather waiting for you,' my mother had said at the Westbahnhof. 'Another part of the family, and you will see what we once were.'

I smiled at her. She had often spoken of the family into which she, the postmaster's daughter, had married. The von Sokorny's, the cousins of 'displaced East European royalty' she called them whenever she dipped into a reverie about what had been the Austro-Hungarian Empire.

'They took away our title, our deeds,' she said. 'In the name of democracy. Socialism, it is...'

She patted my cheek. 'We had many royal friends ages ago. Your godfather is a count. He has kept the 'von' before

Sokorny. He was a general, too. It will be good for your education. Something the Republic can no longer offer.'

I slept fitfully on the night train from Vienna. Not only was it my first trip away from home, there was also the prospect of meeting this 'almost royalty' my mother so admired. Despite my curiosity about meeting my godfather, I was also anxious that I might not measure up, might not belong.

When I arrived at Madrid's Atocha station I was grubby and my clothes were rumpled. I stood up and fidgeted with my collar, then with the back of my hand I tried to smooth the cloth of my trousers. A glance in the compartment mirror showed me that my cowlick had won and that my hair was standing on end. I spat in my hand and tried to slick it down. Royalty! Soon I would see my godfather. And what if he wasn't at the station? I picked up my suitcase and went to the door.

Count Otto von Sokorny was standing on the platform.

'You will recognise him,' my mother had said. 'Tall, slim, blonde hair, perhaps white now; he will no doubt be wearing a monocle, and he has a scar. Do not stare at it.'

The man in the beige linen suit waved to me as I alighted from the train.

'I'm afraid I have not been much of a godfather,' he said as he stretched out his hand to shake mine man to man. 'But I shall make up for that.'

I took the man's hand. It was dry and cold. I imagined the skin of a snake and concentrated on not withdrawing too quickly. 'Nice to meet you at last,' I said. As I looked up at the count's face I saw a smile quiver over the man's thin lips. There was a glint from behind the black-rimmed monocle clamped in the hollow of his left eye and the muscles holding the monocle in place gave his face a quizzical look. A fine scar ran from his right cheekbone to the edge of his mouth. Don't stare. I concentrated on his monocle.

The Count led the way from the platform with long, precise strides. I tried to keep up with him as he ploughed through groups of people stopping to scan train arrivals and departures.

'A car is waiting outside. You are to join me as a guest at the house of the Duke of Avaron, just outside Madrid.' The count's words were clipped, almost in the manner of an order, and as we emerged from the glass hangar of the station, the air became suddenly dry.

The car was a Bentley. Beige, and with a uniformed chauffeur, who swung open the rear door for me to get in. I sank into the deep leather upholstery. I could barely see out of the window.

The Bentley coasted through back streets of apartment houses. Geraniums decorated some of the wrought-iron balconies; washing hung out to dry spanned others. Suddenly the car screamed to a halt. A young boy had run out on the road chasing a ball.

'Idiot!' the Count snapped. 'Why do you take this way?'

The driver did not reply but kept his eyes straight ahead as the Bentley squealed round a corner towards a large park and sped up by a large man-made pond. Majestic buildings raced by as the Count barked landmarks: El Prado, Banco de España. Palacio de Comunicación. Ministerio del... I could not fit the names to the buildings, many of which reminded me of those on Vienna's Ringstraße, as the car sped towards the outskirts of the city, and I was almost thankful as we began to pass what looked like much poorer areas. At least my godfather had stopped shooting words at the street as if the names he uttered would stick to the buildings they were passing. The houses became blockhouses and were smaller and smaller, some with what looked like lean-to roofs propped on one side. As we came closer I saw that the lean-tos were large boards and rusty sheets of metal, and were indeed roofs. Barefoot children were playing in the dust with a skinny dog.

'Gypsies,' the Count said. 'Slums. And they blame the government. Filthy animals!'

I looked at my godfather and saw that the sides of his mouth had turned down. 'That should have been over,' I heard him say. I turned my head and stared out of the window again.

The landscape had given way to a blood-red soil with grey clumps of scrub. Then it thickened into more green, trees and more trees, as the car began gently to climb. Now I saw that my godfather's mouth relaxed, his lips coming to rest in a straight line. It was as if with every degree of inclination he was casting off the last residues from the slums.

'Now you will see the real Spain,' he said. Then his voice dropped to a whisper that I hardly heard. 'Bullfights, blood. That will make a man of you.' I shivered in the air-conditioned cool of the car as the count's voice rose again and he said: 'Look ahead.'

I leaned forward to look out the front window, my head between that of the chauffeur's and my godfather's; a vein at the older man's left temple was twitching.

The car coasted through an avenue of poplars, closely planted, their branches waving gently in the breeze. Leaves sparkled in the afternoon sun as the light hit each one and the car turned and approached a gigantic gate. The doors had been pulled open.

A small cottage stood on the right at the entrance. Its barred windows braced red geraniums. Behind the house, just as the car drew abreast, three dogs as big as calves strained against a wire fence, growling then barking.

'Spanish mastiffs,' Count Otto said. 'Almost as good as German shepherds. But bloodier.' He coughed.

We drove on for another two hundred metres and turned into a circular driveway; the wheels of the Bentley crunched on gravel, spitting it outwards as the car braked into the curve. A large well in the middle of the driveway was resplendent with deep-red geraniums.

'We are here,' the count said. 'The residence of the Duke and Duchess of Avaron.'

'It looks so empty,' I said. There were the dogs, of course, but no other sign of life. 'Who lives in the house at the gate?'

'The caretaker. The servants are here, but they are best not seen nor heard.'

_ I wondered if the count's remark was also aimed at me.

'The duke is away for a few days,' he continued. 'His home is for me to use as I see fit. He and the duchess will be back tonight.'

I looked up at the stone entrance stairs. The front door was open. My godfather must be very good friends with the duke for him to leave him his house like this. Then the dogs barked in the distance and I shivered.

I followed Count Otto von Sokorny through a foyer of black-and-white chessboard floor tiles. On the left, tall double doors stood open. I saw a fireplace large enough to roast a cow, heavy sculpted wood furniture and plush poltroons upholstered in leather. Somehow, living was not what I associated with the room. I thought of my home in Vienna, a three-room flat, a far cry from this house of a friend of the family.

On the right of the foyer the doors were closed. 'The kitchen,' said the count as if answering a question, reading it in my mind. The foyer stretched on through the house and onto a patio bounded by high walls on each side and bordered at the far end by two low buildings. A space in the centre afforded a view of sparkling water in a pool.

'This is where the parties are held,' the count said, his hand sweeping over the square open space with its fountain in the centre and the creepers over the walls. 'It is cool here on our hot summer nights. You shall soon see. Even tonight the duke and duchess will be entertaining guests.' Then he led me to a curving staircase in stone in the right-hand corner of the foyer. 'Your room is upstairs. Come.'

My room was a 'suite' on the next floor: a bedroom, a bathroom and another room decorated with furniture like that I had seen on the tours my mother would take me on through Vienna's Schönbrunn Palace. 'Here you will take your breakfast,' my godfather said. 'The duke and duchess take that meal by themselves. I do not eat before noon.'

I dropped my case on the floor by the bed. I had not spoken one word. The trip, the changes in scenery, the dogs, this giant old empty home, my godfather, Count Otto von Sokorny. I felt weak and sat down on the bed.

'Rest now,' the older man said. 'At ten the house will be full.' Then he left me alone in my room.

At ten there was a knock at my door. 'Shall we go?' my godfather said. I quickly tucked in my shirt and straightened my collar then followed him down the stairs to the patio.

The guests had arrived, and held glasses. They picked at tapas of olives, pickled anchovies, sliced sausage. In among the bare arms of the women and the sleeved ones of the men I saw a priest and two or three officers from the military. Having seen no one earlier on, I wondered if that was all people of this class did in the Spanish summer – drink, nibble and meet outside. I wondered what the ordinary people did. The people I had seen from the car on the way to the house, the ones without champagne and blue blood. I looked at the vein at my wrist. If I cut it, I thought, the blood will flow the same colour as that of those out in the streets.

'I want to see how real people live,' I said to my godfather.

The man flicked ash from his black cigarette. 'We are the real people, Carl. We are the ones who can do things. That is why we are here. Never forget that.'

Why we are here? Where? Madrid?

'Come, Carl. I shall present you to the duke and the duchess,' the count said as he propelled me towards a couple standing by the fountain in the middle of the patio. Although it was only a matter of strides, I felt the distance endless. I was just a puppet, my movements governed by strings held in my godfather's fingers. I wanted to bolt, but I couldn't.

The Duke of Avaron was a tall, thick-set man with a bushy moustache and a shiny bald head. The tall slim woman by his side seemed much younger than him, with her honey blonde hair open on her shoulders.

'So, Otto, this is your heir? The boy you want to turn into a man? You must take him to the *corrida* then. The bullfight, you know,' he said, and then laughed as he held out his hand. I placed my hand in the duke's. It was a mechanical action. 'Pleased to meet you,' I said.

The duke laughed. 'Of course.' Then with my hand in his he steered me towards his wife. '*La duquesa*,' he said as he dropped my hand. *La duquesa* held out her hand, the back curved for a kiss.

'Just graze the back of her hand with your lips,' Count Otto whispered in my ear. I did as bidden and then straightened up, my cheeks flushing hot to my temples. 'Charming,' I heard the duchess say as I kept my eyes down. The presentations seemed endless and I found myself stuttering words about my trip having been long, how I was happy to be in Madrid.

Then the duke laughed again. 'Go now, young man. Go and get yourself a drink.'

I nodded and turned. Before me the room was now full and I felt suddenly trapped. I tried to move around the guests to find a way to the bar, where I hoped I would find a beverage other than beer or wine. Snippets of conversation followed me as I pushed through the crowd.

'That one is Count von Sokorny. He was in Dachau. He knows what it's like.'

'What's he doing here? I thought he was in Switzerland acting as some ambassador or another – a relief organisation – somewhere in Africa.'

'Didn't he help spring *Il Duce*?'

'Shhh.'

I felt eyes on my back as I passed and heard whispers.

'The godson.'

'From Austria.'

'The other side of the family?'

'Not really family.'

'Shhhh.'

What did they mean, I wondered. What did they mean by
'not really family'? I arrived at the bar and leaned in on the
wood, pressing myself against it as if to cling to a safety raft.

'*Naranja*,' I said.

The waiter poured a blood-orange liquid into a tall glass
and held it out to me.

Bullfights and blood, I thought. Even the orange juice is
red.

***

When I finished Katrina was staring at me. It was as if she
wanted to reach out and touch me. 'Carl,' she said, 'when my
uncle was here, when he told me some things about his life...I
couldn't follow it all, but I'm sure he mentioned the name
Skorzeny. Or was it von Sokorny?'

I took her hand. 'Katrina, I think you should stay here
until you leave Vienna. I'll move in with Rudi if you like. I
don't think you need to worry about that motorbike business.
It's been too long.'

'Nothing is ever too long in Vienna,' I say.

'What's that supposed to mean?'

I shrug.

Chapter 36

Katrina Klain

I was due to leave Vienna on the Tuesday after Easter. I'd promised Carl to stay in touch and he said he would send me any news he heard about my uncle or about Zorko. Just before going to the station I went by the American Express office to pick up my mail. There was a letter from Jake.

At the Westbahnhof Carl hugged me goodbye, and then on the train I opened Jake's letter.

Sydney, 15 March 1970

Dear Katrina,

It's been a while. It's been over a year since you left. Promises, eh? Sure, I've been getting on with my life. And I know you've been getting on with yours. You know you stopped writing letters a while back and even after you left UNIDO. You'd only sent a postcard from East Germany, and that was ages ago. I was beginning to think I was engaged to Mata Hari. Are we still engaged, Katrina? Don't answer that. Even at Christmas, just a card. So I guess you'll forgive me if I haven't been much better.

I rang Jane to find out how you were. She said she didn't stay with you too long.

I'm sorry, Katrina. I'm worried about you.

The company wants me to look at markets in Europe and they're sending me to Zurich. It's not far from Vienna. I should be there in June.

Let me know. You can contact me at my work number.

Love, as always,

Jake

The train raced and I wondered what to do. So much had happened. I'd found and lost friends, found and lost family. And now work. It was good Jake was coming. The year had been long up. But I still needed more time. Opportunities were knocking. I couldn't stop now.

'Yoo, hoo.' I wave.

'What do you want?'

I want to make amends, but I cannot tell her that. Couldn't stop now. 'I may have something.'

She looks puzzled.

'An article. *Spiegel.*'

'*Mirror?*'

Rupert Murdoch does not own everything yet. 'An article in the German weekly, *Der Spiegel.* About the diaries your

Carl mentioned.'

'He is not my Carl!'

I can see she is interested. Her eyes are wide and blazing.

'It mentions your father.'

'Another of your nasty truths?'

I may also have a copy of the diaries somewhere...

'Give it...'

'Not yet.'

Click.

In Geneva, Madeleine stood on the platform with open arms.

'You look wonderful, Katrina,' she said and hugged me. 'Let me look at you. Yes. Radiant. In love?'

I laughed. 'That must be it, Madeleine. You look quite fantastic yourself. More of the same?'

Madeleine laughed. 'We shall see. It is much better than expensive makeup, *n'est-ce pas?* You really do like to travel light. Only an overnight bag?'

I shrugged.

'You can share with me, if you like,' she said.

'Only until I get a job.'

The taxi curved up to Champel, on the hilltops overlooking the university. 'A propos of a job, Katrina, I think I may have something for you.'

I beamed as the taxi came to a halt in front of a marbled six-storey building. I looked up. 'They've got trees on the roof terrace. Madeleine, this is luxury.'

'Not quite. But it is a good area.' Madeleine tipped the driver and we entered the mirror-walled foyer.

She ushered me into the bright, roomy flat. From the

balcony I could see over the old town towards Lake Geneva. The only furniture was fruit crates and large cushions. In the bedroom, two large mattresses adorned the feet of a plaster copy of Michelangelo's *David*.

I raised an eyebrow.

'*David* is a gift. I did not want to spend more, as my furniture is still in storage in Vienna, but it is coming soon.'

'Did you think I would come?' I asked. 'What if I'd failed?'

'I knew you would pass,' Madeleine said, and hugged me.

It was like the best times in Vienna. A new place. A new start.

The following week, Madeleine's furniture and belongings arrived. She came home early as often as she could to arrange the flat, but that was not all she arranged.

'I have brought you the brochures from the university. You really must do a crash course, Katrina.'

I nodded. Madeleine was taking over. It felt good in a way.

'And I have a contract for you to start as a trainee next week. It is only for two months, but it is in the German section.'

'The German section? I can't translate into German, Madeleine. Hell! My mother tongue's English.' I tried to keep my fingers from fiddling with the edge of the cushion.

'The English section would not have you with just one language. And even my vitamins cannot get you in there. This is the first time they are using German on an equal basis. You will have the best English. Anyway, you will not get more than a few lines at a time and I am sure you can handle that.' Madeleine waited for her news to sink in. 'Oh, and I have said that you are Austrian. You are, by birth?'

'I'm Australian, Madeleine.' I wondered if I was anything

at all. Is this what it took to get work? How long would I be able to bluff my way through?

'The person in charge of the German group, Peter Held, the East German I wrote you about, he said he would do his best to help you and was looking forward to an *English mother tongue*. His exact words, Katrina. So there is no cheating.'

I gave up. This was how it was going to be. At every turn I needed someone. At least it was a start. I'd have some money coming in, some work experience, travel, even. The contract was only for two months, but something told me it might go on for much longer. First the job. Then the flat. Then I'd call Jake and tell him where I was and then I'd ask him to come. Somehow, I wanted to handle this new start by myself.

The following Monday I accompanied Madeleine to the brand-new conference building. It was low, round and modern, with meeting rooms interleaved like cards, invisible yet available. She led me to an office in the basement. The door was open and a dark, slim man in his early thirties stood as we entered. He wore jeans, a denim shirt and a tie.

'Katrina, this is Peter Held, a good friend,' Madeleine said. She almost purred the word 'friend'. 'You will be colleagues. Peter knows the ropes, he is good with beginners.' She said the word beginner in the same way she said friend.

Of course Madeleine knew people, knew how to lead, guide, sometimes push. I couldn't help wondering just how close the friendship between Madeleine and Peter Held was. He was attractive, different.

'Nice to meet you, Katrina,' Peter said, offering his right hand and giving me a steady gaze from eyes so dark the pupils seemed dilated. His grip was firm as he held my hand an instant longer than necessary and I felt a sudden shivery warmth rise up inside me to my cheeks.

Shit! Don't blush, I ordered my mind. 'Nice to meet you, Peter,' I said.

⊙

'Nice to meet you.'

'Shut up,' she says.

I shrug. 'Let me click.'

Click.

⊙

'Jake, it's not that I don't want you to come, but I want you to come when everything is just right. I've got a job and I should have a flat soon. I'll ring you again as soon as I know. I'll write.'

Jake waited a second. 'I've got a few things to sort out. Let me know. Love you.'

Two weeks later, on a Friday, Jake arrived in Geneva. I ran towards him on the platform and he dropped his overnighter, stretched out his hands. I stopped dead before him and he swept me up in his arms.

'I've got my own place, Jake. A studio. It's just one room – bathroom separate of course.' I stroked his cheek and he turned his face to kiss my palm.

'And you've got a job,' he said.

'Yes. A job. Trainee translator, but I make enough to pay the rent. The flat's not far.' Jake's arm slipped around my shoulders. 'We'll get you settled. Tonight you're all mine.'

'And tomorrow?' he whispered.

'Tomorrow we'll have dinner with Madeleine and Peter. You'll love them both. It was really Madeleine's idea. I don't mind sharing you a little, not often though.' I pecked him on the lips.

Jake held me still, his hands on my shoulders. His eyes plunged into mine. 'I don't want to be shared.'

My studio was four blocks down from the station, just around the corner from Geneva's red-light area.

Jake laughed. 'What would your mother say?'

'I'd never tell her. She'd just imagine King's Cross.'

'Do you mind?'

I look at her.

'It's my story.'

'But I love to...'

'...be a voyeur. Yes, I've noticed. And don't sulk.'

I wanted to impress him. Candlelight. Champagne.

'Ever tried blinis, Jake?'

'With tuna spread?'

'No, with caviar. Take a dollop of these grey pearls.' I handed him a small glass plate with a tiny pancake holding a heap of glistening grey balls. 'Take them gently. Let the taste explode in your mouth...and now a sip of champagne... and now a kiss.'

Jake obeyed. 'I've never seen you quite like this. It's amazing what a French-speaking environment can do.'

'Cliché alert,' I said with a grin.

We sat on the couch and fed each other blinis and champagne, finishing the meal with strawberries and thick Gruyère cream.

Chapter 37

We spent Saturday morning in bed. At every stirring, we found new vigour.

'Jake, we do have to get up some time,' I said.

'Mmm. Scared it'll wear out?' Jake stretched out his arms. I kissed him on the mouth and tugged at his hand.

'All right. Show me your new town.' He pressed his lips to my forehead and swung his legs to the floor.

We strolled down to the lake, turned left at the giant lion statues guarding the Gothic Brunswick memorial, and crossed to the promenade opposite the Beau Rivage Hotel.

'Sissi, the Austrian Empress, was murdered there.' I pointed to a plaque by the side of the water. 'An Italian, I think, and then there was war.'

'That's a bit morbid on such a lovely day.' Jake pulled me

over to the water's edge. The *jet d'eau* shot up across the water on the other side of the lake. 'Know why they built it?'

'You're going to tell me it was because of some engineering feature, aren't you?'

'Yep. To relieve the pressure.' He pulled me to him. We held each other as waves lapped against the rocks. A seagull circled and dived into the chopping water. 'I love you, Katrina Klain.'

I think I am beginning to have a soft spot for her myself.

'Did you say something?' she asks.

I shake my head.

We arrived at La Glycine just after six. It was a rustic restaurant tucked behind the upper part of the station, much loved for its patron's generosity to the arts. Bright abstracts hung between classic scenes of Lake Geneva.

'Look at those paintings, Jake. The walls are full of them. There's guitar music, too, and sometimes cabaret. And they have a wonderful steak tartare,' I said.

'Since when do you eat raw meat?'

'Since I got here. The chef serves it in the shape of a heart, but it's so spicy.'

We were still waiting to be shown to our table when a dark-haired couple came through the revolving door. The woman was slightly shorter than the man, slim. Her hair fell in gentle waves about her face. An ivory angora stole hung over her shoulders, half covering the beige crepe tunic topping midnight-blue trousers. I tugged Jake's hand. 'Here they are. Madeleine, this is Jake. Peter. Jake.'

Jake and Peter sat diagonally opposite across the table, like crossed swords. I noticed Jake glancing often at my colleague from East Germany. He didn't seem to be as interested in Madeleine.

'So how do you like it...in the West?' Jake said.

Peter paused, putting his knife down on his plate: 'It's an experience, in more ways than one.' He glanced sideways at Madeleine, who looked back at him evenly. 'There is much I have to look out for. So much choice. It is quite numbing at first.'

'But no longer at second, Peter,' Madeleine said. 'You manage to close your mouth now.' She laughed.

Peter laughed, too. Part of the joke. Jake watched them both. So did I.

Perhaps you had to come from the same landmass, I thought. It didn't matter the politics. Me and Jake, we were from the other side of the world, yet sometimes I felt he was more so than me. I cut my tartare heart with the side of my fork. 'Jake is surprised I eat raw meat,' I said.

'You don't eat tartare in Australia?' Madeleine asked in mock surprise.

'We're not cannibals,' Jake said. 'Well-done is more like it.'

We all laughed and toasted each other with the clear red wine from the Dole.

I cannot understand women.

As we walked back to the flat, I was quiet. The meal had eased into pleasantness. Madeleine and Peter made a fine couple, I thought. I was glad for my friend and glad that I felt no tinge of jealousy. Why should I be jealous? I had Jake. Would I have been jealous if Jake had not come? Jealous of whom, of Madeleine, of Peter?

'What's up, Katrina,' Jake whispered. 'You're miles away.'

I shook my head. 'Nothing. I was just thinking how good I feel with you here, with Madeleine and Peter.'

Jake gave my shoulder a squeeze. 'I'd like to come and live here, Katrina.'

'You've only been in Zurich a few weeks.'

'We could live together.'

I felt a tingle inside. 'You just like my flat, is that it?' I said.

'More like its occupant. What do you say? I'll try and set things up with Batello. They approached me ages ago in Australia. They have an office in Geneva.'

I felt I was floating inside. He wanted to be with me here. Not there.

I turned to him, and kissed him on the cheek.

'I love you, Jake,' I whispered.

'I'm going to try and get a job here,' he said. His arm drew my shoulder closer. 'I want to be with you.'

And so time flies. Sometimes too fast.

'It was a perfect time,' she says.

As I've said before, perfection is overrated.

Three months later I held the balcony rail of the eighth floor flat. 'What a wonderful view! You can see Mont Blanc all day!'

'We were lucky to get it. Did you see the waiting list?' Jake slipped his arm around my shoulders and we looked over to the *jet d'eau.*

'I suppose you used your,' I drew closer, 'connections?'

'Yes. How else could we have got it? Main thing we have. Let's see how we get it together.'

'Let's keep it natural, make the most of the light, Jake.'

'Swedish furniture would fit well. Simple. Stark.'

'We could play round with colours – pictures, cushions, mats. It'll be lovely, won't it?'

We spent weekends setting up house – painting and furnishing the two-bedroom flat.

Time went by and I felt I'd attained what I wanted. I translated from French now. My work was varied and soon I might be sent off on short assignments. Jake was doing well, working for civil-engineering projects. Family was far from my mind.

Then Jake went to Sydney. 'Just a quick hi to Mum and Dad. Batello's paying.' Nothing more. He'd asked whether he should visit my parents. I'd said no. 'It's the same place, Katrina. Warm. Friendly.'

'But so far away,' I'd said. Geneva was utopia. Everything worked.

No wonder they held peace talks there. A safer place there could never be.

I even heard from Jane.

'Jake! Jane's written at last.'

'That's wonderful, darling,' he said snipping the runners from the vine on the balcony. 'What does she say?'

Sydney, 15 September 1973

Dear Katrina,

I suppose it's up to me to write first but I would love to hear from you. I know Jake is with you. I'd told him I'd seen you when I got back from my trip to Europe. I didn't know he'd be over so quickly. But I'm glad he did go. Your mother gave me your address in Geneva. She said she was wondering when you'd come. She knows it's not easy to commute back and forth across the world. At least yours understands. Mine wouldn't have.

David and I got married just after I got back. The twins are two and a half now. Yes, twins – a boy and a girl, Phil and Prue. We've got a house on the other side of Sydney, out near Pittwater. That explains why your mother didn't know about David and the twins, especially since Mum and Dad moved up north for Dad's arthritis (seems the hot weather hasn't really helped, though).

I'm home, of course. David's doing well with his own accounting business. People will always have to file taxes, he says. I've got my hands full with the house and the garden, and the children. But I do manage the odd game of tennis with Rosemary. Do you remember her? She's married, too. Her second husband. Imagine. They have a lovely house, with a pool and tennis court. Rosemary says she doesn't want kids. I suppose they'd be in her way.

I must stop rambling. Please let me have some news. Hope all is well. Say hi to Jake.

Love, Jane.
PS. The opera house is finished. They say it looks like sails.
Looks more like eggshells to me.

'Seems to have settled down,' Jake said.

I folded the letter. 'I'll have to write her. I'll have to write Mum. Haven't written for ages, not since Dad died.'

'Is that why you didn't want me to go there when I was over?'

'Please, Jake. He's gone.'

Jake shrugged. 'You've got an office now. No more excuses,' he said with a wry smile.

I picked up my mug of tea and went to my office. Mum and Dad smiled down at me from the photo on the cork notice board. I wrote to my mother:

Geneva, 1 October 1973

Dear Mum,

How the time flies. Things are fine in Geneva. The job is interesting, specially since East and West Germany have established diplomatic relations. It seems to seal their separation. Funny how an agreement brings that out stronger than a fight.

I had a letter from Jane. She had twins — two and a half, they are now. I don't think you knew. Do you hear from her parents? They went up to Queensland, didn't they?

They've brought in a ban on driving cars in Switzerland. It's every second Sunday. Because of the energy crisis. It's quite fun really. We went up to Montreux by train to hear Joan Baez sing (reminds me that Jake is so happy Vietnam's over and he won't ever run the risk of conscription again). Anyway, the streets of Montreux were filled with people walking, on bikes, roller skates, even a man on a penny-farthing bike and some people on horseback. Maybe they should keep the Sunday ban. It gives a holiday atmosphere.

Jake is fine. He's doing some civil-engineering project. And I think he likes Geneva. He is even learning French. I'm getting on well at the Conference. Who knows how long it will last? I don't think I can afford to come back yet. Yes, I know you said you'd pay. But I do want to do it by myself. I hope you understand. It's important for me. I love you, Mum.

Your Katrina

What else could I say? I wanted to say more as I thought of white eggshell sails on Sydney Harbour. Don't get emotional. Don't get homesick. Don't rake up the past. Not now that things were working out so beautifully in Geneva.

Don't rake up the past. Interesting comment. Nothing grows in a vacuum. Silence. Silence. Silence is no good in my job. Luckily things always seep out. Even if it does take time.

PART FOUR

INFLIGHT PANOPTICON

IV

Chapter 38

Katrina Klain

1974. The phone rings three times before I pick it up. 'Yes. I am Katrina Klain.' I am silent. Listen. Take a breath. Answer 'Yes.' Then I put the phone down and sit at my desk, staring, as the man's name and disjointed words repeat themselves in my mind:

'My name is Stanislas Zorko.'

(It was difficult to understand him. His voice sounded robotic. He spoke slowly.)

'Your uncle, our adopted son, is dying. Please come to Madrid. He is in a hospital where Sophia Loren was once treated. A hospital of the stars, of beautiful people. A hospital where cancer is never treated. Harald Klain is riddled with cancer. But he must not know. We have taken the greatest precautions. He has not got long. You can say you are passing through and will come back. He will believe you. Come to the Avenida de America 22. Wait downstairs. The chauffeur will take you to the hospital. I will meet you afterwards.'

'My name is Stanislas Zorko...' Stanko Zorko.

Stanislas Zorko the mastermind behind a scrap-metal racket that in the Fifties and Sixties cost the Austrian Government millions. Carl Sokorny had found this out for me. He'd reported that Zorko had been in Dachau with Leopold Figl, who became the first Chancellor of Austria after the Second World War. That friendship of sorts had no doubt facilitated later actions on Zorko's part, like his avoiding extradition from France and his exile in Spain. And where he went, his lawyer, Dr Harald Klain went, too. Carl told me that Zorko had frequented social gatherings in Madrid that Hitler's 'Scarface' Otto Skorzeny had also attended.

Otto Skorzeny had been in charge of a last-ditch operation towards the end of the war where German soldiers were sent behind enemy lines wearing the opponent's uniform and speaking English. Skorzeny's diaries hint that my father may have been one of those soldiers. So many snippets lost in silence, in Vienna, Madrid and even in Australia.

Chapter 39

Harald Klain

Mama died of cancer. I saw her suffer. I am terrified of this creeping monster coming from nowhere to eat me up from the inside out. Oh, yes. Stanko and Monique must have twisted a few arms, as only they could, to get me into Sophia Loren's bed. They knew I would appreciate that little joke. No. Never cancer patients in this hospital. *Ergo*, I cannot be suffering from cancer. Bullshit!

This is not my first meeting with the monster. It devoured Mama's breasts, albeit from the inside.

When you lose your mother, a part of you dies. I wonder if Alfred felt that. I did send him the photos of Mama in her coffin. A macabre Viennese practice, but cheaper than the death mask. She and Papa still lie in the Central Cemetery in Vienna. It has been paid up for another ten years. After that, no doubt, they will become little more than compost, the space they occupied making way for a new clan. And me? Well, I am not going to die, am I? Not in this hospital. No one dies here. They leave here with new noses and bosoms, beautified gangsters, the beautiful people. Ha! They could have fixed up old Scarface here, but Skorzeny made it his hallmark. I managed to pick up his diaries. Hot off the press. Even *Der Spiegel* bought excerpts. Fascinating how publishers latch on to the sales potential of evil. *Plus ça change.*

Operation Greif. There was mention of a Klain. It could have been Alfred. Young men were recruited as a last-ditch effort. The fools. They were to go behind enemy lines in enemy uniform. Cause havoc.

Skorzeny's boys. And then he divulges that one of his boys wet his pants. Doesn't reflect well on him as the *lider*. Ha! No. Alfred would never have wet his pants. Pity. I don't think I will ever be able to ask him. Or if I did, he would most likely kill me. Maybe that would be a better way to die than in this bed where La Loren had a bit of nip'n'tuck. Women!

One woman I would really like to see again is Bettina. Ah, Bettina. What would I say to her? Nothing. I would just look at her. See that slight dusting of freckles, the high cheekbones, the brown velvet eyes. No, not as an old woman. I want to see her as she was when we'd go to the *Tarzan* films together. How I'd swing her high in the trees with me, swing through that post-war jungle, hold her tight with one arm, feel one breast on my forearm, smell the thick scent of her longing as she spread her legs and then closed them around the jungle vines and we swung and we swung and we swung. And in the dark of the cinema in the back row where we sat, she would part her legs. My fingers would enter and she would close on them, forcing them to scoop out a nectar that I would bring to my lips and to hers as our mouths suckled on each other's tongues to the beat of the jungle drums. My God. She's done it again. Ejaculating me into death this time. Ha! I am spent now.

Who is there? It is not a dream. Bettina. I cannot speak. She comes closer. I can smell her. No. Not the smell of our jungle. Something new. Fresh. Am I already in heaven? She strokes my head. I close my eyes. Ah.

The nurse. The nurse is talking to her. No. Don't send her away.

Bettina. I hear the nurse say. 'I am sorry.' No.

Chapter 40

Katrina Klain

I didn't know what to expect, but it certainly wasn't the emaciated face peeping from the white sheets. Harald Klain's cheekbones stood out, but his blue eyes were burning with fervour, or was that what fever did? There was a sweetish smell of an undefinable floral tone. The nurse straightened the sheets of his bed. 'It won't be long now, I'm afraid,' she said.

I was afraid, too. I'd never seen anyone dying or dead. And this was my uncle. I approached. There was something in his eyes. He recognised me. But there was something more. It was weird. His eyes were flirty. Flirty on his deathbed? I stroked his forehead and he closed his eyes. A slight tremor made his mouth look like it was smiling. It was a smile of satisfaction. As if he were pleased with a job well done.

Stanko had told me not to stay long. To act bright and

breezy, say I was on my way to...who knows?

'I just popped in to see you. I'll have more time on the way back from...from Agadir.' Where did that come from? 'Yes. Three weeks in Morocco.' I bent to kiss him. He shivered. But his smile was still there. 'See you when I get back,'I said. I had to get out. Tears were starting to well up in my eyes. He shouldn't see them. I tried not to run.

In the corridor, a big man in his seventies came towards me. He must have been over six-foot tall. Portly. Impeccably dressed. In one hand he held what looked like a microphone. He placed it against his throat. The voice came from there. Metallic. 'My larynx has been removed. Throat cancer. No, don't worry. I had fun. I'm used to it. Technology.'

I didn't know what he meant and put it down to his choosing the words in English.

'Monique is waiting. I will take you to her and leave you girls alone.'

Chapter 41

Stanko dropped me at the front door and snapped his fingers at the concierge. Monique Zorko was waiting for me in the penthouse apartment in the Avenida de America. Her maid showed me up the single step to the small living room where icons of the Virgin Mary adorned the walls and in a corner a life-size madonna, restored from its antique state, beckoned me with an upturned palm.

My hostess was a frail woman, in chic black skirting her knees, perched on the curve of a shocking-pink foam armless settee. She wore two strings of pearls above the high-scooped neckline of her designer dress, pearl earrings beneath her freshly styled grey hair. I gave her early seventies, perhaps a bit more. Her knees were pressed together; her sheer shapely ankles resting pertly above the tiniest of black patent leather pumps.

'Approach, child,' she said, her palm upturned like the madonna's.

I had never been called 'child'. Not even when I was one, but I stepped forward. Monique Zorko's eyes twinkled as she offered me a sofa chair matching her own in form and colour. I sat down but resisted sinking into the full curves of the seat.

'Designed by a young artist. All the rage in Madrid these days.' Her hand swept the room. 'I quite like the contrast with the old,' she said in a low vibrant voice. 'The price is the same, you know.'

Not waiting for an answer, she turned to the doorway where the stout maid waited. 'Jonny, bring us some Sauternes, would you?' Then she turned to me. 'You do like Sauternes, don't you?'

I nodded and she clapped her hands as I had seen the older men in their trim suits do as they beckon to waiters.

'Jonny has been with me an eternity. She adored your uncle. Adored the family. We were a family, you know.'

In a way, I thought. I nodded again, wondering when she was going to say about my uncle.

'You look a lot like him,' she said. Her eyes ran over me as if perusing one of her icons. 'The same blonde hair, the high cheekbones...' She leaned back and looked me over again. 'The same wild streak?' she murmured more to herself than to me.

Jonny came up the step with two glasses of wine on a tray, a bowl of crisps between the glasses. The tray and bowls were silver, the glasses crystal. She placed the tray on a low, massive glass table topping a silvered oak trunk. Jonny's gaze flickered over me. Then she gave Monique Zorko a subtle nod before leaving the room.

'Pure silver,' Monique said.

I wondered whether she meant Jonny and her services or the base of the modern table.

As if to clear away any cobweb of a doubt Monique added: 'The same artist. It's amazing how he can work with the pliability of foam to make it strong enough to support a body and then ply silver to the form of an oak. *Salud*, child.'

I lifted my glass and sipped. Then I placed it back on the tray. 'Señora Zorko...'

'Do call me Monique,' she said. 'We are almost family, aren't we?'

She settled back, her smile waiting for me to act.

'If you call me Katrina,' I said.

Monique gazed at me with a serious look. 'You have his spirit,' she said. Then she sipped once more from her glass. Her hand could hardly cup the bowl as she held the stem dropping between her fingers. 'What were you saying, Katrina?'

I looked straight into her eyes. 'Please tell me about my uncle.'

'Harald?' Monique placed the glass on the tray next to mine. Then she perched on the edge of the settee and slowly crossed her slim legs. It was a studied movement that could only have become natural with years of practice and coquetry. 'Harald. Our heir. God rest his soul. Yes. I know he is dead. Did you know he was mine and Stanko's heir?'

I shook my head.

'He was the youngest. We thought he would outlive us. Now there is only me. Only me.' Her eyes gazed past me. I wondered if the madonna were nodding behind my back, agreeing with me that Monique Zorko was nuts. Her Stanko had just brought me to her. Then her voice hushed as she leaned forward. 'He was my lover, you know,' she said with a mischievous smile. Then she laughed. 'Oh, Stanko knew.' Her laughter rippled like the wave of an *olé*. 'Harald was very close to Stanko,' she said with a knowing wink. 'Very close. Very close.' Her voice hushed once more. 'It surprised me at first. They were so...different. Different as men could be. They used to go off to Toledo together, and then to San Sebastián.' I shook my head. 'Ach, child,' she said. 'They did so enjoy their little boys.' I didn't know where to look, what to do. Should I just cover my ears, ask to go to the bathroom?

Monique uncrossed her legs and leaned forward to take a crisp. A large diamond ring drew attention to rather than detracted from the sprinkling of brown spots of age on the back of her hand. I instinctively surveyed the back of mine.

'Do you smoke?' she said.

'Yes.'

She looked over her shoulder past the step towards the kitchen and cocked her head as if listening for a sound. Rewarded by a quiet rattling of crockery, she leaned forward again and said. 'Give me a cigarette. Quickly.'

I didn't react immediately.

'Hurry, child.'

My eyes narrowed as my hand slipped into my bag and my fingers closed over the flip-top box. I pulled out a cigarette and offered it to her, filter tip forward. Her hand pounced and slipped it by her thigh to nestle there for what I guessed would be an appropriate moment.

'The lighter,' she hissed.

'I have matches.'

Monique rolled her eyes as if I had committed a social sin. 'Then those. Give...'

Just then Jonny entered the room. 'Is there something you need, Señora?' she said.

'No, Jonny,' Monique said. *'Gracias,'* she added as if as an afterthought. When she was sure that Jonny was out of earshot, Monique Zorko slipped the cigarette in her mouth. 'Light.'

There was a sudden smell of sulphur as I lit a match and reached the flame to the tip of the cigarette.

Monique Zorko inhaled. 'I am forbidden to smoke. Imagine! In my own home!' Then she leaned forward and said in a low voice: 'So what is it you want to know about Dr Harald Klain? And which Harald Klain do you want to know about? The crook? The...' Monique Zorko stopped.

'Quite enough for one man, don't you think?' Then she slipped a foot out of her shoe, flicked cigarette ash into its hiding place and told me her story.

Chapter 42

Monika Zorko

'They all think it began in the Fifties and that it was just about money. But it began a lot earlier and yes, it was about money, but it was also about love, hate and revenge.

'I was in my last year of law at Vienna University when I met Stanko Zorko, a bull of a man in more ways than one. He swept me off my feet, literally, and I found in the man, so different from any I had ever known, so different from myself, the perfect match for my body and my mind.

'Stanko had money. Where he got it from I did not know and I would not ask. I loved him. I trusted him. Trust was between the two of us. No one else. Until Harald. But I digress.

'Stanko was not a Jew. Or if he was, he was not practising. Just circumcised. From his time in the Yugoslav army. I sometimes wondered if he was really a Jew; the notion had a certain liberating appeal for me, a way of justifying the taking of risks. I was from a Catholic bourgeois family, should have married a count or some such. My family was outraged when I married Stanko on a weekend away at Trieste. Stanko put up the money for our legal practice and my degrees made it, shall we say, legal.

'Stanko said war was coming, and that in such a climate one could become rich if one were clever. What he meant was import/export. Forgery. Documents.

'I had been out to the university to look for a likely candidate to help out in our law firm. We wanted someone we could train to our mould, or rather someone who could not be trained to anyone else's. That is where I met Harald Klain, your uncle. He was quite a rascal, a charmer, even for his young age. There is no greater tonic than the attentions of a young man. Of course, I played the game. And Stanko? He enjoyed the game, too. When the Nazis came, Stanko fled to Belgrade and I carried on alone with Harald. Your uncle was quite brilliant in court. Stanko and I would meet secretly in Trieste. There was an underground community there with links to Jewish friends. I forged papers that attracted little scrutiny. Stanko managed to keep out of the way and became quite the expert in customs procedures. Then, one day, he was caught. Just one missing signature on an export form and one zealous young Nazi officer. Stanko was brought to Dachau. He wasn't there long, luckily. Luck has always ruled our lives.

'In Dachau he met men who later became highly placed in the new government. No one turns his back on those who have shared one's darkest hours. We just had to wait for Harald to come back. Harald was in a prisoner-of-war camp in England. But you know that, don't you?

'So there we were. Trump cards in our hands. Nothing to lose, and all to gain. I would have my revenge, that of having made my life against the will of my family. Stanko turned the world around, his allegiance being only to himself. Harald, too, had his own sort of revenge. The anti-hero. We all had our games of the mind where we pitted all against a State with stakes in the millions and we knew that never would we be brought to what good citizens call justice. We knew that there no longer was such a thing. Justice was a commodity, like coffee. Coffee, in fact, brought in our first million, and on it went.

'You will no doubt have seen Stanko's name in the news. He enjoyed the exposure. It was like the bravado of the bullfighter for him. Harald always stayed in the background tying up the loose ends. He was, I might say, the real brain behind it all in the end, behind our exile.

'We were a perfect triangle. You had your flower power in the Sixties, but we had our excitants, too, in the Fifties. Harald has probably died by now – yes, cancer – yes, I know he met you in Vienna. But you must understand he could not come back nor could he contact you. Interpol was ever on our trail and only in Spain were we safe. The irony of it: a Jew safe in fascist Spain. A Jew hobnobbing with Nazis, the likes of Count Otto von Sokorny even. The Count, of course, was not really a count, and von Sokorny was not his real name, but the title helped immensely, as they always do. I think he even worked for the United Nations. Harald had him in mind for a deal, but I do not know where that led. There are still people in high places who want silence. But I am too old for them to worry about and my two men are dead or soon will be.

'When we found out that Harald was dying, Stanko was mortified. I was too, but you know how much stronger, how much more tenacious we women are. We tried to keep the truth from Harald, but I think he knew, and just played along. He did so admire Sophia Loren. Stanko had a sudden massive stroke five years ago and I have been alone ever since.

Stanko so wanted an amnesty to be able to die in Vienna. But it was not to be. I shall die in Madrid. There are worse places. Austria made me flee.

Why go back? I know too much. Too many in high places were complicit in our activities. Oh, and the money? I still have some in Germany.

Living well is expensive and there are always debts. I imagine you have already found out that no lunch is ever really free.

'But I think I have something for you. Harald's letters, the few personal effects he kept with him. Mostly papers. It must all still be together in that tooled box of his. 'Jonny!'

Chapter 43

Katrina Klain

Back in my hotel room near the Prado, I spilled the contents of the tooled Moroccan leather box onto the bed. Harald was dead. Really dead. Not just the dead of a long-ago postcard. Not just the dead of a hospital where no one ever came to die. The lies. The lies. Monique Zorko's words had added some lost pieces of the puzzle, now I just had to make them fit. But she had also added some confusion. Stanko was dead, she said. But I had seen him at the hospital. And he had dropped me off at Avenida de America. Monique Zorko, it seemed, already had one foot in La-La-Land. Is that where lies stop, or just disappear?

The three had embezzled the Austrian Government out of 50 million Austrian *schillings* and had never been caught. Interpol had done its best. The press had sent out its reporters. When questions were asked, things suddenly stopped. Had they tried to scare me off in Vienna when Carl Sokorny had taken me in? Carl Sokorny. Monique had spoken of Count Otto von Sokorny. Carl's godfather. A Nazi. Was it too late to go back to Vienna? They were dead. Count Otto, too. It wasn't Carl's fault, nor was it mine. All that was left now were letters and photos. I poured myself a drink from the whisky bottle from the minibar and began sifting through the papers.

There were university ID cards for the years up to the war and the early war years when Harald had attended Vienna University. Or were these samples of Monique's forging hand? A carbon copy of a letter to the landlord in Vienna, imploring him to let Harald's mother remain despite a lapse in her rent payments. Harald Klain's birth certificate. His mother's birth and death certificates. Photos of her in her coffin. I remembered. My parents had received a photo like that in Sydney. Harald had kept dozens. A paper to say that his family tree was in good health. This was signed in 1939 in lieu of the usual family booklet. A postcard of a ship sent from Colombo. The writing looked familiar. It was addressed to Frau Klain c/o Dr Harald Klain. All it said was that Frau Klain senior must have had a secret, otherwise why hate Bettina so? That it was just a matter of time. But it didn't say what that secret was. What was that all about, I wondered. Then there was a letter in the same familiar hand. I opened it and smoothed back the creases.

Sydney, October 1955

My Darling,
I never wanted to write and I swear I shall not write again. This new life must be just that. New. A break from the

past. A clean start. But Australia is so far away. When I think that we are worlds apart now after having been so very, very close. You shall always be in my yesterday – nothing makes this more clear than my being here. But so it must be. One thing, though, that I would like to know is why, when her two sons both loved me so, your mother hated me so. But I want to finish this letter on a note of love. It is best for Katrina, if not for me, that things worked out this way. She will have her chance at a future that was always denied us.

Know, dearest Harald, that despite the way life has turned out for us, I shall always love you.

Your Bettina

I gripped my whisky glass and then took a gulp. The liquid burned my throat as tears rolled down my cheeks.

What was going on? What had been happening? It was all too much. First my father. Then my uncle. Now this. I wanted to go home, but there was no home any more.

I threw myself into my work: *Arbeit Macht Frei.* The world as I knew it had turned upside down.

I remain silent. Just let the film spool. It will soon be over.

She will be landing soon. What is there for me to say?

Katrina watches the screen. I pass her a tissue. She turns to my hologram, takes it and nods.

Write it down. Write it all down. All the lies. All the silences. How they served the love of ordinary people. How they served to protect those whom lies and silence would always protect. Hadn't one Austrian chancellor protected Zorko, and another bestowed the amnesty he had craved? Hadn't one Austrian president hidden behind silence and lies and, with the help of the Americans, even run the United Nations? Hadn't Skorzeny, 'the most dangerous man in Europe', also acted as a UN ambassador while secretly working on his Odessa files? And more recently, a former finance minister evading the courts through procrastination. *Plus ça change.* And in Australia? Had Mum been right? Did we all have to learn from our own mistakes? Lest we forget? Indeed! Had history become just a video game?

Heads would never roll due to friends in high places. I didn't know all their stories, but others did. I had to make a start so that my own lies and silences would not join the many so deep in the archives, perhaps missing the day to become unclassified. I had to write it all down. Now.

***

I board the Wiener Walzer and arrive in Vienna at nine in the morning. From the new Hauptbahnhof with its boutiques and eateries, I go down the stairs to the way out. People are milling around. Men, women, children. Lining up for hot food, blankets. A train ticket. A sign says, *Train of Hope.* Another sign indicates free legal advice. *Free interpretation. Farsi. Arabic.* Another says: *Welcome Refugees.* I slip a twenty-euro note into a collection box and go out into the street.

I cross the road to the Belvedere Palace. I'll walk down. Pebbles crunch underfoot. Egon Schiele, you weren't the only mad one. Halfway down Prinz-Eugen-Straße I wait for an arriving tram to pass. A man stands beside me. He is wearing a hoodie like many now do. I glance at him and step onto the street. He is behind me. I quicken my pace. A motorbike flashed in my mind. I will be quicker this time. Then I fall. A woman comes out of the large wrought-iron door of the publishing house where I am awaited. She holds out an arm. I scream. She screams. The man in the hoodie runs off. I lie slumped over my case, blood streaming onto the ground.

Click.

'I didn't feel a thing,' she says. 'It was all so quick.'

'It made the news,' I say. I could have done a better job. The headline sounded a bit like tennis, obviously influenced by the latest Federer comeback. *Author's passing shot frustrates hoodie attack.* Everything goes so fast these days. A melting pot of sensationalism to appeal to all tastes. Even the tabloids have gone to pot. Facts? They're just a point of view at a given time. Memories make them. Gone to pot. I laugh.

Cut throat at the Belvedere! A woman was found in front of a house opposite the Belvedere Palace. A man in a hoodie was seen running off. Police are calling for witnesses.

'And that's how you came to be where I found you, Katrina. But I am afraid that you have not kept to Rule No. 2, so must stay here with me.'

She smiles.

Perhaps she has resigned herself to this new situation – an old situation considering how long it has all taken. Too many memories perhaps. The facts. Always stick to the facts.

'The facts?' she says. She is reading my mind? 'Facts? They're are a joke,' she continues. 'They are just a point of view at a given time. Memories make them. I laugh. Cannot.' She laughs.

I do not understand. 'Katrina?'

'Why don't you do your click thing one last time?' she says.

'It's all over, Katrina. There are only blanks now.'

'Just once more,' she says.

I will have her with me for eternity. If she wants to see blanks, then so be it.

'I cannot see into the future, Katrina.'

'I can,' she says. She stands up and walks to the door.

'You cannot leave, Katrina.'

She blows me a kiss and says, 'Yes, I can! Click on, Tchaimie.'

'I cannot see into the future.'

'The future is now. Just click.'

She is so sure that she can leave. Can leave me. If I click, will she slip through the door on to wherever? Can she leave me alone with my files and my archives and the ghosts of the past? She may have been right about that cat and its curiosity. But I have to know. Damn her! Damn me!

Click.

I switch off the LED screen, glance at the red caftan on the floor by the door, and pour myself a glass of my very best brandy.

Prosit, Katrina Klain! I say and raise my glass to my beautiful liar.

PART FIVE

LANDINGS

Chapter 44

Katrina Klain

2009. When I arrived in Sydney, I saw the surprise on Jane's face.

What was she expecting? A broken woman? I felt so rested. Had slept so deeply. Films don't usually do that to me. But this one went on for both legs. And now I can't remember a thing, but I feel so serene. It's as is if I know where to go and how, but without really knowing yet. I don't want anyone mucking things up. Crazy?

'Are you all right?' Jane asked as she flung her arms about my shoulders. The older woman next to her smiled. 'This is Rosemary.'

I nodded. But couldn't smile. Rosemary? I stuck out my hand to Jane's lover. Rosemary hesitated and took my hand. 'Sorry,' I said, 'European habit,' and turning to Jane, I said,

'Is she...?'

'In the morgue,' Jane said. 'Behind Sydney uni.'

'Can you take me there now? It's on the way home.' Home. Funny how the word sticks like a bindi-eye in the grass, pricking the sole of your foot.

The building was squat and grey. 'We do our best,' the woman in charge of viewings said. 'Take your time.'

It was cold. Bettina lay under a sheet. Silent forever. I felt nothing. They say that once the soul leaves, just a carcass remains. Bettina was no longer there. There was a smell of emptiness, not even sweet or sour, no disinfectant smell, just void. With one finger, I stroked my mother's cheek and then kissed her forehead. 'My beautiful liar,' I whispered.

I asked for a quick cremation. No service. Yes. I would collect the ashes.

'But what about her things?' Jane said.

'Things! Things! She's gone. There are no things. No reminders. I want no reminders.'

'But Katrina. Think about it. There may be something you'd like to keep. Let's go back to the house.' Jane put her arm around my shoulders.

I turned my head and searched Jane's face. Then I shrugged. 'I suppose you're right,' I said.

***

The white suburban bungalow hadn't changed in the almost thirty years I'd been gone. The letterbox was still out by the stump where the front gate had once been. Every other house in the street had a front fence and gate, but I couldn't remember when the stump with its ivy tendrils hadn't been there. The house used to be my home. Now it was just a house that was mine. I stopped at the front door. Jane handed me the keys.

They trembled in my hand.

'Do you want me to come?' Jane asked.

I shook my head.

'Why can't you accept help from those who love you?' Jane said quietly.

I looked at my friend for a long moment. Mum had prepared me for this, hadn't she? 'I've got to do this myself.'

'We'll go for a walk then and leave you alone,' Jane said.

'I'll sit out here on the patio when I'm done. Thank you,' I said, and slipped the key in the door. The key stuck in the lock with that little hiccup it had had years ago when I'd just make the midnight curfew on my outings with Jake. Jake. The way we were. All over now.

I entered the dim hall that gave onto the small lounge. Mum had always said that one needed a room that was always tidy in case the pastor came by. No pastor had ever called; just the priest who'd been turned away. Turned away with the threat of an imaginary pastor. Trust Mum, I thought. My eyes scanned the room. I moved dully, fingering the corners of the low round table, my eyes now on the old vitrine in the far corner of the room. Its contents testified to a collection of years: in among ornaments whose origins I couldn't remember, I spied a white rabbit in china. I'd paid for it out of my pocket money; it had been a gift for Mum. The rabbit stood between two crystal glasses, the sort with no edges. They bore the portraits of my grandparents, my father's parents, Otto and Alberta.

At first I wandered the house as if I'd been alone in the night in a mirror maze, searching for a familiar path towards the light, bumping my nose against the past. I opened drawers and found papers and bills, my school report cards, and a family photo album. I hadn't wanted to open the album, knowing that the photos were of me as a baby, a toddler with my parents. Those were from Vienna. Then in Australia: horse riding, schooldays. I'd seen them all hundreds of times. There'd been few photos of my parents together since one or the other had always been taking the picture. I still wasn't ready to flip back the pages and look at the photo of my father and my mother with me, their baby, in Mum's arms. There were no recent photos of my parents together, apart from the rare ones where they were in a group.

I closed my eyes and tried to recall the sight of Mum and Dad the day I'd left on the *Achille Lauro*. Mum had worn a floral shift whose cut was intended to make her look slimmer despite the bright colours she insisted on wearing. Her short pepper and salt hair was unruly. Dad, with his neat grey moustache and silvered hair had smiled and taken my forearm in his large hand. The top button of his shirt was done up although he was without tie. Mum had laughed at that: 'Your father is always so buttoned up.' I saw them again in my mind. They were waving goodbye. Suddenly tears welled in my eyes.

I wandered through the house. I felt that I had to be looking for something, but didn't know what. I went to the hall where Mum had placed a small vitrine for her collection of china. She had collected coffee cups and saucers she'd bought in bric-a-brac shops with *Antiques* on the door. The vitrine had come later. I opened the door. I remembered the pale-blue and white cup Mum had as a girl and had brought to Australia. I looked, but couldn't find it in the vitrine. Had she sold it? Was it broken, like the ashtray I'd given my parents? I pursed my lips at the thought. She wouldn't have sold such a precious piece. It had sentimental value. It was a link with her youth, her home even. A link with Germany.

I went to the dining room. The bright yellow and blue of the plates of the Spode gift I'd bought my parents from my first pay cheque at David Jones flashed through the glass-fronted dresser. It was bright-blue and yellow on white, fantasy birds and strange fruits. My parents were proud and had filled the glass dresser with the twenty-four-piece set. But they'd never used it.

'Why don't you use it?' I'd asked.

'We don't want to break anything,' Mum said. 'It's so beautiful like that.'

On the bottom shelf, half-hidden by the doors of the dresser, I spied the Meissen cup on its saucer. Had Mum really brought it all the way from Germany? Could she have afforded such a piece of china back then? She'd said they had nothing. Nothing was such a big word. I opened the door and took out the cup. The saucer lay on what looked like a piece of bright cardboard. I lifted the saucer and took the postcard with the snow-covered peaks. A black and white photo was tucked beneath it. A young woman between two men: one dark, my father, the other blond with the same high cheekbones. I wondered if the other man might be Harald, my uncle. I stared at the postcard; it looked familiar. The photo, I'd never seen before.

I jerked my head towards the hall. The light had suddenly brightened as if drawing me out to the sunroom. That room had always been my favourite. It had been the real living room. Through the glass walls the sun lit up the pine of the floorboards and caressed the hand-woven rugs. Beige linen curtains draped over one large windowpane. But the others were drawn back. My eyes searched the floor. There it was.

Peeping out from behind the drapes in front of the window that had never opened. My plaque. Just as I'd last seen it. A chocolate-brown ceramic plaque with letters raised in beige relief.

I must have been about ten when I'd made that plaque. I remembered how Mum had praised my handiwork. I wanted to have it on the outside wall next to the front door.

'Don't think it really fits there,' my father had said. Mum hadn't said anything. She'd just placed the plaque on the floor in the corner of the sunroom. EMOH RUO it said.

'That's all I'm taking,' I said and picked it up. Underneath were two yellow envelopes and a small package. One was addressed to my father, the other and the package were addressed to Mum.

***

Outside on the patio, I sat down on the wrought-iron chair and waited for Jane and Rosemary. I pulled out the letter addressed to my father. It was handwritten. The British queen's head in profile; priority-mail orange. Who did Dad know in England? I slid a nail into the flap of the envelope and slit it open. The letter was typewritten, but I could hardly read it. Whoever had typed the letter had hit the keys hard, for the 'o's had made holes in the paper, yet the other letters were faint as if the ribbon had been almost worn out.

Turnham Green, 15 October 1987
Dear Mr Alfred Klain,
I am writing to you on the off-chance that this letter will find you. I have been searching for your brother and you for the last twenty years. You may not remember hearing about

me, but I was your brother Harald's friend. We met during my stay in Vienna at your father's hotel in 1937/8 when you were in London. Harald and I became very close. You must have known that towards the end of the war Harald was detained in a camp in England. He wrote to me, but I was unable to contact him there. After the war I lost all trace of him. Two years ago, I heard of a Jewish newsletter with subscribers all over the world. I sent them a letter requesting anyone knowing Harald's whereabouts, or yours, to contact me. A man in the USA answered with an address he said was Harald's, but my letters to your brother all came back unopened. Your address was sent to me by someone in Australia. I would appreciate hearing from you and receiving any news you might have about Harald.

Sincerely,

Kenneth Browning.

I re-read the letter. My uncle in America? He couldn't have been. Dad had never mentioned America. He'd always said his brother was dead. And what was this Jewish connection?

I opened the letter addressed to Mum.

Turnham Green, 5 December 1987

Dear Mrs Klain,

I am sorry to hear about the passing of your husband, Alfred. I did not know his brother, Harald, very well. It was only for a brief period during my youth that we had a friendship. Yet it was an intense one – perhaps because of the times. I have tried to capture that period and thought the best way was to tape you my story so that you would be able to see Harald and myself when we were young. I hope the tape is all right. I had to try many times. Did it record correctly? Does it make sense? Does it tell the story I wanted to tell?

Towards the end of the war Harald was in a POW camp in England. I tried to visit him, but was unable to do so. For many years I refused to buy goods 'Made in Germany', yet a part of me knew that a friendship had been forged in that time long ago and that there is good in the world.

Please forgive this old man's ramblings. Perhaps I, too, am trying to make sense of my past.

Sincerely,

Kenneth Browning

I took out the tape and slipped it into the Walkman I'd bought in Singapore on the way out. I heard a cough and the clearing of a throat. Then the slow precise words of an old man.

'I was finishing my apprenticeship in the kitchen of the Rembrandt Hotel in Brompton Road. It was 1937...' The tape crackled. There was a cough. The voice became softer, almost inaudible. I turned up the volume. What the voice was saying was vague, disjointed in places, repetitive; yet, at times it was full of emotion.

For a moment I wondered how he could have a name like Browning. Then I dismissed the thought. Names were names and they could be changed in small ways, or even completely.

As Jane and Rosemary came down the drive, I switched off the tape and slipped the Walkman and letters into my tote.

Jane put an arm around me and said: 'You should try and unwind. Everything's going to be all right.'

I nodded. I couldn't listen to the tape now. I had to say farewell to Bettina.

'When are you having the service?' Jane asked.

'There won't be one. She's being cremated as soon as possible and I'll collect the ashes.'

Jane's face said it all. 'But...'

'I have to do this alone, Jane.'

A soft rain had been falling and the grass glowed almost turquoise in the light of the sun straining through the veil of clouds. The smell of damp earth and eucalyptus drew me back to my childhood.

I closed my eyes and sifted through my photo memories. Vienna. The photo of me as a baby in Mum's arms. My father stood proudly by my mother's side. Then one of me alone with Mum, my head pressed close against Mum's thighs. I couldn't remember Dad's presence in those early years either. But I'd seen the photos: a man in a hat and coat, posing by my mother's side. The child pressing back against his knees had pale blonde curls. Was the child pressing back to stop him from leaving? From going to a place far away? I remembered – it must have been just six months later – we were on a ship. We were going to join the man in the photo.

That must have been when Dad had left for Australia. Then in Sydney, at the beach with him. He looked like he was holding in his stomach. Stiff almost. Soldierly. Mum had told me that he'd been a pilot, had served on the Russian front. When I'd asked about the war all Mum had said was, 'We'll explain it all one day'. Then the years passed and little was said.

Mum was German, that much I knew, but Dad had always insisted he was Australian, that the past was over. He'd been born in Vienna, as I had. Yet he said he'd never been German. When Hitler annexed Austria, he'd become German overnight. Was that what he meant by the past being over? My parents had told me that they'd come to Australia for me. They'd not wanted to bring me up in Austria. Austria was the past. Germany was over. It was all so confusing. What was it that they'd said? I sat and tried to remember.

In the back garden the passionfruit was in bloom. Bettina had buried Alfred's ashes there, she'd said, when I'd made that quick visit. 'He wanted them in the bush, but the Council did not allow it. Dogs, they said.' Dogs? The dogs would go mad? 'He always said I spent too much time in the garden, so now he will be close to me.'

I took a trowel and added a handful of the passionfruit soil to Bettina's ashes then I tipped everything into a plastic bag and went down the bush at the back of the house. I followed the path my parents had walked with me as a child, and probably later together for many years. Down by the creek I snipped off a corner of the plastic bag to let a meagre stream trickle out as I walked. The last ashes trickled out just at the point where they would turn to go back home. A kookaburra laughed, but there was no rain. It was as if Alfred were calling her. Or was it perhaps Heinrich, or even...?

Bettina had always said she wanted her ashes in the bush. And to hell with the council and the nanny state, more worried about the possible madness of dogs sniffing an ash flake. Don't cry, Katrina. Reminds me of Argentina. Did not Harald go to Argentina? Or was it Colombia?

The following Monday, I saw the family solicitor, and instructed him to sell everything. All I'd take was the *Emoh Ruo* plaque, and an envelope with papers, letters, and the tape. I signed all the necessary papers, bade Jane and Rosemary goodbye and boarded the Qantas flight for London and then on to Geneva. Flying out over Sydney Harbour, I could no longer control myself. I tucked my body into the window seat and, covered in my blanket with my back to my neighbour, I tried to cry. It was the last time I'd see Australia. The thought, like hot desert winds, dried any hope of tears. Home was gone. I would have to make my own. I didn't need things to remind me. Didn't need photos.

With the money from the house I'd buy a home. A home? Where? I browsed the pages of the in-flight magazine. A page fell open on the Swiss Riviera, the Jura range as a backdrop. I'd never noticed Geneva from that angle, the Jura always running second, in my mind, to the mighty Mont Blanc range. Suddenly, I saw things with new eyes. I'll buy an old house in the countryside. Down by the lake. Or up in the vineyards. Do up the place. Mum would have liked that. She wouldn't mind an old flat. A small one. Memories were engraved in my mind, in my heart. Regrets, too. All the questions I could no longer ask. And what about Kenneth Browning and why he was looking for my uncle? He must be about Dad's age, I thought. Eighty-something. The war had been over for over fifty years. Death had claimed my father, but had it been strong enough to sever the links between Kenneth Browning and Harald Klain? Had it severed my own link with my uncle?

I ran a hand through my hair. My fingers caught in a knot. I'd forgotten to tie it back at the nape the way I usually did.

I stared out of the window as the plane circled Sydney Harbour, dipping then rising from the green blue of the ocean up past the scribbly lines of white cloud.

This man from England had come into my life and pulled

me into his past. Was he also pulling me towards a new life? I wanted to go forward.

My fingers gripped the plaque in my bag. Then I let go and pulled out the Walkman to listen to Kenneth Browning's tape.

Chapter 45

Kenneth Browning

It was the happiest time of my life. The saddest time, too. It was 1937 and I was seventeen.

I had arrived from England to work for eight months in a grand Viennese hotel. I was excited. I would at last see the world. Get away from Turnham Green. Go further than London.

It was early May when the train puffed into the grey hangar of Vienna's Westbahnhof. The other passengers bustled by as I lugged my knapsack down the high steps of the train and stood lost on the platform. Suddenly, a large hand clamped on my shoulder. I started, almost jumped, turned and saw a tall stout man with red shiny cheeks.

'Kennes Brrowning?'

I nodded. 'Kenneth,' I said.

'I am Herr Klain,' the man said. 'Velcome to Wienna.'

He picked up my knapsack in an easy swing. The knapsack dangled and Herr Klain's arm directed me outside. His other hand held my shoulder.

The spring sun was blinding as Herr Klain hurried to the black-hooded taxis gleaming in a line. Then he tucked me and my knapsack into the back seat of the first car and took his place beside the driver. 'Elisabethstraße. Gösserhof,' he said.

Herr Klain's head scraped the car's ceiling. I could hardly see between him and the driver, so looked out of my window at the road rushing past.

'Do you speak some German?' Herr Klain asked and turned his balding head towards me.

I shook my head.

'Ah,' Herr Klain said. 'That will be good practice for my Harald then.'

'Harald?'

'My son. He has your age. My other son has taken your place in London.' Then Herr Klain settled back in his seat and looked straight ahead until we pulled up in front of a hotel. A man in shirtsleeves and a black bow tie, a long dark green apron over his black trousers, pulled at the shining brass handle of the heavy glass door.

'*Grüß Gott, Herr Klain,*' he said.

Herr Klain nodded and ushered me in past the oak-beamed foyer to stairs curving upwards.

'Our apartments are upstairs. You shall have your own room,' he said. 'You shall share Harald's bathroom,' he added.

Lugging my rucksack, I followed in Herr Klain's long shadow.

At the top of the stairs a fair-haired boy lounged against the banister.

He greeted with a half smile. '*Grüß Gott, Papa.*'

'Harald! This is Kennes,' Herr Klain said and caught his breath.

I nodded.

'Come, boy,' Herr Klain said to Harald. 'Prove your English. You must learn something in that expensive school I send you.'

'Welcome to the Gösserhof,' Harald said as we reached the landing.

He held out his hand.

I almost lost my balance as my rucksack slid to the floor.

Disengaged, I grasped Harald's hand. 'Good to meet you,' I said.

Harald smiled that half-smile again.

'Show Kennes to his room,' Herr Klain said. 'Get acquainted.'

The room was long and narrow. The width of a cupboard and a bed. The door opened outward. There was one window on the far side.

Looking out on the cobbled street, I dropped my rucksack under the sill.

Harald leaned in the doorway.

'One needs not much more in this house,' Harald said. 'It is enough to have a place to come back.'

A strange thing to say, I thought, but nodded.

'The bathroom is next door. I have made place.'

'Thanks,' I said. Then I smiled. Harald smiled back, but still stood in the doorway. And he stood as I unpacked my two shirts, three singlets, underpants. Harald watched me unfold them and flatten them out in the cupboard. I didn't know what to say so said nothing, hoping that he'd leave me a moment to adapt. When I had nothing more to put away, I faced Harald. 'And now?' I said.

'Now I show you my town,' Harald said. 'Come.'

Harald took the stairs two by two and I ran after him. 'What's the hurry?' I said.

'You must make the hay while the sun is still shining,' Harald winked then laughed. We raced out the door, past the man in the green apron. I had a strange and wild feeling of freedom. Suddenly Harald stopped. 'Take a deep breath,' he said. We both stood with our hands on our hips and filled our lungs. Then we both buckled over with laughter, but I didn't know why. 'Come,' Harald said and raced ahead.

A group of four or five boys in dark blue shorts and shirts with kerchiefs around their necks, the ends held together in a leather toggle, swaggered towards us. They must have been about ten or twelve years old.

'Your cub scouts?' I said.

Harald raised his eyebrows.

'You know. Camping. Hiking. Hiking in the Vienna Woods?'

Harald nodded. 'Yes. Cub scouts,' he said. 'Of a kind.' As the boys drew abreast Harald quickened his gait. I was almost out of breath as we stopped at a fountain in the middle of a crossing. Cathedral spires threw long shadows down upon us. I shivered. Harald splashed his hands in the water and then splashed his face.

'It's cold,' I said.

'But good.' Then Harald stared at me. 'Are you a Jew?'

I splashed my hands and wet my face as he had done.

'Why?'

'You have a big nose.'

'So do you.'

We both laughed out loud. 'Come on,' Harald said and slapped me on the back. 'Race you back to the hotel.' He was off and me behind him, trying to keep up. At a block away from the Gösserhof, Harald stopped. 'Walk now. We must be serious.'

My friendship with Harald grew with the weeks. On Mondays, when I had my day off, Harald would dash in to show me new places. One day we sneaked into Saint Stephen's cathedral and hid in an empty confessional booth off the main altar.

'Tell me, my son,' Harald said. 'Have you sinned?'

I giggled.

'Sshhh,' he said.

'How can I tell you if you say "Sshhh"? No,' I said and stifled my mouth. 'Have you...my son?' I tried not to laugh.

'Not yet,' Harald said. 'Not really.' His voice was earnest. Then he nudged me. 'Let's go.'

Daytime in the hotel was spent learning how to fold napkins, lay tables, always under the critical eye of the headwaiter. The napkins had to be folded like a hat with a peak and they all had to be exactly the same. The other waiters watched silently as I struggled to get the folds right.

One day, the headwaiter led me to a huge tank of live fish – the fish were all trying to stay at the bottom. 'Take a carp,' he said.

'How?'

'Just put your hand in the tank and...take a carp. Catch it.'

I rolled up my sleeves and grabbed for the slithery form. I managed to catch it. Pulled it out. The fish thrashed, slipped from my hands and landed on the sawdust-strewn floor. The waiters roared.

'Pick it up,' the headwaiter said drily. 'Rinse it and give it to the chef.'

Behind his back I heard snickering.

The hotel waiters had set up a soccer team. I burned to join in.

'Why don't you play?' I asked Harald.

'They are rough. You should keep away.'

'But it's a game,' I said.

Harald shrugged.

When I asked Herr Klain if I could play on the staff team the older man's face grew sad. 'I do not think you should,' he said. 'They are rough.'

I wanted to play badly. 'Let's go once, Harald. Just once,' I said.

The next Monday afternoon we changed into shorts and jerseys and went down to the field a few blocks from the Danube Canal. Six of the seven waiters were already there. Three against three.

'*Können wir mitspielen?*' Harald called out.

The waiters stopped and looked at us, one of them pointed to both sides. Harald went to one, I to the other. Then the game started. The ball came towards me and I braked it with my toe. I started dribbling towards the goal. I was in control. Suddenly I felt a thwack in my side. A word spat by my ears as I crashed to the ground. '*Sau Jude!*'

Harald was by my side and pulled me to my feet. 'What did he mean?' I said.

'Let us go,' Harald said and walked me away. Behind us, again I heard snickering.

'I said it was better you did not play,' Herr Klain said. 'You are a Jew.'

I stared at Harald's father. Harald sat on the stairs, his elbows on his knees and his head hanging down.

'Kennes,' Herr Klain said, 'it is sad, but some of our waiters, they are good boys, yes, but...they do not like Jews.'

'But how do they know?' I said. 'I look just like you. Like Harald.' I tried to find some relief and looked over at Harald. 'I have a nose just like his.'

Herr Klain put his arm around me and reached out an arm to his son.

'It is unfortunate,' he said.

The next Sunday and all Sundays thereafter Herr Klain insisted I accompany the family to Mass at Saint Stephen's. I soon forgot the soccer incident. Harald and I would exchange grins as we knelt and glanced over at the confessional boxes.

One day, Herr Klain took me with him to one of the neighbouring villages in Burgenland to place his wine orders. Glasses of golden wine were passed around in the damp cellars.

'Sip,' he said.

I saw him drink, but didn't see him spit the wine out. I took bigger mouthfuls. I swallowed.

'The boy does not know how,' the wine-seller said.

'You're supposed to spit it out, Kennes.' Herr Klain spat

in a bowl.

'Like this.'

I nodded.

'He will learn,' Herr Klain said to the wine-seller.

'That type never learn,' the man said. 'Just like those types in the village we are stuck with.' Two other men tasting wine in the cellar mumbled agreement. The words came to me in a haze. I wondered what they had meant. I noticed the men didn't spit out their mouthfuls, so I swallowed mine.

As we came up from the cellar to the fresh air, my head started to spin, and my legs wobbled.

Herr Klain laughed as I tried to walk a straight line. 'It is to taste wine,' he said. 'You are supposed to spit it out. Not get drunk.' And he clapped me on the shoulder. 'You will learn, Kennes.' I was euphoric again. I wished Harald were there.

On what was to be my last trip to the wine-seller's, though I didn't know that at the time, we saw a family at the entrance to the village. A man in a slouch hat squatted on his haunches, smoking. A child sat on the ground, drawing in the dust. A woman in long dark skirts and a bright headscarf stood behind a makeshift stand piled with corncobs. She was pulling back the dried leaves that form the cobs' husks and plaiting them to expose the yellow pearls of corn. I had seen bunches of corn like that hung out to dry on the outside walls of the cellars and when I'd asked, Herr Klain had told me that the dried corn was to serve as pig fodder in the winter.

As we passed in Herr Klain's old Ford, I turned my head, kept watching the family. The two men from the wine cellar appeared out of nowhere and sauntered towards the threesome. They kicked down the stand. Herr Klain kept driving, slowly. I watched through the rear window as the child buried its head in the woman's skirts, as the man stood and his arms encircled his wife. The two men laughed, it seemed, and walked off. All the while Herr Klain had been silent then he stopped the car in the middle of nowhere.

'Kennes,' he said. 'I do not think you should stay.'

'But I still have months to go,' I said. 'I like it so much here. You. Harald. I love Vienna.'

Herr Klain sighed. 'It is best you go back to England.' His voice was cold. Final.

Harald came with his father to see me off at the station. 'Now I bear hug you,' he said, 'and I will write.'

Herr Klain swung my rucksack in the overhead strapping and dropped back to the platform where Harald and I stood. Then he hugged me. '*Leb wohl, Kennes,*' he said and his hand patted my face.

Tears prickled my eyes as I stood at the window waving at the large figure of Herr Klain and the slender Harald by his side.

I must have fallen asleep just after Linz. I awoke to screams as the train pulled into Salzburg. Two uniformed men in khaki, a red band flashing on their left arms were shoving three or four of the other passengers before them. It was a family I had seen board the train in Vienna. I had wondered if they were from one of the Burgenland villages near the Hungarian border where Herr Klain and I had tasted the wine. They were dressed in a similar way, almost like gypsies, but the woman was without the bright colours and the clinking gold baubles. Why would gypsies travel by train anyway, and where were they going? I had fallen asleep thinking they couldn't have been gypsies.

I looked out of my window. One of the uniformed men was barking something at the huddling group of four. The other turned to the train driver and raised his right arm straight in a stiff salute.

I stared out past the platform as the train pulled off to the border.

'Farewell, Harald,' I said as tears rolled down my cheeks.

Chapter 46

Katrina Klain

It was 25th December 2009; it would be Boxing Day when I landed in London. The walls of the plane were sprigged with plastic holly and fir branches. Red baubles peeked out from the green that was fastened with yellow ribbon. A miniature Christmas pudding sat in its small now-opened box, its red tinsel trailing on the empty tray. I'd tuck it into my bag, keep it for later, for the hotel when I'd wish myself well and sip the extra miniature bottle of cognac the stewardess had served with my coffee.

So many hours still lay before me: a stopover in Singapore to stretch my legs. And then sleep, I hoped, more to make the time pass than to ease the fatigue of my pent-up excitement.

The cognac had been a surprise. The second bottle, anyway. I fingered the tiny bottle, more for its form than its content, yet the taste of the warm, mellow liquid I'd just savoured had triggered scenes I imagined from Kenneth Browning's tape.

The tape was still in the Walkman. Over and over I'd played the beginning, trying to visualise Turnham Green, Vienna, my grandfather's hotel. My hand gripped the gift bottle, enclosed it. All my father had told me about that time was that he'd been to London, had worked in a hotel. He'd spent Christmas there. His first alone. He'd sought a church. It had been closed to him. A private service.

I pulled down the shutter against the brightness now leaking into the black sky as the plane began its race against sunset. The past was finished, Dad had once said; yet from time to time things had slipped through, but had become screened out through the flurry of my growing up. I tried to remember, to peel away the years; it was like peeling the brittle skins of an onion, knowing that once I cut to the flesh, tears would surely follow.

The lights in the plane suddenly dimmed. The film was over. I'd not even noticed that one had been playing on the overhead screens.

I pulled the airline blanket up to my neck.

I remembered the last time I'd visited. Mum had been preparing dinner in the kitchen; there'd been a smell of cabbage and caraway seed.

I'd been going through some old papers, looking for anything that could be of use in Geneva. Dust motes flickered in the yellow glow of the desk lamp as I took out a worn tooled-leather folder. Deeds for the house. Dad's will. A yellowing piece of paper the size of a postcard. A small hole was worn in the middle where it had been folded in four, just big enough to slip into a wallet.

I'd taken the paper and read: *Alfred Klain has been cleared of all suspicion relating to war crimes. Signed. US Forces. Dachau. 1945.*

My heart had thumped as I folded the paper and placed it back in the folder. Later, Mum told me that a reporter had come. Had thought Dad was an old Nazi, and that was when Alfred had brought out the paper. He had been in Dachau, as a US POW; at the end of the war, the Americans had brought suspected Nazis there to make them see what had happened.

Emaciated bodies, some naked, some half-clothed in grey-striped pyjamas, slaughtered, dumped in heaps in the agony of their twisted limbs, open mouths and still staring eyes. Had this been what he'd seen?

Or had the cadavers by then been taken away for the semblance of a human burial, the only trace of what had happened, the stench of the ground freshly scrubbed with ammonia? Did the Americans show him the place where human guinea pigs were infected with malaria, where their bones were transplanted, where they were castrated and sterilised? Or did they show him nothing at all and just lock him up in a cramped cell where the floor reeked of a smell no disinfectant could cover, so that his imagination would do the job of ravaging his mind and his heart?

I slept fitfully and woke to the wail of an infant protesting the descent to Singapore. My fatigue of crossing through the first time zone with the promise of more to come made me dizzy as I followed the trail of passengers into the transit lounge. There was just enough time to go through the gate, circle the garish duty-free shops with their mixture of French perfumes, alcohol and tobaccos. Bolts of shot silk in fuchsia and emerald were draped like curtains before a theatre of carvings and trinkets, and distracted me from joining the queue in front of the women's restroom. I would go later.

Back in my seat, I settled in for the seemingly endless night. I closed my eyes, but could not sleep as my mind searched for things my father had told me.

When Alfred came back to Vienna, he had found everything gone. The empty rooms of the flat above the hotel had been boarded up. He never mentioned what had happened to the family fortune.

My mother, Bettina Strasser, whom he had married on finishing his training as a young officer, had worked in an ammunitions factory in Stuttgart, he'd said. At the end of the war she'd managed to make her way to Vienna. She'd managed to find him. That was all he'd said. Mum had just nodded that it was so.

The city had been cut into four, like Austria. Alfred and Bettina had fled. Anywhere. Anywhere that would take them. Australia. Alfred had said the past no longer existed. Their new life, the only one, was Australia.

Perhaps Kenneth Browning knew more about the war time, even if it was from another perspective. I'd written to the old man to say I'd be in London between Christmas and New Year, that I'd phone him on 26th December. In Australia, nobody did anything on that day except go to the beach. I wondered what people in London did. Meet the descendants of friends from their past? What if he wasn't home? My hand closed on the gift bottle of cognac now in my bag and my fingers traced the tinsel of the plum pudding. I'd go to Turnham Green. Retrace Kenneth Browning's steps. With or without him. Then I slept.

It was still dark, and light snow was falling when the Qantas flight landed at Heathrow. My hands trembled slightly as I tightened my plaid scarf and pulled up the collar of my brown, three-quarter length Drizabone coat. The coat had been perfect against the rain of Sydney winters. In Vienna and Geneva, it had kept the wind out. Now, with a thick jumper beneath, it kept my body warmth in. But I felt underdressed among the thick woollen coats, the furs and the anoraks of the other passengers spilling from the airport.

I'd taken a bed and breakfast in central London, hoping that I could lose myself in the festive lights of the city for a day before trying to contact Kenneth Browning. All I could focus on was a meeting with an old man in Turnham Green, wherever that was.

The next day I phoned. 'Is that Mr Browning?'

'Yes. Who is this?'

'Katrina Klain. From Australia. Did you get my letter?'

'Yes, of course. You must come here.'

'I was hoping you'd say that.'

'Pardon?'

'I'd love to.'

'Take the tube at Victoria Station. Stay on the Victoria Line. I'll pick you up at Turnham Green station. Two o'clock.'

'Two o'clock.' An hour away. 'Thank you, Mr Browning.'

As I hung up I realised that I'd forgotten to describe myself, had forgotten to ask what Kenneth Browning looked like. Yet I was sure I'd recognise him.

At the exit at Turnham Green station I looked left and right at all the passing cars, but not one of the drivers looked my way.

It was five to two. The snow had melted and the road glistened with a wet that would freeze to black ice if the weather report were right. I shivered. My coat had been enough to keep me warm when I'd been striding through the bright lights of London's bustling streets. But here I was off-centre, standing and waiting, the cold seeping in through the sleeves and under the hem of my coat. I shivered again.

'Miss Klain?'

I turned. A short, stocky man with white hair and a moustache stood behind me. He wore a thick, dark-blue coat and a scarf. He leaned on a walking stick.

'Mr Browning?'

The man nodded. 'My car is around the corner. I thought it must be you. Your coat does not look warm.' He turned and waved me to follow him. 'I thought we could go to a tea room. There's one not far, but too far for me to walk.'

I followed the old man to a grey Morris Minor. He opened my door, waited for me to get in, then made sure that my door was properly shut before he went back to the driver's side. The sky was like thick grey felt as we pulled away from the curb. A horn honked, but Kenneth Browning just drove on.

Chapter 47

Ye Olde Tea Room five blocks down from the station had leaded window panes that glowed from behind bunched scarlet curtains.

We took a small table by one of the windows.

'Tea, and cucumber sandwiches?'

'Yes, please,' I said.

The waitress, a plump, motherly soul, went off with the order. Was she the owner? I wondered. 'It's so amazing to be sitting here with you,' I said.

Kenneth Browning smiled wistfully, then laid out an array of laminated cards, the sort that hold tablets. He looked at the fob watch on the gold chain at his waistcoat and popped five or six of the pills out onto the table. Green, red, white capsules. 'They keep me alive,' he said. As he moved in his chair, his walking stick fell. I got up and leaned it in the corner behind him.

'Thank you,' he said. 'A wound from the war.' The way he said it, I felt that it must have been one of many.

'I'm sorry I can't tell you more about my uncle,' I said. 'But I have this.' I pulled out the photo.

Kenneth Browning's eyes took on a new lustre. He adjusted his glasses and stared at the photo. 'Yes. That is Harald. Is the dark-haired man your father?'

I nodded. 'The woman is my mother.'

'You look like both of them,' Kenneth Browning said and surveyed my face. 'But you have your uncle's blonde hair.'

I laughed. 'It's funny how things stay in a family. I bet some great grandparent was blond. Mr Browning...I've been meaning to ask you....'

Just then the waitress owner came with the tea and sandwiches. Kenneth Browning pushed his pills aside with the back of his hand to make room for the cups and a small pot. After pouring for both of us, and adding milk to his own cup, he popped the pills in his mouth. I waited for him to swallow and wash them down with his tea.

'Take a sandwich,' he said. 'They are very good here.'

I gingerly took a triangle of white crustless bread. It was soggy with its soft dough and the moisture of the cucumber slices. I thought of the lettuce and Vegemite sandwiches I'd swapped at school for the brown bread salami ones I'd brought.

'What did you want to know?' the old man said.

I put the half-eaten triangle back on my plate. 'How come you didn't know my father?'

Kenneth Browning took another sip of his tea and then took a sandwich. Chewing slowly, he said: 'I did, in a way.

Your father worked at the hotel that arranged my time in your grandfather's in Vienna.'

'So you never actually met him?'

'No. But I heard a lot about him.'

'From his brother?'

Kenneth Browning shook his head. 'Your father lived with my family. A rented room. He was very close to my sister.' The old man pulled a black and white photo from his wallet. It was creased and had pinked edges. 'That's me with my sisters, Agnes and Leah. They are both dead now. The pretty one is Agnes. She never married. She was quite a few years older than your father – about twenty-seven back then. He had what they called a crush on her – and I think she was in love with him.'

I stared at the old man. I couldn't imagine my father as a young man, one who had had a crush on an 'older' woman, one with whom that woman had been in love.

Kenneth Browning cleared his throat. 'Of course the things that she told me, and they were very few, they led me to believe that perhaps she was in love. He had to leave suddenly. His father was ill. And then the war broke out. Agnes died ten years ago. I wonder now if she had been waiting for him to come back.' He cleared his throat again as if the sound would wipe away invisible tears. 'That's all in the past. Pure speculation.'

I suddenly felt sorry for him. I didn't want to open old wounds, even if they were not strictly his. I sipped my tea. It was strong, despite the cloud of milk I'd added. 'Can you tell me anything about my grandparents?'

'Your grandmother was a noble woman. Perhaps too immersed in the business. But a real lady, if somewhat aloof. I didn't really have much to do with her though.'

I looked past him at the waitress owner and tried to imagine the opposite. A dark, wiry woman, hair in a bun, a high collar perhaps?

'Your grandfather...'

'I can visualise him from your tape,' I said. Yet he had seemed like a stranger, not my grandfather, or how I'd imagined him to be.

'It was just a short time,' Kenneth Browning said.

'And what about Harald? You said you tried to find him.'

'Harald. Harald was a prisoner in England. He was in Romsey and had sent me a letter and a map so that we might meet. It was 1946. I contacted the War Office, but they told me that unless I was a relative I could not visit a POW. Years later I started looking for him. Perhaps it was for old time's sake and I owed him the meeting I was unable to keep. His father, your grandfather, had been good to me. I felt I had a debt towards him. When I started my search for him in earnest years later I thought he had gone to America. But then the trace ended. My letter to your father was my last chance.'

I took the old man's hand and held it a moment.

He looked at me sadly and said: 'I wonder if without realising it, I was also looking for him as a way of finding out where your father was and how his life had turned out. Perhaps I was doing it for Agnes' sake, for her memory. It's not always clear why we do all the things we do.'

I shook my head. No, it wasn't always clear, at least not at the outset. And that was all, I thought. Yet somehow I felt that the end of Kenneth Browning's story was the beginning of my own. 'Where should I start, Mr Browning, to try and find out more about my family?'

Kenneth Browning turned his hand and patted mine.

'Vienna. Start where you would any search. There are archives, people to ask.'

'Archives?' I thought of Carl Sokorny and the material he'd found in the archives. The newspaper clipping. My uncle. Zorko.

'It will take time. There will be false leads and there will be pain. But if you persevere, I am sure you will also find joy. I have had joy in meeting you, Harald's niece.'

I suddenly felt sorry for Kenneth Browning. His search had led him to me. And I had little to give him for it. Just a vague resemblance to a friend from his youth.

'In the past, Katrina, there is much to discover, if you have time and use that time wisely. It can lead to your future. Mine now is gone. I am an old man.'

'I'll let you know what I find, Mr Browning,' I said.

Kenneth Browning nodded slowly then waved to the waitress for the bill.

Chapter 48

2010. Geneva. I unpacked the 'EMOH RUO' plaque. I was alone. There was no 'Ruo'. But it was all I had. I'd thought about going back to Vienna to follow Kenneth Browning's advice. I could even look up Carl Sokorny, for old time's sake. I hadn't been very lucky with men. The career, the haphazard quest for answers I wanted but was afraid to hear.

The intercom sounded. *Pacquet!* When the postman comes by, it means hurry up.

The packet the postman handed me was well-travelled with addresses in Vienna and Berlin struck out. It was postmarked in London.

I frowned and ripped it open. Another packet was inside, which was sealed and marked in black. Katrina KLAIN. There was a letter.

London, January 2010

Dear Ms Klain,

I am Kenneth Browning's daughter and I am sad to say that my father passed away just after Christmas after a long and rich life – not devoid of suffering, however. I know he had met you and that he was a friend of your uncle's before the war. Among his things I found the enclosed packet with your name on it. It was sealed and I have left it as found. I thought you should have it.

Best wishes,

Agnes Browning

I ripped open the packet. Inside was a letter addressed to Kenneth Browning and an ochre-covered booklet.

I traced a finger over the Gothic script: *Ahnenpass*. Above the word was an eagle clutching a swastika in its claws. A genealogical record. The sort the Nazis made each family carry during the war. It was in very good condition. New almost. Guarded safely, then forgotten or destroyed.

Carl Sokorny had worked in the archives in Vienna. He'd told me that the real truth was in those booklets, but that they were kept in the family. They didn't have any in the public archives. They had to go back until about the middle of the 1800s to prove a family's lineage. To prove there was no Jewish blood. There's no name in the front, but there are names and birth and death dates in the back. The name was Klain. It was all very neat.

I slipped the letter from the slit envelope that was addressed to Kenneth Browning. It was from Mum. I stared at the two sheets of lined paper. They were written on both sides.

Sydney, 1987

Dear Mr Browning,

I do not mean to burden you, but there is something I would like you to know and you are the only person I can tell. Do with it what you will. I cannot give it to my daughter, Katrina. Too many years of silence have gone by for her to understand. And to what end? It is our own generation that must come to terms with our time.

What I am writing to you is a confession of sorts. I have carried this secret alone for too many years. And, apart from Katrina, you, as a friend of Harald Klain, may be the only person alive to find my secret of interest.

I must first make something clear. I was in love with Harald Klain. We met in Vienna just after I married his brother. Yes, I know I was married, but love does strange things. My husband had to carry the burdens of his past and I must carry mine. Harald Klain is the father of my daughter, Katrina. Alfred, I discovered, was unable to procreate – a consequence of the war. An ironic fact since he had wished that I bear many babies for Hitler's new Reich. Alfred believed to the end and then his world crashed. He never knew that Katrina was not of his seed, although I think perhaps he did suspect. People will close their eyes to what they do not wish to see. Perhaps my mother-in-law suspected something. She always hated me and let me feel it. This was the woman who looked after you as best she could when you were in Vienna. You said yourself that she was preoccupied, preoccupied with the business, I imagined. I never really understood why she hated me and years ago – we were already in Australia – I wrote to Harald, my last letter to him, asking whether he knew why it was so. It was only shortly before Harald's death in 1974 that I received an answer to my question. He had written to bid me farewell. He had seen Katrina in Vienna, but was already racked with cancer. I am glad that he was able to see his daughter. Before that he had come to Vienna to see his dying mother and he had asked her why she had hated me.

This may interest you, Mr Browning. Frau Klain senior hated me because she thought I had overheard her praying. You may wonder what is wrong with that. Mr Browning, she was praying in Yiddish, not German. My mother-in-law was a Jewess.

She, too, had confessed. She confessed to her son, Harald, on her deathbed. Her life, too, had been a lie. You can see from the booklet that there is a blank against her grandmother's name. Herr Klain senior was a wealthy man with connections in high places. It was not difficult for him to ensure that the family papers did not reflect any inappropriate lineage. He had taken his precautions very early. In the name of love. What we don't do in the name of love, Mr Browning.

When Alfred Klain senior fell in love with a young Italian girl from Trieste, he made her swear to renounce her Jewish faith and marry him in the Catholic Church. She was in love and so she obeyed. She also swore that any sons would not be circumcised. Vienna has a long history of anti-Semitism, Mr Browning; it was surely thanks to their mother's promise that the boys' lives were saved. So you see, the closeness you had with Harald Klain had deeper roots. Of course, there is no final proof of all this. That would be in the booklet. My mother-in-law's origins would have to be corroborated by the authorities of her home town in Italy. But to what avail? I am not a genealogist. And I wonder if it really matters any more. I even wonder if it would change anything for Katrina. She may be better off not knowing all this. Just in case, though,

I shall leave your tape and original letter in a place where Katrina might find them should she ever come back. She left to find her own way. Sometimes to go forward one must go back. Sometimes not. I have never blocked her from knowing anything, but I have also never encouraged her to find out.

We came to Australia to start a new life. But I think the Klain family does owe you a link with their past. Your friend, Harald Klain, was a good man. He just swam against the current.

Forgive me if old wounds have been reopened. I shall not write again. I thank you and remain,
Sincerely,
Bettina Klain

I dropped the letter into my lap. My cheeks were wet.

I am the only one to know the whole story. Is it the whole story? Kenneth Browning and my mother knew nothing about the embezzlement, about Zorko. Monique Zorko may have suspected that Harald Klain was my father. The truth about Alfred is best left alone. My uncle is my father and I am Jewish. Does that change anything? I don't know. I don't think so. Not any more. So many before me have lived their own lives. I want to live mine, now.

Chapter 49
Katrina Klain

2015. My parents are dead, their ashes scattered on their favourite Sydney bushwalk; Jane lives in Australia with her Rosemary, and Jake, I hope is now happy in a life from which I may have kept him. Madeleine, ah Madeleine, perhaps she has gone the way of so many from a privileged system, possibly still alive and well in a duty-free country. Fritz, I was far too naive for him, as I was for the international conference circuit, and Peter Held? A good man from the lives of others. Perhaps, not knowing where I was coming from never allowed me to go anywhere with any man. Belonging or not can be a sorry state. But the stories are there, grounding me.

I still leaf through those snapshots in my mind. Recently, I came across something more about the *Achille Lauro*. She was built between 1939 and 1947 as the Dutch ship, *MS Willem Ruys*. The man after whom she was originally named was taken hostage and killed in the war.

I'm still trying to piece things together, still exploring why it is that I care.

Perhaps it has something to do with the ship that took me away from what may have been home so many years ago. That ship was the *SS Neptunia*. The year was 1952. We sailed through the Suez to a new life in Australia. Memories.

Memories? They're the bits you feel and the bits you're told, and they all come together in your mind as sound bytes and snapshots. Some you lose, and some become parts of someone else's memories. Some bits just disappear, and you end up looking for them for the rest of your life, not knowing why, because all you can do now is to care or to break down.

I pack an overnight bag and board the Intercity train from Geneva to Zurich. At Zurich station I sit with a glass of white wine and wonder if I am going mad. So much time had gone by. Write it down. Write it all down. All the lies. All the silences. How they served the love of ordinary people. How they served to protect those whom lies and silence would always protect. Hadn't one Austrian chancellor protected Zorko, and another bestowed the amnesty he had craved? Hadn't one Austrian president hidden behind silence and lies and, with the help of the Americans, even run the United Nations? Hadn't Skorzeny, 'the most dangerous man in Europe', also acted as a UN ambassador while secretly working on his Odessa files? And more recently, a former finance minister evading the courts through procrastination. *Plus ça change.* And in Australia? Had Mum been right? Did we all have to learn from our own mistakes? Lest we forget? Indeed! Had history become just a video game?

Heads would never roll due to friends in high places. I didn't know all their stories, but others did. I had to make a start so that my own lies and silences would not join the many so deep in the archives, perhaps missing the day to become unclassified. Forever the "deads". I had to write it all down. Now.

I board the Wiener Walzer and arrive in Vienna at nine in the morning. From the new Hauptbahnhof with its boutiques and eateries, I go down the stairs to the way out. People are milling around. Men, women, children. Lining up for hot food, blankets. A train ticket. A sign says, *Train of Hope.* Another sign indicates free legal advice. *Free interpretation. Farsi. Arabic.* Another says: *Welcome Refugees.* I slip a twenty-euro note into a collection box and go out into the street.

I cross the road to the Belvedere Palace. I'll walk down. Pebbles crunch underfoot. Egon Schiele, you weren't the only mad one. Halfway down the Prinz-Eugen-Straße I wait for an arriving tram to pass. A man stands beside me. He is wearing a hoodie like many now do. I glance at him and step onto the street. He is behind me. I quicken my pace. A woman comes out of the large wrought-iron door of the publishing house where I am awaited. She holds out an arm. I scream. The man in the hoodie runs off. I walk through the door with my manuscript.

It was all so quick. The headline sounded a bit like tennis, obviously influenced by the latest Federer comeback. *Author's passing shot frustrates hoodie attack.* Everything goes so fast these days. A melting pot of sensationalism to appeal to all tastes. Even the tabloids have gone to pot. Facts? They're just a point of view at a given time. Memories make them. I laugh. Cannot stop laughing.

Chapter 50
Carl Sokorny

2016. Vienna. Browsing the shelves at the Morawa bookshop behind St Stephen's Cathedral, a cover catches my eye. No picture, just letters. Red. *ALL THE BEAUTIFUL LIARS.* In black: Katrina Klain.

I open the book, read the opening, the ending. Acknowledgements. I see my name. Turn to the index. They are all there. All the big names. Most dead now. Some still alive. Some still jealous of their secrets and those of their fathers. At the end of the book, like an epilogue, there is a glossy photo of a newspaper cutting:

The reporter Jaimie Stadler was found dead in his apartment. He was known for his sports and war reportage, and predominantly for his coverage of scandals, including the never-solved Zorko Affair.

I remember a headline from 2009. A thwarted attack near the Belvedere Palace. A man in a hoodie was seen running away. He was never identified.

Back in my apartment, I unlock a filing cabinet. I take out folders of notes and clippings: minutes of parliamentary meetings, translations of overheard telephone conversations, police reports, cuttings from long-defunct newspapers and ones still in print, *WieWo, Express, Neues Deutschland, Bild*, even old issues of *Die Krone* and *Der Spiegel.* I place them all in a neat pile on my desk next to Katrina Klain's book. She had not contacted me, but I kept on collecting. Collecting and waiting with the ghosts of her life.

The phone rings three times. I pick it up.

'Carl? Carl Sokorny?' a woman's voice says.

I answer and smile. 'Katrina Klain?'

END

A note of thanks

I had the first ideas for this novel in the early Nineties. A working title back then in the pre-web days on Compuserve was *Cutlet*, little ham, or a foreshadowing of future cuts. A couple of years later, after having been awarded a mentorship with Carl Harrison-Ford by the NSW Writers' Centre then headed by Irina Dunn, the title changed to *Tillandsia* and I found an agent in Australia who has been nurturing me until just recently.

Tillandsia languished and I turned to literary short stories, novellas, erotica, another novel, but my first one kept nagging at me. In 2000, I was fortunate to have been mentored by the late Timothy Findley via the Humber School for Writers in Toronto. The title changed to *When the Walls Came Down* and Tiff, as he was affectionately called, told me it might take twenty years or so, but that I should persevere, yet do

314

other things. I would come back to the novel in stories and watch it change and develop, just as I did as a writer. Some of the extracts and stories found homes online at the *Richmond Review* and *Gangway*, and in print in my collection *Back Burning*, published by IP Australia in 2007.

For research on the Zorko affair, I wish to thank the good people at *Kurier*, who many years ago let me have excerpts from print media reporting the matter. I am grateful for feedback over the years from the late Patrick Sandes and individual members of the novels writing group on Compuserve's literary forum, where I met up with members of what was to become Alex Keegan's online Boot Camp. Feedback was also received from my writing mate in Geneva, the mystery writer, Donna-Lane Nelson and from members of the Geneva Writers' Group. In 2015, I participated in an online self-editing course run by Debi Alper and Emma Darwin, where I received great encouragement, and in 2016, *All the Beautiful Liars* was placed third in the Yeovil Literary Prize.

I thank Zoe King, who then went through *Liars* and gave me structural advice, and I am so happy that Dan Hiscocks of Lightning Books was a person I was then able to touch with this work. My thanks also are due to Clio Mitchell, my editor at Lightning Books, who guided me in a sensitive manner to make the book one of which I am proud. I am also grateful for the cover art by Ifan Bates and for the panopticon logo by Gerfried Mikusch.

I am forever grateful to Margaret Kennedy for having believed in me, and my work, since first signing me so many years ago, for this freed me to concentrate on my craft.

Thanks also are due my 'Schubis', Tanja Mikusch and Corinna Geppert at the University of Vienna, and Sheila

Perlaki at Shakespeare and Company Booksellers, Vienna, who agreed to cast fresh eyes on my *Liars*.

I am grateful for permission received from the Estate of Timothy Findley, to use words from Timothy Findley's novel, *Famous Last Words*, (first published in 1981, copyright by Timothy Findley) as an epigraph to the present work. I am also grateful to Angela Readman for permission to use words from her poem, 'Those Things We Do Not Say'.

My husband, Günter Linsbauer, and our daughter Maarit never stopped believing in me and supporting me, though at times, I imagine they did have serious doubts.

So many people have contributed to this journey of twenty-five years. Thank you, all.

About the author

Following a language degree in Sydney, Australian Sylvia Petter trained as a translator in Vienna and Brussels; she became an international civil servant in telecommunications policy before starting to write fiction in the '90s in Geneva where she was a founding member of the Geneva Writers' Group.

Based in Vienna since 2006, she holds a PhD in Creative Writing from UNSW (2009). Her stories have appeared online and in print since 1995, notably in *The European* (UK), *Thema* (US), *The Richmond Review*, *Eclectica*, *Reading for Real series* (Canada), the anthology, *Valentine's Day, Stories of Revenge* (Duckworth, UK), on BBC World Service, as well as in several charity anthologies, and flash-fiction publications.

Her latest book of short fiction, *Geflimmer der Vergangenheit* (Riva Verlag, Germany, 2014), includes 21 stories drawn from her English-language collections, *The Past Present* (IUMIX, UK, 2001), *Back Burning* (IP Australia, Best Fiction Award 2007), and *Mercury Blobs* (Raging Aardvark, Australia, 2013), and translated into German by Eberhard Hain, Chemnitz.

Writing as AstridL, several erotic stories appeared in anthologies in the US (Alyson Books) and the UK (Xcite) and subsequently in her collection of 17 erotic tales, *Consuming the Muse*, (Raging Aardvark, Australia, 2013.)

In 2014, she organised in Vienna the 13th International Conference on the Short Story in English.

Sylvia works part-time at the University of Vienna in education science, and blogs on her website at sylviapetter. com, where there is more on her and her writing.